# D-DAY IN PARADISE

# MAX CATTO

# D-DAY IN PARADISE

WILLIAM MORROW & COMPANY
New York, 1964

# Part One

He that will enter into Paradise must come
with the right key.

THOMAS FULLER

# 1

Captain van Eyck felt his ship lurch through the gap in the reef, felt it slide flat-footedly across the lagoon, and knew it was time to dress himself in a little authority and go up on deck. He put on his braided cap, not bothering with shoes or socks: he didn't need that much authority. He drank off the last of the bottles of beer he'd been timing with computer-like accuracy to last since Tahiti. And then he went barefoot up on deck.

His engineer, China Tom, was just ahead of him in the gangway. The Captain said severely, "You must give way to your superiors," trying to block him off with his fat bulk. China Tom gave him an Oriental look. He giggled nervously, squirming by like a tadpole. No manners. Let up for a minute and they will take over the ship. You have to make them respect the dignity of command. Keep pushing them. In time a little of it will sink in. In about two thousand years.

A bottle rolled softly down the gangway. Captain van Eyck, who had the love-hate association with his ship that a man has with the slovenly wife to whom he is hopelessly tied, thought: these Papuans. They won't lift a hand to keep it clean from Christmas to Christmas. Come to think of it, it

3

nearly *is* Christmas. After thirty years in the South Pacific the Captain still connected it with a great muffled white silence, the hiss of skates on frozen Dutch lakes, pines topped with bonnets of snow, and he went up on deck to be met by a fissonable blue sky and a sun whose scorch literally hit him like a hammer on the head.

Some Christmas. The world is upside-down, he thought.

The *Heinrich van Reyn* was riffling the sheen of the lagoon. The Captain looked back at the surf steaming about the reef through which they'd just passed. He looked at the native in the wheelhouse. Finally he looked at Kanaka Tom, his Melanesian first-officer, thinking critically: it is his duty to take her in. Kanaka Tom saw him coming. He smiled, unhooking his leg from the rail. He crossed the deck to make a little light fastidious water over the side. It was less an act of nature than an act of derision.

I am a good Lutheran, thought the Captain, and I try to love my black brother, but they make Christian charity a bitter pill.

He had two Toms on his ship, but it was hard to address his first-officer intelligibly as Tom Melakaluza, or his engineer as Tom Wai P'su Hai: after a kind of sensible arbitration the Captain distinguished them by renaming them Kanaka Tom and China Tom. He knew that they had certain names for him which he ignored. Command makes a man lonely. It wasn't easy these days to pick up even second-rate mates and engineers.

The frigate birds soared frantically over the reef, and the Captain stood smelling the island, watching the line of the beacon, and then, looking up at the native in the wheelhouse, he said humourlessly to Kanaka Tom, "If he keeps this course he'll run us straight up the village street into the post office."

"What can he hit? Just the wharf," Kanaka Tom said.

"Don't talk like that."

"How do you want me to talk?"

4

"I own this vessel."

"You have my sympathy," Kanaka Tom said.

The Captain bridled. He wanted to defend his ship, but she defeated him before he could open his mouth. She was old, old, old, and she had a sour, gangrenous smell. The disease of rust had pitted her plates, like chronic acne. The Captain wondered with despair what kept her afloat but the crabbed obstinacy of the aged. The engines were shot, but they took the *Heinrich van Reyn* where she had to go. It was a miracle. The Captain thought, there are too many miracles about this ship. I will deserve my reward in heaven. She will still be sailing when I get there.

"Take the wheel," he told Kanaka Tom.

"The helmsman can manage."

"Get up into the wheelhouse."

"That is an order?"

"You want it in writing?"

Kanaka Tom said insultingly, "You *can* write?"

"Hold your tongue. And anchor in the harbour. There is another ship already at the wharf."

Kanaka Tom went up into the wheelhouse, and there was no perceptive difference in the course of the ship, ploughing straight for the point of the jetty, then the engines shuddered and the *Heinrich van Reyn* made a crabwise turn, losing way, and finally the anchor chain ran out and the ship grew still. They raised Safu-Tura about twice a year. The Captain stared at the island. He thought, they smell sweet in books: but get within nostril-range of them and they're as rank as copra on the turn. The palms trailed daintily down to the sea like ballet-girls dabbling their toes, and the sun fried them, and the beach dazzled his eyes like polished brass. Lovely, he thought: but don't get too near. A pirogue stole across the lagoon and, touching his big belly with envy, he watched the wonderfully muscled black body of the native with the fish-spear poised to strike. The tricolour drooped over the customs

5

house in the windless air. He stared at the frame warehouses and the thatch huts of the islanders and the villas of the French *fonctionnaires,* then at the church, only half of which was sanctified: the other half was a cinema open twice weekly. They made God compete with busty celluloid attractions. The Captain knew that at the back was a corrugated iron *pissoir.* The French never let you forget that the spirit was wedded to the flesh.

Then he stared intently at the ship tied up at the wharf. A three-masted auxiliary schooner. He had never seen it before.

"What's its name?" he said to China Tom. "You have good eyes."

China Tom peered across the intervening water and said, "*Le Rossignol.*"

"That means nightingale."

China Tom, whose French was better than the Captain's, said gravely, "Now is that so?"

What was it about the schooner that affected the Captain like a bad smell? Perhaps it was the suggestion of rotting canvas, the senile twist of the bow. He noticed that even the arthritic masts leaned out of true. It must be older than Methuselah's mother. There is a ship that wants to die, the Captain thought.

"It doesn't look much like a nightingale."

"No," China Tom said.

"A mess."

China Tom glanced back along the deck of the *Heinrich* and didn't say a word.

Still, the Captain thought, it'll be company. Somebody to talk to. Kanaka Tom came down off the wheelhouse and called for the dinghy, and the Captain said to him, "Are you going ashore?"

"Yes."

"Be back on watch at ten."

"What is there to watch over?"

6

"Your ship."

"Yours, not mine." Kanaka Tom had very large white teeth and the mop of his wire-hair sat on his head like a big black nest. He laughed too much, and every laugh needled the Captain, which was what Kanaka Tom wished. Barbarian.

"Don't get drunk," he said. "And keep off the women." The dinghy went banging over the side.

Kanaka Tom laughed again and the Captain knew that he wouldn't see him for two days, and then he would turn up red-eyed and sated, all the sexual vinegar in him gone. A pulsating animal. Two Papuans got into the dinghy with him and the three went rowing fast across the lagoon. They will make another eight women pregnant, the Captain thought. They live on their senses. One day they will pay for it. If only I could be sure.

He said to China Tom, "They make you feel ashamed."

"Not me," China Tom said.

"You're going, too?"

"Of course."

"What for?"

"What would you think?"

There was a nice Chinese lady who ran the post office, which was also the laundry, also the house of assignation, and the Captain knew that that was where China Tom would be for the next two days. The Captain pressed his great belly, which made physical relations for him so awkward, feeling a curious glandular stir.

"I had a better opinion of you."

"If you will forgive me, Captain," China Tom said softly, "the only opinion of me that matters is my own."

He went below and when the dinghy came back he reappeared in his heavily creased white suit, pomaded and shaved, his thin black hair greased back, and he looked at the Captain and chuckled again, hiding his bad teeth delicately with his hand. He could spend his money better on

7

a dentist. With a queer frustration the Captain watched him go ashore.

He had a bath, shaved with care, changed into his shore uniform and put on socks and shoes. Then he, too, in his lonely dignity, went ashore.

He took another long look at the schooner from the jetty, wondering whether to pay a formal call on its master. It was as scarred as an old bruiser. It smelled of more than salt and decayed rope: it had the actual smell of a bad life, and that put the Captain off. A native rose from the deck, wearing only a *nambu*, the finger of fibre cloth that covers no more than the essential masculinity, and gave him a hard look. Another time, perhaps. The Captain went down the straggling street, keeping in the shade of the palms, touching the sensuous frangipane as he passed. No doubt about it, these islands are feminine. And sensuous is the word for them, he thought. . . .

A police sergeant emerged like a scalded cat from a house, clapping on his *kepi*. A woman's screech pursued him across to the *gendarmerie* and he answered with the iron disdain that only French husbands have. He saw the Captain. He stopped to squint at him in the sun. "Oh, it's you. *Bienvenu*," he called out.

"Well, we're here again," the Captain said.

"When did you get in?"

"We just anchored."

"You don't get any thinner."

And you don't get any sweeter-tempered, the Captain thought. The sergeant was a small, dry, embittered man. There was a half-mad glint in his eyes and the Captain knew exactly why. "How are things going?" he asked.

"As usual. Listen to the bitch riding her broomstick."

"And how *is* your wife?"

"Nothing wrong with her vocal cords."

The sergeant's wife came into the doorway and saw them

8

and laughed. She was a bold, handsome woman. It was something about her black lustrous eyes. She's too healthy, the Captain thought uneasily: meaning that her bosom was too expansible. It made men look at her twice, three times if her husband wasn't present, and those who knew his exact hours of duty sometimes did more than look. A woman like that makes me glad I'm a bachelor. Carnivorous. She would put me in an early grave.

"Well, how are you, Julie?" he asked.

"I try to keep happy," she said.

"Also half the male population of the island," the sergeant said.

"*Taisez-vous,*" she said.

"You are addressing your husband."

"I would like his usefulness occasionally proved to me," she said.

The sergeant went all hooked like a bat. "Is that a slight on my physical dignity?"

She looked at him, then winked, and he felt momentarily that he'd left his fly undone. She gazed down the street, cooking in the sun, watching the black children mounting the palms for wild bananas. Then she yawned, taking a deep breath so that her buoyant front dilated, and laughed again and went inside.

"What do you do with a woman like that?" the sergeant asked.

"Satisfy her. Or hit her," the Captain said.

"One day I will catch her at it."

I hope I'm at sea when it happens, the Captain thought.

Then a few fishermen came in out of the sea, chanting noisily, hauling a big pirogue out of the surf, and without stopping they rushed the pirogue up the beach and right across the road. The sergeant stiffened. "They *know* they mustn't do that," he said . . .

"What's the harm?"

9

"The road is for traffic."

"There isn't any traffic."

"There will be one day. Regulations are meant to be kept."

. . . and he went over to shout at them; they watched him obtusely, and he became twice as enraged. They had blossoms in their hair, which gave them a feminine appearance despite their muscles and the shark bones in their ears. The Captain thought happily, this is one speck in the Pacific where bureaucracy hasn't a chance, and he continued down the street to the bistro and went inside.

It was deeply shaded by rattan blinds from the sun. The Captain, peering blindly about, caught first the drool from the phonograph of accordion music—the French can make even the squeeze-box sound martial—then the keen smell of anis that in some way reminded him of neglected drains: the buckled zinc: the vituperative voice of the *patronne* somewhere behind—the Captain had an instant sense of familiarity. It might have been just another bistro off Rue Blanche. What made it so disconcerting was the coconut-bearing palm framed in the window. The name of the bistro was the Coucou Rouge, and the bartender's name was Jojo. He looked emptily at the Captain as if he'd last seen him only yesterday afternoon. A lot of tides had flowed across the Pacific. It had been at least four and a half months.

"Well, isn't someone going to say hello?" the Captain said.

"Hello," Jojo said.

"It's been a long time."

"That's right. What will you drink?"

The Captain made a joke. "On the house?"

"If you want a free soup-kitchen," Jojo said unsmilingly, "I can recommend one in Paris. It's only eight thousand miles."

"Beer, then."

"With that waist-line?"

10

"Beer," said the Captain, "and without the personal remarks. I can always get those from my crew on board."

His eyes had now become accustomed to the shade and he saw a thick bull-necked man sitting at a table in the corner, wearing a peaked cap. The master of the *Rossignol.* This'll save a lot of protocol: I won't have to send my formal card on board. There was quite a din above the burble of the accordion, popping noises and excited giggling, and the Captain saw a few natives in jeans playing a pinball machine. It clattered and winked lights and shot down aeroplanes and profitably ate up coins. They weren't locals. These must be the *Rossignol's* crew, he thought.

He was very surprised to see Kanaka Tom and China Tom playing with them.

He looked at the master of the *Rossignol,* who winked at him, then beckoned, and the Captain took the froth off his beer in one vast gulp and went across.

"Captain van Eyck," he introduced himself, and sat.

"Captain Malaise," the bull-necked man said. They shook hands.

Captain Malaise. Captain Sickness. What a name for a human being, the Captain thought.

"Another beer to follow?"

"You're very kind," Captain van Eyck said.

Captain Malaise shouted to Jojo, who normally moved with the lethargy of the aged. He came smartly across with the beers. It must be something in the rasp of that thick peremptory voice.

"I saw your old coffin come in," Captain Malaise said.

Coffin. Captain van Eyck thought offendedly: now I wish I hadn't sat down.

"Not many ships call here. I was very pleased to see that wooden morgue of yours," he said.

Captain Malaise chuckled. "Now we know where we are. Nothing like a couple of insults to clear the air."

11

"Where are you from?"

"From wherever the wind and my stinking old engine fetched me."

"Such as?"

"Such as mind your own business, and I will mind mine." Captain Malaise laughed to take the sting out of it and drank off his beer. He watched Captain van Eyck closely over the glass.

He had small unwinking eyes and they slipped over Captain van Eyck with a kind of humorous malice: I do not think I am going to like this man, the Captain thought. His hands were hard and red, chipped at the knuckles—the Captain's eyes were momentarily fascinated by a frightful white scar that crawled like a living worm under his chin. He had an overmastering urge to look under the chin to see where the worm had escaped, and Captain Malaise laughed as if it were a favourite party trick, rolling his neck so that the scar appeared to writhe. This is an animal, thought the Captain, who suddenly felt afraid of him. He was very strong, thick about the shoulders. He smells bad, like his decaying old ship.

"Dutch?"

"Rotterdam."

"I am out of Brest," Captain Malaise said.

Hell more likely, the Captain thought.

"Where are you heading?"

"Christ's Island," Captain van Eyck said.

"I never heard of it."

Probably not of Christ, either, Captain van Eyck thought. Why am I so uncharitable? He is a man. My brother in God. He must have some redeeming feature. It is going to be very hard to find.

"What do you carry?"

"You ask a lot of questions," Captain van Eyck said.

"The only way to get a lot of answers. If you don't want to tell, you must have something to hide."

12

Captain van Eyck said, "Why would I have anything to hide?" and started working himself into a huff. "Guano. Phosphates. Stores for the islands. Anything that will fill my holds."

"There's no money in it."

"That's my business."

Captain Malaise grinned, "You don't seem to have one."

And Captain van Eyck put down his glass, the taste of the beer suddenly gone bad. He thought, this is where I leave. Then: perhaps better not. This ox of a man is capable of making a disturbance. The small hard eyes sparkled, the white worm of the scar writhing with amusement. It had been so badly sewn that the Captain could see every surgically botched stitch.

"You're not very polite."

"Forgive me. I was neglected by my finishing school," Captain Malaise said.

He waved to Jojo. The bartender opened two more bottles and they fizzed lightly as if they'd been brought to the boil. Then he went back to the magazine he'd been reading at the bar. A nude projected unreal breasts from the back. On an island that had no missionaries to cover up the local mammaries one would think he'd seen enough of breasts. The dazzle of the sun bit into the bistro and the over-hot air grew stale. A goldfish swam hopelessly in a bowl. Captain van Eyck felt rather imprisoned, too. The pinball machine in the corner clattered and flashed zooming aeroplanes like a neon advertisement all over the dial. Captain Malaise's crew whispered with Kanaka Tom and China Tom as they played. The tattered jeans robbed them of a native's dignity. They looked coarse. With that master of theirs to set an example I'm not surprised, Captain van Eyck thought.

Suddenly Captain Malaise called out to them sharply, "What are you talking about over there?"

13

They went silent.

"Stop jabbering behind my back. Do you hear? I will kick your testicles through your teeth if you open your mouths again."

They watched him, giggling nervously. Then went back to playing the machine.

"Primitives," Captain Malaise said intimately to Captain van Eyck. "Always bang them about a little before breakfast. Never let them get out of line."

"How do you keep a crew?"

"With the toe of my boot."

"There are better ways."

"You stick to yours, I'll stick to mine."

"They're human beings, too," Captain van Eyck said.

"Who told you that?"

Captain van Eyck hadn't meant to sound pretentious. It was dragged out of him, "We're all children of the same God . . ."

Captain Malaise stared at him seriously, as if suspecting a joke, then said, "You're an even bigger fool than you look."

"I don't have to stay and listen."

"Who's holding you down? *Allez-vous promener*," Captain Malaise said with classic French simplicity, meaning: so clear off.

"You have a very brutal attitude."

"I've learned a very brutal philosophy. All men are animals. White a little less so than black. I treat them all on the animal level."

I am going to stop being Christian and hate this man, Captain van Eyck thought.

But Captain Malaise was no longer paying attention; he'd tilted his head to listen to his crew, who were whispering and giggling again with Kanaka Tom and China Tom, and suddenly his face went ugly and he shouted, "What are you saying to those men?"

14

There are silences that crackle: like ice. One of the natives started, "Captain—"

"What did you tell them?"

"Nothing, Captain."

"You want a leg or two broken? Get back to the ship. Go on, all of you. You don't set foot ashore again."

They watched him, and for a moment Captain van Eyck sensed rebellion; they stared nostalgically at the pinball machine that was flashing its last fit of insanity as the coins ran out. There was some exchange of money with Kanaka Tom and China Tom. They all went shuffling out.

"What's the harm in them talking?" Captain van Eyck asked.

"They're fools."

"That's still no reason."

"You want another? They don't even breathe without my permission," Captain Malaise said. He changed the subject. He was as resilient as a ball. "You're interested in a little business?"

"I already have a cargo."

"This one will pay."

The wages of sin if I know you, Captain van Eyck thought. But he couldn't resist asking, "What?"

"Never mind what. The Indonesian islands. The risk is small. And it isn't too far."

Gun-running, Captain van Eyck thought. This man *is* on the animal level.

"No, thank you," he said.

"You've guessed?"

"You have that kind of face."

"Open. And honest. You won't think it over?"

"No. I have sailed these seas for thirty years, my needs are small, and I sleep well at night because I keep my conscience intact."

15

"One day the bottom will fall out of that can of rust you call a ship. You won't be able to eat your conscience then."

"I won't starve."

Captain Malise said, "Not for a while. You can always live off that superfluous fat." The horrific white worm of the scar started pulsing merrily under his chin; Jojo watched it with fascination. Captain Malaise began to roar at his own joke and Captain van Eyck, feeling an enormous offence, went red and walked out.

He stood sweating copiously in the sun. He watched the reef, hazed and rainbowed over the opening where the Pacific was trying to crash into the lagoon. What a remark. I am not as fat as that. The lagoon lapped like silk, and a fish flashed into the air, and the palms on the beach slept, leaning over as sentries sleep on their feet. Not at all as fat as that. Finally the pinball machine in the bistro stopped clattering and Kanaka Tom and China Tom came out.

Kanaka Tom looked at the Captain and said, "I'm going to take a little walk."

"You don't have to tell me where," the Captain said in a hard voice.

"Good." The pair set off briskly along the beach. Then Kanaka Tom paused and came back. He said softly, "You know what those niggers told us?"

"No." Those niggers, Captain van Eyck recalled, had been a shade or two lighter than Kanaka Tom.

"That Captain of theirs has a man in chains locked up in the forward hold."

"It wouldn't surprise me." Captain van Eyck winced. "Let it remind you what a good master you have. He treats his natives like . . ."

"Not a native. A white man."

Captain van Eyck felt as if he'd received a small bang in the stomach. "That cannot be true."

"That's what they told us."

**16**

"A white man?"

Kanaka Tom laughed ironically, repeating something the Captain had said earlier, "You want it in writing?" and he tapped China Tom's arm urgently and both of them went off.

I don't believe it, the Captain thought. They gabble like children. Anything to shock. I wouldn't accept a Melanesian's word that wasn't supported by three eye-witnesses and a Justice of the Peace. Just the same. He looked back into the bistro where Captain Malaise was refreshing himself with another bottle of beer. The Captain thought strangely: what a bladder that man must have. He watched his first-officer and his engineer vanish in the distance, Kanaka Tom into some hospitable native thatched hut, China Tom into the laundry. It had a department upstairs that pandered pleasurably to sins that no laundry could wash away.

There was nothing to tempt the Captain but the beach, and he went down to the shade of the palms, making a nest for himself in the soft warm sand, hoping the hermit crabs and the flies would let him be. And he pulled his cap over his eyes and fell fast asleep.

❀   ❀   ❀

He woke to a frenzy of scratching, his head on fire, for the sun had passed over the palms and the flies were eating him alive. He made himself tidy and went towards the market; he ate a few red bananas straight off a stall, deafened by the clack and the chaffering, watching the split black-toothy faces that were still as foreign as Tibetans to him. He could just see the *Heinrich van Reyn* round the wharf. My old familiar unsinkable enemy. A little venomous smoke belched from the flaked funnel. Who is that wasting my oil? he thought. The bananas just stirred up his appetite, so he ate a little *varo*, the cooked sea centipede that tastes exquisitely of lobster; averting his glance from it, for God, who balances

17

all things in nature, had given it the eyes of a Frankenstein and a revolting number of legs.

Then he walked absently towards the *gendarmerie*. The door was wide open. The police sergeant sat with his feet on the desk, reading a magazine.

The Captain looked at the cover and thought, why are they all so preoccupied with it? It must be something to do with the heat.

"You, is it?" The sergeant closed the magazine, bosom down.

"You're not very busy."

"I run a good island. I don't allow trouble. When I begin to be busy I shall be falling down on my job."

There was an iron-barred cell behind him. A Polynesian slept contentedly on the floor.

"A drunk," the sergeant said. "Every Sunday after church. He comes here to sleep it off. Beer?"

"Home-brewed?"

"American. Canned."

The Captain let it drip tepidly down his throat. His eyes rested on the schooner tied up at the jetty, and he knew exactly why his feet had led him here, and what he had to say. He began tentatively, "That ship. *Le Rossignol*. You know her master?"

"We have had a drink."

"I heard a strange story."

"If you've time to waste you'll hear many strange stories. All of them untrue." The sergeant was watching his wife, Julie, narrowly through the doorway. She stood gazing with a kind of expectancy down the street. "What did you hear?"

"That he has a white man chained up in the hold."

"Who has?"

"Captain Malaise."

"Who told you that nonsense?"

"His crew said something to my first-officer . . ."

18

"That Kanaka?"

"Yes."

"Don't you know they love melodrama? Infantile blacks. They go behind a tree to relieve nature and make a gigantic adventure out of it. Why would Captain Malaise want to keep a white man in chains in the hold?"

"I don't know."

"Neither do I. Because it's absurd." The sergeant wasn't very interested. His mind jumped like a faulty watch. "Why does she just *stand* there?"

"Who?"

"My wife. Just looking at the street. Who does she expect?"

"Certainly not me. So you think it's silly?"

"What's silly?"

"What I heard about Captain Malaise."

"Of course. He's a rough diamond. One has to be with a crew like his. But not a bad sort." The sergeant's mind switched again, "Why *does* she stand there?"

"Ask her."

"She laughs."

"And you don't want to ask Captain Malaise about it?"

The sergeant tore his avid eyes away from his wife with irritation and said, "What's the matter with you? You must be mad."

"I'm sorry. You're probably right."

"You should grow up. And not listen to the gossip of moronic natives." The sergeant's eyes slid back to the door, but before he could speak the Captain said cruelly, "Why don't you throw that drunk out of the cell and lock *her* up?" He went out.

Julie called over to him demurely, "How is he?"

"On the hot seat."

"Good," she said, and the Captain walked off.

Suddenly he was violently hungry. He had a very vocal stomach: he could hear it grumbling, could feel the eager

19

little butchers sharpening their knives down there. He went back to the bistro. He was startled to see that Captain Malaise was still there, and made a right-about turn, but it was too late to retreat. "Come in and join me," Captain Malaise called out to him heartily. He was having dinner. "I hate eating alone."

Before him was a vast platter of rice heaped over fried bananas, covering something that looked like a steak. He has some eager little butchers down there, too, Captain van Eyck thought.

"What's that?" he asked. His tastebuds started flowing.

"Superannuated horse. Very tasty," Captain Malaise said.

"I'll have the same," Captain van Eyck called out to Jojo. He didn't know whether to be stiff and formal, or show his resentment by saying nothing at all.

"Now this is nice," Captain Malaise said. "Try this." It was hard to think it was the same man who'd insulted Captain van Eyck so brutally earlier. He poured out a glass of *calvados* for him. "*A bon santé.*"

"*Salud,*" Captain van Eyck said.

"Have you had a pleasant day?"

"It's good to be ashore," Captain van Eyck said.

"People don't realize what loneliness a seaman suffers."

"That's true."

"Nor what responsibility rests on a ship's master."

That's true, too, Captain van Eyck thought. The *calvados* started warming his veins. He began to look at Captain Malaise with a little more charity. What's the use of being starchy? So he just isn't a gentleman. He cannot help that.

Captain Malaise smiled at him disarmingly and said, "You're still annoyed with me, aren't you?"

"Well," Captain van Eyck hedged.

"Forgive me. I'm just a rough mariner. I forget myself. I have what we call a *langue vulgaire.*"

Vulgar is the word. Still. "It's quite all right," Captain van

Eyck said. The food was good. He mellowed. He felt that he ought to make a gesture, too. "Anyway, they *were* talking," he said in a low voice.

"Who?"

"Your crew."

"Why should I care?"

"You seemed to object to it at the time."

"Oh, that," Captain Malaise shrugged. "I have to put up with enough of their silly clack on board, I just don't like them babbling in my ears when I'm trying to relax."

"They told my first-officer and my engineer that you have a white man chained up below."

"Idiots," Captain Malaise said. He filled his mouth. "Anything for sensation. They'll say whatever comes into their—" Then Captain van Eyck's words seemed to penetrate and his mouth opened, showing unmasticated food. "They said what?"

"That you have a white man locked up in your forward hold."

Captain Malaise said bewilderedly, "Why would I want to do that?"

"I don't know."

"In this climate? A man could die of heat stroke."

"Yes."

"It would be inhuman. I may not be one of nature's aristocrats, but I'm not a brute." Captain Malaise made a wry face. "Why would they say a thing like that? Spite." Then, even more confused, "With labour so scarce would I keep a good white man locked up? I would *use* him."

"That's so." Captain van Eyck stared hypnotically at that fat white scar. It fluttered at him with a kind of personal reproach.

"What do you do with these black morons?" Suddenly Captain Malaise looked straight at Captain van Eyck and said with surprise, "You didn't *believe* them?"

21

"I didn't say so . . ."

"But you did. I can see it in your face."

"Please." Captain van Eyck sweated violently. His appetite went.

"Is that what you think of me? How could you?"

"I assure you . . ."

"Captain, my forward hold is empty. There is nothing in the bow but the chain locker. You owe it to me. Come and see for yourself."

"No, no."

"Yes, now. This minute. If it's the only way to set your mind at rest."

In his great embarrassment Captain van Eyck said rashly, "I told the police sergeant I didn't really believe it," and then thought too late: why don't I learn to shut my mouth?

Captain Malaise said strangely, "You went and told the sergeant? Without telling me first?"

"I'm sorry."

"Was that nice? It debases a man's standing. I am not rich, and my good name is all I have. It wasn't a friendly thing to do. What did the sergeant say?"

"That it was crazy."

"Of course."

Captain van Eyck felt terrible. "Can't we forget it?"

"Only if you come and look my ship over. It isn't the *Queen Elizabeth*. It'll only take a few minutes to search it from bow to stern."

"You make me feel awful."

"I insist." Captain Malaise started tugging him compulsively to his feet.

"Forgive me. I can't say how much I regret it . . ."

"Apologies are cheap. I also have feelings. It will take me a long time to forget this."

Captain van Eyck stared wretchedly at the leaping reproach of the scar and said, "For the last time. I appeal to you. Please."

After a long while Captain Malaise looked at him, then smiled begrudgingly, and said, "I can't bear malice. It's too ridiculous, anyway. What's the use of getting worked up?" His face shone suddenly like a field of stubble after the rain. "Let's have another bottle."

"It's such strong stuff."

"I know a man when I see one. You have a head as steady as a rock."

Captain Malaise called for a bottle from Jojo, and they sat talking pleasantly for almost an hour: about Quinn's bar in Papeete, and the one in Tahiti's Les Tropiques. Captain Malaise seemed to be well connected with bars. The *calvados* ran to Captain van Eyck's head and when presently Captain Malaise rose and said, "Well, I have to get a night's sleep," he was actually afraid to get up. "This was wonderful. We must do it again," Captain Malaise said. "Are you by any chance a card player?"

"Yes."

"I'm delighted. You must come aboard and give me a little game." He shook hands formally with Captain van Eyck, paid his bill, and went. How mistaken we can be in people, the Captain thought. The ones with the worst faces turn out to be the most genuine of all. Jojo had gone back to his magazine.

The Captain looked at the cover and said, "Why do those things amuse you?"

"What things?"

"Breasts. Bardot with a towel. Bardot without."

"I'm a Parisian. It's my only link with civilization," Jojo said.

"I see," the Captain said. He didn't really. When he thought of civilizaton he thought of the tulip fields of Lisse, of Rembrandt, and the hump-backed bridges over the canals

23

at Delft. It took all sorts to make a world. And, of course, the French were always the French.

He paid and went unsteadily back to his ship. He glanced without hope in Kanaka Tom's and China Tom's cabins to see if they were back—they weren't—there must be something to this business of letch, he thought. And he got into his virginal bunk and fell instantly asleep.

❀   ❀   ❀

He woke. It was quite dark. He looked at his watch. It was two o'clock. The *calvados* seethed in his stomach. The steak lay there heavily; the superannuated horse hadn't yielded it an hour too soon. He twisted, with the taste of lime in his mouth, trying to make himself comfortable in his bunk. It was no good. He put on his dressing-gown and went up on deck for a breath of air.

The night sky had the luminous glow of a black pearl. The stars blazed: they filled the Captain, always ready to be religious, with awe. There wasn't a light on shore. And the silence was impressive: just the soft lap of the lagoon and the intermittent croak of sleepless gulls.

Then a strange thing happened. The Captain was watching the black twisted shape of the *Rossignol*, and suddenly a faint glow began to crawl in the forward portholes of the schooner, as if someone were carrying a candle or a lamp, and it went all the way along to the bow porthole and flickered there. It was ghostly. The Captain thought: there's nothing in the bow but the chain locker. So why? The candle stayed there, as sinister as a murderer's eye, and the Captain went up into the wheelhouse for his binoculars, but all he could see was the round of glowing glass in the bow, a jumping shadow or so: and for a moment he thought he could hear a bitter cry. Then the candle retreated and finally the *Rossignol* was once more dark.

24

A gull screamed. The Captain went back to his bunk. Presently he fell asleep, but it was broken by a bad dream: he had the queer sensation of being bathed in cold candlelight, and just before he woke up with a cry he dreamt that a gull was frantically beating its beak against the glass of his port-hole, and when his unwilling eyes turned to look at it he saw that it had the face of a man.

It was dawn. He was wet with sweat. Neither Kanaka Tom nor China Tom had returned. He bathed and dragged his Papuan cook up to give him breakfast. Why should he sleep if *I* can't? he thought.

      ❂     ❂     ❂

He went up on deck. The dawn sky was a glory of pink and saffron, the gulls were yelling, and the Captain thought, I never want to hear those creatures again. Then he stared. Other strange things had happened in the night. A small fleet lay just outside the reef, and though they were silhou-etted against the rising sun, spidery with radar bowls, the Captain made out a light cruiser, two attendant destroyers, a fat supply ship, and a cluster of blunt, grey landing-craft with droppable bows.

The lagoon was a fine natural anchorage and he wondered why the fleet chose to stay so unapproachably outside. He got his binoculars and studied the flags. It was peculiar. He made out an Australian, two American, one British, a Filipino flag, and another with a crescent and stars that he thought was Pakistani but couldn't be sure. What a very mixed bag. And the grey silent shapes lay there, guardedly, like dowagers shunning publicity, nothing on board moving, and the rising light didn't make them seem more companionable, and the Captain thought: what very odd things have happened this night.

25

# 2

The sun leapt over the palms. Life came to the town. It was like watching a flower unfold. Shutters tossed wide, mattresses flung out to air on sills, cats ejected for nature's call: the heavy iron shop grilles that would have guarded the Bank of France went crashing up. Look at it, thought the Captain: there is the Boulevard Malesherbes and the Cannebière of Marseilles. He could almost smell across the lagoon— he couldn't control his taste buds—breakfast coffee and yeasty croissants.

He waited for something to happen, the early breeze tickling the huge tent of his robe. It'll go like this, he thought. The shopkeepers first. Rubbing sleep from their eyes, staring at those quiet grey ships outside the reef. Then the housewives peering out of shutters, pointing, calling husbands from toilets, more and more faces crowding the windows, a little mob in shirts and held-up pants gathering on the beach. And the natives watching from the thatched huts.

That was exactly how it went. In that order.

The Captain focused his binoculars on the *Rossignol*. He saw Captain Malaise come stretching up on deck in long woollen combinations, like something out of an antique Keystone comic, saw him stare curiously at the fleet. The night-walker. What had he been doing at two in the morning with a candle in the bow?

At that moment the gig of the *chef de douane* shot out from the harbour and made for the fleet. He may come back with a little hot gossip: and maybe he won't. Navies are notoriously silent. The Captain saw the police sergeant waiting impatiently on the jetty, and when the gig came back he and the *chef de douane* disappeared into the customs shed.

Then the natives took off. Trade being trade. The pirogues slid across the lagoon, laden with mangoes and bananas; they passed the gap in the reef and circled the navy, standing picturesquely in the canoes, shouting their wares. Sprinkling the sea with blossoms. There were a few women amongst them. Semi-exposed; the potent breastworks of the islands. That'll draw the sailors, the Captain thought. Oddly enough, it didn't.

The ships remained very quiet, only an officer or two moving about the decks, one could hear a bugle, the clank of machinery as the fleet went about its private, terribly private, business: it was hard to believe that the glamour of the South Pacific was calling so uselessly down there.

Presently the canoes came back. The market opened. Life shrugged and went on. The Captain thought, why am I so hungry? And he dressed and got one of his Papuans to row him ashore.

❁        ❁        ❁

He saw Captain Malaise sitting outside a café by the beach. He tried to avoid him by walking quickly through the fruit stalls but Captain Malaise shouted out, "I've ordered breakfast for you."

"I've had it."

"Have another," said Captain Malaise. "There's a big man

27

to feed there," sliding his eyes guilelessly down Captain van Eyck's front.

He *likes* being rude, the Captain thought. He sat. He looked sidelong at Captain Malaise. He hadn't shaved. The white wormy scar seemed strangely quiet. It hasn't fed yet, thought the Captain: when it's had its coffee it'll start jumping again.

"Well, what do you think of that?" Captain Malaise asked.

"The ships?"

"The navy is here."

"Oh, there's always a navy somewhere."

"In these seas? A mixed outfit like that? It's very queer."

"Why should you care?"

"I don't," Captain Malaise said carelessly. "So long as they don't come chasing me."

And I'll bet there have been times when the possibility has worried him, Captain van Eyck thought. Brigand. Captain Malaise dunked his roll with great concentration, and when it had soaked up most of the coffee he poured the rest into the saucer and drank from that. He watched Captain van Eyck closely over the lip. He was like a butcher studying the carcass he intended to slit with his knife.

"I am leaving tomorrow," he said.

Good, Captain van Eyck almost said.

"There's no trade here. I wonder how a man with an old iron tramp like yours can manage to exist."

"Small honest profits."

"Who are you fooling? You're talking to a business man," Captain Malaise said.

It came snappily out of Captain van Eyck, "I hope you're a better business man than you are a liar."

"What?" Captain Malaise had his head down to the saucer and he managed to drink and keep his eyes frozen on Captain van Eyck's face.

"I happen to know that you do have a man locked up in the

28

hold of your ship," the Captain said. He didn't, of course, but he thought: there's no harm in trying it on.

"What makes you say that?"

"Never mind."

"You didn't believe me?"

"Who would?"

Suddenly the small still eyes started glowing and the Captain thought, he actually *enjoys* being caught out. The white scar became very animated and the Captain was sure that it was enjoying it, too. "So what?" Captain Malaise said.

"So nothing."

"What can you do about it? I shall be gone in the morning."

"I didn't say I was going to do anything about it," Captain van Eyck said. But his curiosity got the better of him. "Who is he?" he asked.

"A man. With two legs, two arms," Captain Malaise said.

"White?"

"Quite white."

"Do you know what he must be suffering down there? In this climate?"

"A little privation is good for the soul. It gives a man a foretaste of death, which we all have to come to," Captain Malaise said.

He got off this pious announcement without a flicker. He wasn't in the least frightened. He called for another bowl of coffee and Captain van Eyck lost his hunger as he started the messy process of dunking and saucering again.

"What did he do?" he asked.

"Do? Nothing."

"Then why is he . . ."

"Because I own him. I bought him," Captain Malaise said.

Captain van Eyck thought with incredulity: either I'm not hearing properly, or I have wandered into the wrong century. This is an authentic Arab slaver talking.

"Who *owns* a man these days?" he asked.

"I do. In a way."

"What way?"

"Is it your business?"

"I could lodge a complaint . . ."

"Try it."

"Where did you get him?"

Captain Malaise thought about it, his eyes alive and cautious; the scar seemed terribly excited, as if bursting to share the joke, and Captain van Eyck watched it frozenly, telling himself: this is part of last night's bad dream. I will never drink *calvados* again.

"In Vietnam," Captain Malaise said.

"North or south?"

Captain Malaise made an upward jerk with his thumb as if to say: the north.

"Dealing with the Reds?" Captain van Eyck said stiffly. "That can get your ship black-listed."

"Trade is trade. Put it another way. *Pecunia non olet.* Money doesn't stink," Captain Malaise said.

"So?"

"So I was in Nam-Dinh. There'd been some fighting, there's always fighting up there, and they'd taken a bundle of prisoners." Captain van Eyck didn't want to ask whether *they* were Chinese or Vietnamese. "Bundle." What a word. As if they'd captured a laundry consignment. "They shot a few," Captain Malaise said rather absently, maybe because his mouth was full. "They sentenced the rest to moral regeneration in a labour camp," winking to make himself understood. "You know? In the paddy-fields. The mines. I was talking to the lieutenant at the camp; he knew I was short of deckhands, and he said if I wanted to pick one out I could have him if I'd compound his sentence with a fine." Winking again, "They can always lose the odd prisoner. If the price is right. He had a white man, a mercenary, some kind of hired soldier, and I said I'd look him over, and how much? Three hundred

30

dollars. Strictly American currency. So I took a look at the man and beat the lieutenant down to two hundred."

"Your humanity does you credit."

"Naturally." Captain Malaise looked Captain van Eyck straight in the eye.

"You're a horror."

"Now you're spoiling a beautiful friendship," Captain Malaise said.

This is really a very bad man. I demean myself by just sitting here with him. Captain van Eyck couldn't get up. His buttocks wouldn't let him. He wanted to hear the rest.

"I hope you got a bargain."

"Well, I didn't. All I got was trouble. The man won't work. He resists my legal authority," Captain Malaise said.

Captain van Eyck wondered if he'd heard the word correctly. "*Legal?*"

"I paid his fine, didn't I? He is mine."

"Every man is his own."

"That's what you think. I'll break his spirit for him. I'm not a philanthropist. I have invested two hundred dollars in him. I intend to get my money's worth."

That was where Captain van Eyck should have stopped asking questions. This isn't my business. There's enough misery in the world. But his tongue ran away with him. "Why is he chained below?"

"You think I'm crazy? He'd only decamp at the first port," Captain Malaise said.

"What's his name?"

Captain Malaise said evasively, "All I bought was a strong back. I didn't ask to see the label." He laughed. "He's very *roux*," he said.

"What's that?"

"Red of hair. My black imbeciles admire it. That is what they call him, Red."

"Poor man."

31

"Why pity him?"

"He is human."

"A matter of opinion. I told you, he's nothing but a *mercenaire*. A common soldier-of-fortune." Captain Malaise fished out of the coffee a piece of bread that had escaped him and said holily, "To bear arms for money. It's a filthy trade."

"And yours?"

"You're getting rude again."

"Go to hell."

Captain Malaise beamed, "Why not? We will no doubt meet there," and got up.

He was happy. The scar was also happy. Captain van Eyck could just see the *Rossignol* through the fruit stalls, and he stared from the twisted bowsprit and the out-of-true masts to Captain Malaise, thinking: they've grown to look exactly like each other. Corrupt. He was sure that somewhere the *Rossignol* had a very excitable scar, too.

Captain Malaise was watching the silent grey ships beyond the reef and he said, "I don't like navies. Always poking their snouts into trouble. That lot means trouble for somebody, believe me. Those guns. Look at them." He seemed to admire them in a greedy competitive way. "I don't mind running a few cases of rifles, but at least I'm a peaceful man. I never use them myself." He knew that he was making Captain van Eyck feel sick and he jabbed in the needle a little. "That's where all our money goes," he said, pointing to the fleet.

Captain van Eyck wondered when either of them had last paid taxes.

Captain Malaise laughed, and he went off, the laughter booming across the market, stopping to shout back, "Don't forget that little card-game. You must come aboard tonight."

Captain van Eyck, who treated cards as a religion and chose his playing companions as fastidiously as a millionaire chooses mistresses, muttered to himself: not while I'm con-

32

scious. Brute. His eyes went back to that porthole in the bow of the *Rossignol*: a window in a coffin, he thought.

He had some argument with the *patron* of the café, for Captain Malaise had forgotten to pay. He bought a flower in the market and put it in his buttonhole to restore his self-respect. The heat was frightful. The lagoon looked greasy; the birds squatted limply on the beach like a black rash in the shade of the palms. As the Captain passed one of the thatched huts of the islanders Kanaka Tom came stumbling out. He was red-eyed. It wasn't possible for a man that black to look pale; the nearest word the Captain could apply to his skin was grey. Kanaka Tom stared at him wildly, not recognizing him for a moment, reeking of *kava*, then said belligerently, "It's no use. I'm not coming back."

"Not in that condition." A native peered out of the hut. The Captain could hear giggling. He caught a glimpse of shining exposed flesh. "Who are those women?"

"My friend's wives. He has two. He has asked me to kindly help out."

"You have no shame."

Kanaka Tom roared, "I'll tell you what I have had, though," and started informing the Captain anatomically. You'll never teach them modesty, thought the Captain, letting the crude laughter bounce off his plump back. They're steeped in original sin. He made for the *gendarmerie*, and when he got there the sergeant's wife was standing in her doorway on the other side of the street. She still had that expectant expression. What *was* she looking for? Terrible woman. The Captain could guess. She watched him approach, her coarse eyes travelling up and down his podgy figure, and as she chuckled he knew she was thinking the same kind of anatomical thoughts as Kanaka Tom.

"Julie, is your man busy?" he asked, and then wished he'd phrased it rather differently, for she laughed.

"Man? Is that what you call him?"

33

"Don't start that. Is he in the office?"

"Hush. Don't disturb him," she said mockingly. "He's become very important. He may be telephoning God."

"What are you talking about?"

"He's just seen the *chef de douane*, who's been out to that navy there, and they're both full of great secrets and all swelled-up like frogs."

She meant her voice to carry. The sergeant came out of the *gendarmerie*. "Be quiet, there," he cried.

"Make me."

"You have no respect for my position."

"I respect only one position," she told him, and the Captain winced as she described it. That was pretty anatomical, too.

The sergeant dragged the Captain inside. "She wants everybody to hear." He stood there, a small bitter frustrated man. He said, "One of these days I'll assert myself," and the Captain thought, no, you won't, she's too much woman for you. The sergeant knew it, too. His face went sour and he sat. "Did you want something?"

"Not so fast. You know what those ships are there for. I hear you had it straight from the horse's mouth."

"That's no way to refer to the *chef de douane*."

"Maybe not," the Captain said.

"Who told you?"

"Julie."

"The woman is dangerous."

"Oh, never mind that," the Captain said impatiently. "Come on."

"It's highly confidential. I don't know if I ought to tell you." That means he doesn't really have anything to tell, the Captain thought. Ninety per cent fiction, ten per cent fact. The sergeant put on his *kepi*. It made him look official. The Captain looked at the pinched bureaucratic face and knew why Julie despised him. He began to despise him, too. The ser-

34

geant said, "Still, you're a responsible ship's master. And you'll soon be gone. Just don't talk about it."

"Who do I have to talk to? Kanaka Tom?"

The sergeant twisted to stare out of the window: at the unobtrusive naval vessels, far out beyond the atoll, that seemed to shun the island like lepers. There might have been no life on board; only a faint smoke hazed the stacks. It struck the Captain that he hadn't seen an officer, not a single enlisted man, come ashore. Strange. Maybe the island had nothing to offer. Only the fetid beauty of the Pacific and a few brown "sleeping girls." The sergeant said, "They are SPUD."

It took the Captain a few moments to realize that he was referring alphabetically to something more important than a vegetable.

"South Pacific Union for Defence," the sergeant said.

"Oh, that. Stop throwing military shorthand at me," the Captain said. "What are they up to?"

"The *chef de douane* only hinted at it. It's top security. He was very discreet." The Captain wondered how the *chef de douane* knew about it if it was so top secure. "He had to go aboard the Filipino ship and you know how they talk. They're going to establish a rocket base. Maybe something even more frightful," and the sergeant expanded his fingers significantly to make the familiar nuclear mushroom shape.

"Not *here?*"

"God forbid. There'd be a revolution. No. They've just pulled in to repair an engine. They're going a long way south. The farther south the better. We'll all sleep better in our beds when they've gone."

"It's an affront to civilization."

"The whole shape of civilization is an affront. We should be glad we live off the beaten track," the sergeant said. "Let the world blow itself to pieces if it wants to. So long as we survive. We must keep our noses clean, not make too much noise

35 S 1252984

to attract attention, and hope nobody takes any notice of us in our little island paradise." True, the Captain thought. This jaundiced fool occasionally talks sense. Then it occurred to him that the fleet would soon be approaching another island that was also off the beaten track: it probably kept its nose clean, too, but it wasn't going to be spared the visitation. "That is why I run a tight, well-ordered little community," the sergeant said, "everything just so and ship-shape. No trouble-making allowed."

And that reminded the Captain. "I did come to see you about something. There *is* a man in the hold of Captain Malaise's ship."

The sergeant looked at him opaquely, then began to make meaningless scrawls on his pad as if he were busy.

"I told you . . ."

"I heard you," said the sergeant. "So what?"

"You mean you *knew*?"

"Of course I knew. I heard the rumour before your ship pulled in. I went to see Captain Malaise about it and he admitted every word."

Captain van Eyck said with bewilderment, "But you told me it was nonsense."

"In the hope you would accept it as nonsense. If you will forgive me, Captain, you have an interfering feminine mind."

"Interfering" wouldn't have annoyed the Captain; but "feminine" did. "What are you going to do about it?"

"Nothing."

"A man rots down in that ship and you're going to do nothing?"

"That's right."

"You have to do something."

"Who says so?"

"As a matter of humanity . . ."

"I'm a police officer, not a humanist. If I concerned myself every time a ship's master had a little disciplinary trouble I'd have no time for my own affairs," said the sergeant, staring hard at the Captain as if he wished he'd take the hint and go. The hell with you, thought the Captain. Try and shift me. I weigh more than the *Heinrich van Reyn*. "Anyway," the sergeant went on carelessly, "I happen to know the man's history."

"What's that got to do with it?"

"A lot. I do not wish him to land."

The Captain said, "Why not?" thinking, this isn't my affair: I mustn't get involved.

"He is a mercenary." The Captain opened his mouth to say, "I'm getting tired of that word," but the sergeant interrupted him coldly. "A professional soldier. A hired man, I've met his kind before. The army is his mother, and when the army no longer needs him he's left without roots. Without human loyalties. That type breeds trouble." The sergeant seemed to have every kind of trouble on his mind. "He trades in blood. There is no blood on this island, nor likely to be, and if he wants to find some let him go and look for it somewhere else."

"Has he done something wrong?"

"Not that I know of. Or even care."

"It seems a little hard."

"Does it? Well, there's another reason." The Captain thought there was. "If I once let him land I might never get him off."

"How's that?"

"He was with *la légion étrangère*. In its mistaken wisdom," the sergeant said with his pale foxy smile, "our *patrie* grants its enlisted children rights of citizenship. He fought in Algeria. He was one of the maniacs they dropped on Dien-Bien-Phu. And not even a Frenchman. Can you understand that?" The sergeant couldn't. "Not out of patriotism. Not for love of his native land. The *Rossignol* leaves tomorrow. Let it take him with it. We'll all be spared a headache."

"Since when is a human being a headache?"

"Captain, I am so busy. Stop talking like Jesus Christ."

The Captain had ten expressions on his tongue, all rancid, but none of them would have affected the sergeant's acid-proof hide. He got up. "Do you know his name?" he asked.

"A man enters the *légion* with no name, no past, and no predictable future." The sergeant made some more meaningless scrawls on his pad to hurry the Captain off. "I'm not an inquiry bureau. Any more questions?"

"Yes. What'll happen to him?"

"How should I know?" Meaning: why should I care? "He'll probably escape at some other port."

"If Captain Malaise doesn't kill him first."

"*If*," the sergeant admitted the possibility almost pleasantly, another faint smile cracking his face. "Good-bye."

The Captain went out. Julie was still standing in her doorway across the street. He thought, she has my sympathy. To have to sleep with that dehydrated ferret. Maybe she didn't? Women seemed to have got themselves some peculiar rights these days. He went over to her and said, "I'm afraid your husband isn't a very sweet man."

"He is eight parts of an obscenity," she said. She told him in literal French what a hundred per cent obscenity was. Then she looked at him curiously. "What's wrong?"

The Captain told her.

"It is not nice." She turned and stared at the bow of the *Rossignol* at the wharf. "That is no way to treat a man," she said. "What is he like?" A typical woman's question.

The Captain said exasperatedly, "What can that have to do with it?"

"Young?"

"I've never seen him. All I know about him is that he's *roux*."

"Red. That is intriguing." The Captain gave her up. As he started to walk off the question that had been dogging him

**38**

for a long time burst off his tongue. "Why *do* you stand there?"

"Why would you think?"

"Julie, don't force me to tell you what I think."

"I'm waiting for something special to come walking up the street. Something with large shoulders and a humorous smile and an aptitude for the bed."

"And it hasn't come yet?"

"Only some very temporary substitutes," she said.

      ❖      ❖      ❖

The Captain went for his evening meal to a fisherman's café where he wouldn't be likely to meet Captain Malaise. The sky was carpeted (an upside down sort of word) with stars. The dusk scented. Belching happily, he walked back to the wharf. And a very strange thing happened. As he went by the customs-shed a man slipped swiftly out of the shadows. He tried to pass the Captain. But the Captain had recognized the uniform. "Good evening," he said heartily to the American lieutenant.

The lieutenant was young and his blond face wary. His brass gleamed. He tried again to get by the Captain, but the alley was too narrow and the Captain too plump.

"I am a fellow seaman," the Captain said affably, pointing across the harbour to the *Heinrich van Reyn*. It lay like a fat hulk, silhouetted against the last flush of the sun. The American lieutenant looked at it curiously and didn't seem impressed. He tried again to walk round the Captain, but the Captain had hold of his arm.

"Which is your ship?" he asked. We have to be hospitable to these young officers. They are away from their mothers too soon. "The cruiser? Or one of the destroyers?"

The lieutenant looked at him vaguely.

"I have never been aboard one of those modern naval

**39**

vessels," the Captain said. "My dinghy is handy. Perhaps you would like to take me over and show me round?"

This time the lieutenant gave him a very sharp look.

"The equipment of those miraculous monsters," said the Captain, who'd drunk a little too much and felt full of good will. "Radar and everything. It is wonderful. I steer by smelling salt. It all fascinates me. It would be nice to see what it is like."

The lieutenant made rather an odd sound, staring behind, then forward, almost as if to escape, which surprised the Captain.

"Would you join me in a drink?" he asked.

Giving him a queer darting glance, the lieutenant shook his head.

"Shall we sit down somewhere," said the Captain, "and compare notes? Tell me where you have been and where you are going," but he never finished what he was saying for the lieutenant slipped out of his fingers and was gone.

All this security, the Captain thought. It makes them unfriendly. What a pity. It is ruining the comradeship of the sea. And I still don't understand it. Did I say something wrong?

❈          ❈          ❈

He went round the corner of the warehouses and walked, a plump fly, straight into the spiderlike arms of Captain Malaise. "Where did you get to?" Captain Malaise cried. "I looked out for you over dinner."

His breath smelled of liquor, and over his shoulder Captain van Eyck was conscious of the dark twisted shape of the *Rossignol* at the wharf, creaking like an old timber yard. He thought absurdly, I know what that ship is: a witch. That long bowsprit is her broomstick. He tried to get free, but Captain Malaise had his arm hooked. "Come on aboard," he said. "Let's make it a celebration. How about that little game of cards?"

"Some other time."

"What other time? This is my last night."

"There's no one on watch in the *Heinrich van Reyn* . . ."

"You think anybody'd want to steal it?" Captain Malaise laughed. He couldn't even utter a pleasantry without being insulting. His thick hands were very compulsive; Captain van Eyck wanted terribly not to go aboard the *Rossignol*, but he was on deck before he could protest. A couple of Polynesians squatted in the well. Captain van Eyck was aware of dark eyes watching him, like hostile animals, and a very ancient stench. Captain Malaise led him steeply down to the cabin and lighted a lamp. He brought out a bottle. He said breezily, "Sit down."

The cabin was plastered with pin-ups. Every ship, Captain van Eyck thought, looking at them furtively, has the usual kind of pictorial art stuck about: but this is pornographic. He sat, and though he tried to manoeuvre himself into a position in which he wouldn't have to stare at blatant sexuality, every bulkhead was revolting. "Fun, eh?" Captain Malaise said.

Fun. A lavatory-wall collection of erotica.

"Better than Rembrandt," Captain Malaise said.

He filled two glasses and produced a pack of cards. He became suddenly rather businesslike. He watched Captain van Eyck in a peculiarly speculative way, and the Captain knew exactly what was going through his mind. He's going to fleece me. Down to my shirt. He thinks. Captain van Eyck was the best card-player between Papeete and the China Sea and he felt coldly offended. Like a grandee forced to defend himself against a peasant with his sword. This man is gross. He'll try to get me drunk, and then he will cheat. Well, I've warned him off. But he insists. The Captain said diffidently, "It's been a long time since I played . . ."

41

"Oh, it passes the time."

"That pack is rather filthy." The cards were repellent. Captain van Eyck hadn't time to check whether they'd been pricked at the corners: to correct the vagaries of chance.

Captain Malaise looked surprised. "You're very squeamish."

"Forgive me."

"One doesn't expect ships' masters to be so fussy. It's all right." Captain Malaise broke the seal of another pack. He didn't look very troubled: it was going to be a swift and easy and profitable ride. "Shall we start the pot going?" he said.

"You mean with money?" Now Captain van Eyck managed to look surprised.

Captain Malaise grinned, "It adds spice to a game."

"You think so? Very well." Captain van Eyck said with some *naïveté*, "How much, then? A dollar a point?"

It was rather a lot, and Captain Malaise was momentarily startled, then he laughed, "I don't mind." Captain van Eyck could almost hear the exultant whirr of that tortuous brain. He is obscene. I will take the first game, because he will want me to, so that I will get big-headed, then I will let him have a couple to encourage him, then I will take the rest. He will start to cheat, of course, after the third and I will have to stomach my revulsion and watch it, and correct his finagling by perhaps cheating a little myself. You cannot play a rogue fish with gold-plated hooks.

And that was how it went. After three games Captain Malaise became red-faced and churlish; then sweaty; the cheating began as Captain van Eyck had anticipated, after the third, and it became so flagrant after a while, that Captain van Eyck had to protest reproachfully, "Captain, you are dealing from the bottom of the pack," and Captain Malaise looked at him like a baffled beast, watching the money sliding magnetically over to Captain van Eyck's side. He said once, in a savage burst, as if it were a breach of the rules, "You're not drinking."

"It inflames the lining of my stomach."

"—the lining of your stomach."

Captain van Eyck made it very surgical after that, and suddenly Captain Malaise had no more money. Two hundred and eighty dollars lay in Captain van Eyck's lap.

*       *       *

Captain Malaise said heavily, "You know what I think? You cheated."

"What are you suggesting?" Captain van Eyck hadn't had to steer the cards in their legal direction more than twice.

"I don't understand it."

"Who understands luck?"

"You'll have to give me my revenge."

"Now?"

"I have no ready cash. I'll write out an IOU."

"Next time we meet, Captain."

"I'm sailing tomorrow. How do I know when we'll meet again?"

"How do I know when I'll get my money?"

"You Dutch crook."

Captain van Eyck said, "If you're going to be offensive," and half rose to go. Suddenly he knew what had made him play; he hadn't let the real reason rise above the surface of his mind. He said softly, "Perhaps you have some security to put up?"

"Such as what?"

"Suggest something."

"You should trust me."

"We're travelling to opposite ends of the Pacific. Trust isn't a thing you can stretch over three thousand miles," Captain van Eyck said. And he waited.

Captain Malaise couldn't take his eyes off the money. He said, "Are you short of deck-hands?"

43

"Who isn't?"

"I'll put up one of my Polynesians."

"I've seen them. Dissolute bums."

"I trained them personally."

Captain van Eyck stopped himself saying, "That was what I meant." He said instead, "But I might take a chance on the one you have below."

Now he waited even longer. The sour malignant eyes became shrewd. Captain Malaise said, "The red one? Why would you want him?"

"Why would you?"

"How much would he count for?"

"What did you invest in him? Two hundred dollars."

"I have sweated out my guts instilling a little respect for authority in that man," Captain Malaise said. "It should count for another forty."

This chaffering is disgusting: it smells of an Arabian bazaar, Captain van Eyck thought. "All right. Two hundred and forty," he said. It doesn't make any difference, anyway. It'll all come back. "But I'd want to see him first."

"What for? I assure you he's all in one piece."

"I'd have to be sure."

"I don't mind. Who cares?" Captain Malaise took down one of the lamps and lighted it. He warned Captain van Eyck ironically, "It's a little smelly down there. After all, you're such a fastidious man."

He led the way on deck, rousing one of his personally-trained Polynesians—they fell asleep very easily—with a kick, shouting to him to remove the hatch. They went down into the hold. The dark wooden cavern made Captain van Eyck instantly uneasy: this isn't like an iron ship at all, he thought. He could hear the whispered conversation between the *Rossignol* and the evening tide; the gurgle of water and the pistol-cracking of planks. They went forward, Captain Malaise lighting the way with his lamp. They entered the for-

44

ward hold and Captain van Eyck recoiled from an ammoniac wall: a latrine smell. It would have taken very little to make him go back. Captain Malaise said simply, "Human beings aren't very sweet." He let the lamp shine ahead and Captain van Eyck saw a man resting on a straw palliasse. He might have been asleep; but his eyes, thinned against the lamp, glinted. He was quite still. A jug of water lay at his side, and as Captain van Eyck's eyes became accustomed to the gloom he saw with incredulity—and shock—the thin chain that ran from the man's elbow to a staple high up near the porthole, then down to his ankle. I have walked into an old horrible century, he thought.

"He isn't very talkative," Captain Malaise said. "You don't want to give them too much nourishment in port. It only fills them full of blood."

What *am* I doing here? Captain van Eyck thought. I am ashamed.

"I come down some nights to keep him company. And we have some pleasant chats," Captain Malaise said.

The man watched him. The mad excruciated face frightened Captain van Eyck.

"Mind you, it's all on one note. He says he will kill me," Captain Malaise said. "He's very ungrateful. I saved him from a Viet labour camp and those are the thanks I get."

I won't be able to stand this stench much longer, Captain van Eyck thought.

"Well, you've seen him. He's able-bodied," Captain Malaise said.

"I want to talk to him," Captain van Eyck said.

"Talk, I don't mind."

"You inhibit the conversation."

"I what?"

"I don't like you standing behind me like a jailer. Go away."

Captain Malaise hesitated. "It's still a bargain?"

"Yes. Go away," Captain van Eyck said.

45

Captain Malaise walked back a little way and waited with the lamp.

Captain van Eyck said softly to the man on the palliasse, "I would like to help you."

He *wasn't* very talkative. Only the chain sounded.

"Please," Captain van Eyck said.

Then the man spoke. "What did he mean? Bargain?"

"Nothing. How long you been here?"

"Four days."

Captain van Eyck flinched. "However did you come to this dreadful state?"

"Didn't he tell you? He bought me in Nam-Dinh."

"Yes."

"For a hundred dollars."

"What a liar he is. He told me two hundred."

"I *will* kill him," the man said.

"It isn't safe. Don't let him hear you."

"He knows it." The man watched Captain Malaise, straining to hear, back there with the lamp. "If he doesn't kill me first I'm going to kill him." Was this the kind of conversation they held in the still of the night? "If I had only a minute to live and make my peace with God he knows what I'd do with it. I'd kill him," the man said.

Captain Malaise heard it and shouted, "Have you finished? You're talking too much."

"Will you be patient a little longer?" Captain van Eyck said to the man.

"Why?" He could still be sarcastic. "What are you going to do? Call out the *Garde Nationale?*"

"Just be patient."

"What else can I be?" The man let the chain rattle. It was like holding a conversation with a dangerous animal. As Captain van Eyck moved he said, "Would you do me a kindness? Leave me a cigar."

"Of course."

46

"Don't let him see. He'll take it away. And some matches."

Captain van Eyck slipped a cigar and a paper packet of matches surreptitiously under the straw. "It won't be long."

The man laughed, "Not long here is for ever," and Captain van Eyck went. He shoved past Captain Malaise and climbed up on deck.

Captain Malaise said, "You won't have any trouble. Don't let him worry you. He's been in the army long enough to accept discipline." They went back to the cabin. Captain van Eyck gave him two hundred and forty dollars. "Now I'll have my revenge," Captain Malaise said.

Captain van Eyck looked at him coldly. He didn't think it necessary to dissimulate any longer. He shuffled the pack like a master, concertinaing them magically, and dealt the cards with such deftness that they rippled like quicksilver from his hands. It gave him enormous pleasure to see Captain Malaise's jaw drop. He wasted no time. Within thirty-five minutes all the money was back in his pot.

＊    ＊    ＊

Captain Malaise said in a thick voice, "I see it. I have been taken for a ride."

"Is that another unpleasant suggestion?"

"They have a name for you in America. A hustler."

"Whatever that means. I played fair," Captain van Eyck said. He put away the money.

Captain Malaise's eyes followed it as a ferret follows a fox to its hole. "I'll send him across to you in the morning," he said.

"No. Turn him loose."

"You said what?" Captain Malaise seemed to hear this from a very long way.

"I'll be over early. I want to see him walk off along that wharf."

**47**

Again puzzled, "Wouldn't that be a great waste?"

"Perhaps to you."

"Well, he's yours. You won him. Whatever you say."

Captain van Eyck wanted only to get off the *Rossignol;* this ship besmirched him. "When are you sailing?"

"With the evening tide," Captain Malaise said.

Captain van Eyck said, "Well, then. Till the morning," and made some kind of perfunctory farewell and went. He rowed himself back to the *Heinrich van Reyn.*

Last night had been a disturbed one, with those very bad dreams. He went to bed early. He lay in his bunk, reading the Bible, lingering with satisfaction over those texts, "Remember the afflicted in their time of need" and "Charity covereth a multitude of sins." He dropped off with an almost holy glow.

But the night was as disturbed as the last. Again that nameless dream: of the gull frantically beating its beak against his porthole, bearing the face of a man, begging behind the glass, and finally that lost sad cry. The Captain woke in a flurry of sweat. It was growing light. He thought sullenly, Kanaka Tom and China Tom have probably slept well after a night of debauchery: why am I persecuted like this?

He showered and dragged on a robe and went up to the coolness of the deck.

The dawn theatrical as always, the sky mad with colour, the faintest breeze stirring the fronds of the palms, and those terribly reminiscent gulls screeching for food. They were circling the *Rossignol.* The Captain's eyes were dull from lack of sleep and the gulls drowned the putter of the *Rossignol's* auxiliary engine—he didn't immediately see the ship slipping away from the wharf. He thought with bewilderment: but I told him I would be over early. And next: he said he would be sailing with the evening tide. Then he understood.

He saw through his binoculars Captain Malaise bustling about the deck, and knew that he was departing like a thief in the night—the dawn, then—and began to shout at the top

48

of his voice. But the gulls drowned him, too. His Papuans came up blearily to see what was wrong, and Captain van Eyck stood there, vulnerable and ludicrous in his thin robe, a slipper lost, beating hopelessly at the rail, watching the *Rossignol* tack about the harbour and her canvas go up.

# 3

May she sink before she clears the reef, he thought: but you
didn't curse a ship, even one as corrupt as the *Rossignol*. And
she carried an afflicted man. Captain van Eyck felt suffo-
cated with futility. His knuckles hurt from banging the rail,
and his Papuans were looking at him as if he were mad—he
was, quite mad—he was screaming at an empty wharf and a
silent beach touched with long shadows by the sun. But his
voice had carried across to the *Rossignol*. Through the binoculars, his hands shaking, he saw Captain Malaise turn and
stare towards him and grin. Where *was* God? At early breakfast? He should be watching.

Through the fringe of the lens he saw Kanaka Tom and
China Tom squatting on the wharf. They must have returned
during the night and found no dinghy: and slept where they'd
dropped. They were staring curiously at their Captain. He
put on his slipper and motioned to the dinghy for someone
to fetch them.

One of the Papuans found his tongue. "Something is
wrong?"

"Yes. That ship is leaving."

"Let it. It stinks."

"There is a man on it."

"Many men."

"You don't understand. Be quiet."

The *Rossignol* had tacked about, her crooked bowsprit almost pointing at the gap in the reef, a light haze about her puttering auxiliary; there wasn't enough wind to flap the heavy canvas.

Kanaka Tom and China Tom came aboard. "What's upset you?" China Tom asked.

The Captain pointed across to the *Rossignol.* "They're clearing off."

"I am not blind, Captain."

"You know who's on it."

"Oh, him. The story's true, then?"

"Yes, it's true."

"Why should you care? What makes him your business?"

"I"—the Captain was about to say, "won him," but it seemed distasteful—"I redeemed him," he said.

Kanaka Tom looked at him sidelong. "Like Jesus Christ?" he asked.

"Hold your blasphemous tongue, barbarian," the Captain said.

And then Captain van Eyck felt a cold dramatic shiver: almost he persuaded himself that there was something biblically miraculous about what happened next. Spectacular and deeply fulfilling and right-to-the-instant timed. The *Rossignol* slid by the *Heinrich,* the auxiliary hacking obscenely, and the Captain watched her with hate. Because of the racket of the engine he wasn't immediately aware of the sudden hubbub that broke out on deck. Then he saw the native crew running. Heard them shouting. Smoke, as black as sin, was oozing from somewhere forward, and Captain Malaise turned and stared at it vacantly, then roared. The crew dragged off the bow hatch, recoiling from the great belch that literally exploded from the hold. The engine stopped. And the *Ros-*

51

*signol* lost way. Captain van Eyck watched a thin lick of yellow-grey flame poke up like a released devil, saw the bow porthole gleam with fire. His first shocked thought was: that old wooden hulk will burn like tinder. And then: serve her right. And next, with horror: but there is a man chained down there.

And finally, with understanding: *he* did it. He must be mad. To immolate himself. It burst out of him, "I'm responsible for that."

China Tom gave him a strange look. "You are?"

"He asked for a cigar. Matches. He has set the ship alight."

China Tom said softly, "I'd do the same."

"You'd have to be insane."

"Yes, with despair," China Tom said.

"That animal"—meaning Captain Malaise—"will let him fry."

"He daren't. We know the man is down there. So does the *gendarme*. You'll see. He'll have to pull him out."

And, in fact, it was happening as China Tom spoke. The *Rossignol* lay in the glassy lagoon, her canvas pink with the glow that was crawling out of the hold. A tall plume of smoke rose as straight as a pencil into the windless air. And there was suddenly life on shore. Captain van Eyck could see the street behind the warehouses, windows opening and people running, the wharf lined with the *petit bourgeoise* of the town, the shopkeepers clutching their pants, the women their robes. His hands still trembling, the Captain saw the police sergeant among the crowd. He heard Captain Malaise bellowing thunderously. He was beckoning; the black crew was reluctant; he had to shove them. Two of the natives dropped into the hold and presently the Captain saw the glass of the bow porthole smash and thought: they couldn't have done a worse thing. The draught will fan fire along the whole hulk. That was what it did. Flames blew out of the hold, and it

52

was exactly as if their explosive force popped the crew out of the hatch like corks.

They emerged hopping with pain. But carrying something.

They dropped it, charred and smoking, and the Captain, his eyes glued magnetically to the binoculars, saw a man rolling over and over on deck. His shirt burning. I will be ill, he thought: I cannot bear to watch. But he went on watching. One of the crew flung a bucket of water over the man. Then another. And Captain Malaise kicked him. Screaming. The man lay quite still, and Captain van Eyck thought: this is the ultimate in horror. Is this how God makes miracles?

He heard Kanaka Tom say with pleasurable excitement, "Holy Joseph, just look at that."

"The man is dead."

"No, he isn't."

"You're sure?" The Captain was no longer watching.

"Pretty sure."

"Anyway, suffering."

"Well, maybe that," admitted Kanaka Tom.

The *Rossignol* was drifting over to the wharf, where the island's obsolescent fire-tender waited. One of the sails had ignited. The flame swallowed it like tissue. Then the Captain heard a busy efficient purr and saw a fire-float from the navy out beyond the reef—he'd almost forgotten its existence— come slipping swiftly across the lagoon, its jets squirting; it circled the *Rossignol* for a strategic position and doused the bow. The fire retreated. The smoke became vile. And through the fumes Captain van Eyck saw Captain Malaise still kicking the man who lay smouldering softly on the deck.

And he thought then: this is the *real* miracle. For the man rose. Captain Malaise watched him deliberately, with an animal's anticipation, and then plunged at him bull-like (that was the kind of animal he was, a bull), and the man with the burned shirt embraced him—actually embraced him—and chopped him down. One of those pseudo-scientific gestures: locked hands and a clinical swipe over the neck. Captain Malaise, looking amazed, sat on the deck. He got up. The man kneed him as he came. Then struck him, the natives watching passively (not a very loyal crew) while he held Captain Malaise against the mast. He began like a trained butcher —was gladiator a better and crueller word?—to maul him. The army teaches men the refined savagery of the Roman ring, Captain van Eyck thought. The jets from the fire-float sprayed them impartially, and they stood there messily, wallowing in water, one propped against the mast, the other working on him insanely; Captain van Eyck fancied he could hear—he couldn't really catch anything above the hiss of the jets—Captain Malaise's anguished croaks and his executioner's vengeful pants.

He wondered how an underfed and exhausted man could do it. There are great reserves of strength in hate, he thought.

It was nearly all smoke now. The *Rossignol* hit the wharf while her Captain was being destroyed. The island's hoses took over. The naval fire-float sped indifferently back across the lagoon, as if a small piece of business had been well done, and Captain van Eyck saw now that it flew the Pakistani flag.

He waved to the dark-skinned officer at the wheel who woodenly ignored him. How terribly secretive they are, the Captain thought.

The *Rossignol* lay at the wharf, bow heavy; the hoses from the jetty merely poured more water into her swilling belly and Captain van Eyck felt: they'll sink her if they don't stop. The fire was out. But she will never be the same ship. He was wet with perspiration. He could see Captain Malaise humped on the deck, the red-haired one stamping on him ruthlessly—and then exhaustion took the man: he simply folded up as if caught irresistibly by sleep.

China Tom gave the long sigh of the entranced spectator. "Well, there's still some justice in this world."

54

"It was too frightful."

"Not to me," China Tom said.

The Captain didn't want to demean himself in front of his Papuans. He went to the other side of the ship to be sick.

When he came back there was only an oily blur in the sky; the sun was mounting swiftly, and most of the crowd on the wharf had gone. Now the police sergeant intervened. He went on board the *Rossignol* with two native *gendarmes* who'd just arrived. He stared for a few moments at the red one buckled up in the thwart—rather malevolently, Captain van Eyck thought—then bent over Captain Malaise. Seen through the binoculars he was like something bloody abandoned in a knacker's yard. Captain van Eyck wondered if he was dead. But after a while he saw Captain Malaise stir. The police sergeant spoke to him. He beckoned peremptorily to the native gendarmes.

A launch had come round and they dropped something sacklike into it. Captain van Eyck guessed what it was. Then the launch came puttering straight across to the *Heinrich van Reyn* and the Captain thought with alarm: why are they coming here? What has it got to do with me?

*　　*　　*

The police sergeant came on deck like a small baleful snake. He stared at the Captain, teetering up and down on his toes, and the Captain—who had begun suddenly to dislike him—thought: I know why he does that. He's trying to make himself sexually taller. Julie's too big for him.

The police sergeant said bitterly, "So you had to interfere."

"I don't know what you're talking about."

"Didn't I warn you to let well alone?"

"You have no right to . . ."

"Shut up. I am very angry."

So am I, thought the Captain. (He didn't want to look over

55

the side to see what was in the launch.) And rather frightened, too.

The police sergeant shouted down to the native gendarmes in the launch without consulting the Captain, "Fetch him up," and they came over the side, still lugging the man sackwise, and dumped him diffidently on deck. The Captain still didn't want to look at him. His first revolted and unChristian thought was, he reeks like a gutted factory. He was afraid to open his mouth. Then he heard China Tom's shocked hiss. The after-dawn sun was as cruel as a gold scalpel and out of the corners of his eyes—very reluctantly—he saw three things. Red hair that seemed to have become doubly incandescent from the fire: areas of charred shirt and blistered flesh: and bloodied knuckles. (My God, what had they done to Captain Malaise?) Kanaka Tom, who wasn't the most delicate of human beings, drew away. And the Captain didn't want to see any more.

He said in a manufactured huff to the police sergeant, "What have you brought him here for?"

"He has nearly killed Captain Malaise."

"Is that my fault?"

"Yes, since you ask me, it is. You had to stick your nose in. Now keep him. He's yours."

China Tom was listening intently. He gave Captain van Eyck a very peculiar look.

"I don't want him."

"You should have thought of that before."

"Get him off my ship."

"Malaise told me. You played for him. And won him. That is why I am telling you: take him. He is yours."

The red-haired one, slumped like a disowned bag on the deck, was listening also. No muscle had moved in him. But his eyes were very bright and angry. And they were fixed on Captain van Eyck.

56

The Captain said, strangled with discomfort and a false sense of outrage, "It was only so that he should have his freedom . . ."

The police sergeant said sarcastically, "You expect me to believe that?"

"Why shouldn't you?"

"He's a valuable piece of labour."

"I am not a slaver."

"It isn't the story I got from Captain Malaise."

"Then he's a liar. I told him he was to let the man walk off along that wharf . . ."

"After I warned you?" the police sergeant shouted autocratically. "*I* told you he wasn't to land."

Whichever way you act, the Captain thought, charity always rebounds in your face like a ball. Next time I'll pass the unfortunate on the other side of the street. He stared helplessly at the police sergeant, thinking: I'm going to hate this little monster for the rest of my life.

The red head was still bent in the Captain's direction, and he thought: he makes me nervous. I wish he would look somewhere else.

"What do you want me to do?"

"Keep him."

"I can't use him."

"Neither can this law-abiding community. He's a dangerous animal." (Oh, come, the Captain pouted. Maltreated, yes. Afflicted. But dangerous? The Captain felt the prick of the man's bitter eyes, fixed on him unswervingly, and thought suddenly, perhaps he is.) "Was it necessary to warn you twice over? I know his history," the police sergeant said. And again, trying sexually to increase himself, up and down on his toes. "These rootless soldiers. Always trouble. A mercenary." (Oh, that *word!*) "We don't have to accept the le-

57

gion's discarded human refuse." The red-haired man was so still that the Captain, on edge for his every movement, thought he couldn't have heard. "You won him . . ."

"No, no," protested the Captain. What *is* the use of Christian kindness?

"So take him. I don't intend to let him land."

"Take him where?"

"Anywhere. Drop him overboard if you want."

"You cannot force me."

"No," the police sergeant said with soft ferocity. "But I'll tell you what I *can* do." He was like a small inhibited rodent, and the Captain almost burst out, damn Julie. Why doesn't she keep him happy? Everybody has to suffer because he's deprived. "Captain Malaise has been criminally assaulted. I can hold you as a material witness. If necessary for six months. Clap a restraint warrant on your ship. Life moves slowly in these islands . . ."

"It would ruin me." The Captain was appalled.

"It would be serving justice."

"—justice."

"Is that a nice thing to say to a conscientious police officer?"

"I'm due in Christ's Island in a week."

"They will miss you," the police sergeant said.

"All right. Leave him here." The Captain stared malevolently at the man. "Let him rot." The eyes were still watching him, without kindness: but the police sergeant had put him in a flurry of panic, and he no longer cared. "I'll get rid of him somewhere."

"I knew your discretion would get the better of you," the police sergeant grinned. "Where do you want him put?"

The Captain glanced at China Tom, who shrugged slightly as if to say: not with me. Kanaka Tom wrinkled his nose at the man on the deck and pretended not to be there. No charity anywhere. "Put him down in the galley," the Captain said.

The police sergeant motioned to the native gendarmes and they went forward to pick him up. It all happened so quickly that afterwards the Captain couldn't quite sort out the sequence of events. The man let himself be lifted: then stamped on the gendarmes' bare feet and drew them together and knocked their heads. Those bushy Stone Age skulls, of course, could feel no pain; but a wise instinct told them it was better to sit down and pretend to be dazed. The police sergeant cried, "Stop him," as the man rose, and the red hair burned, and in that instant of fright the police sergeant must have wished that discretion had got the better of him, too. The man said to him wryly, "The Legion's discarded human refuse. I nearly died three times for *la belle France*," and clapped the *kepi* down over his ears, and yanked his tunic over his head so that for a moment the police sergeant seemed to be enfolded in a sack: then simply threw him into the sea. The Captain had never seen such practised violence. The man was looking at him and the Captain thought with a mental croak: now me. He blurted out defensively the first triviality that came to his tongue, "I gave you a cigar." The man stopped and the corners of his mouth twisted. He went over the side and the Captain saw him striking out for the shore.

They fished out the police sergeant. He stood dripping on deck, shrunken, and the Captain—curiously hysterical—thought: how Julie would laugh. They watched the man swimming to the shore. The police sergeant beckoned wetly to the launch, but it was too late; they saw the man reach the sand and run through the palms.

"He can't go anywhere," the police sergeant said. He was smaller than ever, but more malignant, and he looked about for his *kepi*, but it floated in the sea. "Nobody will hide him.

Nobody will feed him. Not even the natives. They know better. In the end I'll have him," and the gendarmes got up, still pretending to be dizzy, and the Captain thought: I wouldn't be in their shoes for anything. But, of course, they wore no shoes.

❀    ❀    ❀

The Captain was surprised that by midday they hadn't picked the man up. The police sergeant was right; no native would harbour him. The Captain stared at the island, sweltering in the hard glamorous sunshine—this is the Max Factor quality of light—thinking: where can he run? The hinterland was raw jungle. Behind that ravines and dry scrub. Hunger will defeat him. The Captain still trembled from the morning's shock and he said to China Tom, "I'm glad we're not saddled with him. It would be too terrible. He is a very violent man."

But even as he spoke he knew it was a rather prim and unfortunate remark.

China Tom gave a hollow grin, pursing his lips. What right has this little yellow man to disapprove of me? the Captain thought. Kanaka Tom went to the side for one of his obvious acts of nature. It was his way of showing disapproval.

Having said what he'd said the Captain had to go on. "You saw what he did to the police sergeant."

"I was very happy to observe it," China Tom said.

"We have to respect authority . . ."

"Captain, forgive me, you are making me slightly sick."

"Is that the way to address me?"

"I was minding my own Chinese business. I would rather not address you at all."

"Because I oppose violence?"

China Tom said softly, "Every man has his frontier of

60

violence. It is easy to push him across it. You just have to threaten him hard enough."

Oriental imagery. The Captain sniffed.

"I dislike his trade. He is a professional soldier."

"You would prefer amateur soldiers?"

"You are being deliberately obtuse . . ."

"Who made his trade for him? People. Like you and me. We demand to be defended."

"There is no war on . . ."

"So it is safe to assume the halo of peace. To despise him. And when tyranny approaches you cry out for him again."

"I have nothing more to say to you."

"Thank you for your kindness," China Tom said.

Kanaka Tom came back from the side. "I have something to say, Captain. You are a . . ." and the Captain rose, pretending not to hear the expression. ("Fat hypocrite.") Why lose dignity getting involved with that Melanesian primitive? I would discharge him if labour weren't so scarce.

As dusk fell the Captain went ashore. One of his Papuans had told him that they still hadn't picked the man up. Now I *am* worried for him: he has been buried down in that ship on hunger rations. He can actually starve.

The *Rossignol* stank at the wharf. The charred bow, the smashed glass of the porthole, the dribble of water still percolating from her seams: it will need more than water to wash away that evil ship's sins. Nobody was on her. The Captain walked on to the bistro and saw Captain Malaise at a table. He no longer frightens me. He went inside.

He ordered a beer and sat down by Captain Malaise. He was shocked by the ravaged face. The eyes that peered at him with cold enmity were puffed; blackened; the lips split. He will buy no more cheap labour in Vietnam, Captain van Eyck thought. He stared uneasily at the Captain's bound knuckles, and Captain Malaise said, "He has broken my hand."

61

"Yes." Nothing excused it. China Tom should see it. *This* was violence.

"He will pay for it."

"No doubt," Captain van Eyck said.

"It was unprovoked."

He cannot really mean that seriously, Captain van Eyck thought.

"Does it please you?"

"*Me?*" said Captain van Eyck. "What are you talking about?"

"You are to blame."

(He knows about the cigar? The matches?)

"I wish I had never met you. You and your false ideas of humanity. You are a disaster. Everything was all right until you appeared," Captain Malaise said. "I should not have played with you."

I catch it from all sides, Captain van Eyck thought.

The sullen swollen eyes watched him. "Now will you do me a favour?"

"If it's possible."

"— off."

"Willingly."

"If he hadn't stamped on my legs I would kick that fat malodorous Dutch arse for you," Captain Malaise said.

Any moment he's going to get abusive; I'd better go, Captain van Eyck thought. He left the froth of his beer untouched and went.

He was eaten up with curiosity. Where could the man be hiding? Surely they'd found him by now. The Captain walked to the *gendarmerie*. He looked through the window. The police sergeant was out. And as he stood under the quiet palms the sensation stole over him that something else was missing: something about the street was wrong. Julie was no longer standing in her doorway. It was as if a permanent

**62**

fixture, like the statue of a local dignitary, had gone. Perhaps (this made him grin) what she had been waiting for—the large shoulders and the aptitude for the bed—had at last come walking up that street. He went over and knocked on the door. He waited a long time. It seemed that she, too, was out. Suddenly she appeared. She was rather pink and her eyes sparkled and she panted as if she had run a little way. This isn't the same Julie, thought the Captain: that glow of triumph . . . something tells me that she has finally shut her husband out of her bed.

"You, is it?" She kept the door open only a crack.

"I have been knocking a long time. Where were you?"

"In the house. What do you want?"

"Your husband is out. Perhaps you can tell me. Have they picked up that man?"

"What man?"

"The red. You haven't heard about him?"

"Oh, that one. They're out looking for him. With the dogs."

"*Dogs?*" The Captain winced.

"And a posse of shopkeepers. The wild west has come to Safu-Tura." She made to shut the door. "Is there anything else?"

"Julie, I'm worried about him."

"My husband?"

"The man. He hasn't been eating too well. He can lose himself back in the hills: I wouldn't like him to starve."

She laughed. "Don't worry. He's tougher than that."

"How do you know?"

"Oh, it's just a feminine instinct."

"There isn't a man who'll lift a finger on the island to help him."

Again her eyes sparkling. "Then perhaps some woman will."

"Can I come in for a minute?"

"What for?"

"I'm tired. A cup of coffee wouldn't come amiss."

She said demurely, "That wouldn't be nice. I am a married woman."

"You're not usually so formal."

"Tell that to my husband. Here he is."

The police sergeant came trailing down the street, followed at a discreet distance by the two native gendarmes with the dogs. A straggle of the shopkeepers some way behind. They all looked tired. No, they haven't found him, the Captain thought. The police sergeant stared with mixed frustration and exhaustion at Julie and wiped the sweat from his face. "What's amusing you?"

"Have you had some good sport?"

"We'll find him." The police sergeant spat out dust. "Don't worry. He can't get far. The island is small."

"So are you."

"I forbid you to insult me."

"I'm sorry for the poor dogs. They haven't been able to get their teeth into human flesh."

"I'm only doing my duty."

"Hoping to find him alive. There isn't much joy in taking revenge on the dead."

"Bitch."

"Better a bitch than a ball-less sadist."

"Neighbours are listening."

"They all know you're ball-less."

Jojo, the bartender of the Coucou Rouge, was with the crowd. He dragged a shotgun. He gave the Captain an embarrassed grin. "It's a waste of time. My feet are blistered. He must be a long way off by now."

"No," the police sergeant cried. A spasm crossed his face. "I feel it. He's nearer than you think," and the Captain, who happened to be looking at Julie—anything to avoid looking at the police sergeant—saw her eyes glow, and her mouth tighten as if she were afraid to laugh. What is it she reminds me of? A bottomless pool. A man would be mad to plunge in her. What a troubling woman she is.

It hadn't been a very fruitful afternoon. He went back to his ship.

Kanaka Tom and China Tom had gone. Good riddance. I have no communion with those self-indulgent debauched minds, he thought. He could guess where they were. That Chinese lady's salon-of-pleasure, operating blandly over the post office and the laundry, should be closed down. They will be fit for nothing. But he knew they'd come back, eyes shining and refreshed, and he thought: it's all wrong. The Bible says the wages of sin is death. Dusk came. Then the stars. Then the moon, aglare like a lamp, shimmering humorously over the lagoon. He sat listening to his Papuans singing and dancing in the well of the deck—what had *they* to be happy about?—and went lonelily to his virginal bed.

Kanaka Tom and China Tom returned the following afternoon. Looking serene and healthy. Animal glands, the Captain thought. I'm glad we are leaving in the morning: it's time they simmered down. But I have to talk to somebody. I will lose the action of my tongue. He went across to them and said conversationally, "So they still haven't found that man?"

"No," Kanaka Tom said.

"He's in great peril," the Captain said.

China Tom looked at him. Then at Kanaka Tom. He snickered.

Callous, the Captain thought. He said, "It isn't amusing. He's lain out in the hills nearly two days. He's a violent man, but we have to feel for all human beings . . ." and then saw Kanaka Tom's face go sly. The thought occurred to him: they *know*. It broke out of him, "You've heard something?"

"Of course."

"What do you mean, of course?"

65

"Nothing escapes my people. Not a coconut drops off a palm unobserved. They know where he is."

"How can they? He's lying like a beast far off in those hills . . ."

"He's lying not thirty steps from the police sergeant's bedroom," Kanaka Tom said.

The Captain waited: feeling confused and vaguely cheated.

"He's in the shed at the bottom of the garden. He's been there all the time," and Kanaka Tom began to laugh, watching the Captain's face.

"Who is harbouring him? Julie?"

"Of course," Kanaka Tom said.

*     *     *

"Why would she want to do that?"

"Why would you think?"

"She's insatiable. How could a man degrade himself . . ."

"Oh, I don't know. She's a very attractive woman. Better than lying up in the hills." Kanaka Tom's face shone indulgently. "It'd be a double pleasure for him, wouldn't it? To hide out in the sergeant's garden. And be shacked up with his wife."

"Do you have to be so coarse?"

"Must be that Harvard education I missed."

"It's still debasing."

"Not when you feel police dogs snapping at your arse," Kanaka Tom said, still coarse.

The Captain thought, I must be out of date. I believe in the old-fashioned virtues. Honour. Chastity . . . only it occurred to him that enraged dogs showed no special tenderness towards chaste men. I still wouldn't do it. I have my self-respect. The Captain pictured luridly what must have gone on in that shed at the bottom of the garden. He saw

**66**

China Tom watching him keenly . . . He wiped the expression from his face.

"The sergeant will go mad when he finds out."

"He hasn't found out yet," Kanaka Tom said.

And, in fact, he didn't find out until later in the afternoon. The Captain was tempted to walk past the *gendarmerie* with the secret itch of knowledge that at the bottom of the garden behind the house—sexually comforted—the fugitive lay. He went to the Coucou Rouge for his last meal instead. He would now face four days of his Papuan's cooking at sea. Captain Malaise (was he turning the bistro into a hospital ward?) was there with his swollen face and bandaged knuckles and hurt leg. Captain van Eyck sat on a stool at the bar, feeling the stab of enmity in his back. He chatted with Jojo, the bartender, for a while. Presently he saw Jojo's ears prick; he held his hand up for silence and they heard a distant shouting, many many voices, the wild racket of a car engine, and, as it faded, a prolonged human screech that the Captain recognized as the police sergeant's. His stomach went cold: this is it, he thought. They hurried out. Shopkeepers were streaming down the street. Jojo ran towards the *gendarmerie*. The Captain, who wasn't built for running, followed with less haste. He caught up with Jojo in the midst of a gabbling crowd. Jojo said, "They've flushed him out." His eyes shone. "Where do you think he was?"

The Captain grunted non-committally: he didn't need to be told.

"Where is he now?"

"He's made off in Labouche's jeep."

The Captain peered up at the winding road that lost itself in a dirt track that climbed the ravines; Jojo pointed to direct his eyes and the Captain saw a whisk of dust, a jeep spurting ahead of it, rocking, turning bends, as dramatically as a toy; it vanished as he watched into the heat-haze of the hills. A truck shot out from behind the *gendarmerie* and the Captain saw the police sergeant in it, the convulsed staring face, the native constables by his side, and heard the fretful animal yapping in the back. This is not civilized, he thought.

He heard Jojo tell the priest, "He killed one of the dogs. He's lost a lot of blood. How far can he get?"

There was a dry embittered croak like a raven. Captain Malaise had come up. "Kill him," he called after the truck. He stood teetering on his hurt leg. "Kill the bastard. Kill him for me." The puffy discoloured face was as frightful in the harsh sun as a Hallowe'en mask.

"Be quiet." The priest said, shocked, "He is your brother in God."

"Speak for yourself."

"He is hurt."

Captain Malaise said, "But not enough." The mad voice raved after the truck, "Kill the bastard. Kill him for me," but it had long since disappeared. Captain van Eyck went back to the Coucou Rouge. Men hadn't changed much since they came down from the trees.

He waited until dusk. He heard the truck return with a tired grating engine. Lights flashed. There was a lot of excited talking in the street. Presently the police sergeant came in for a drink. He was strangely exalted. The Captain looked at him and the police sergeant said, "He's dead."

The Captain felt his stomach squeeze.

"He went over into a ravine," the police sergeant said. The priest rose with a bitter whisper and went out. "We'll start looking for what's left of him in the morning. When the ants have finished breakfasting off him," the police sergeant said.

The Captain said cynically, "You didn't by any chance throw him over?"

"The dogs did. There was blood all over the place."

"It seems to have made you happy."

"I did my duty."

"With a little personal incentive. It'll look good on your record."

"Since you say so."

"Now you've only to tell Julie."

And the police sergeant's face went pale. He said in a choked voice, "That bitch. I'll settle her once and for all . . ."

"No, you won't," the Captain said. "She carries a long knitting needle in her girdle." (Only a woman could think of such an uncomfortable place.) "She would stab you to death."

"Who told you that?" The police sergeant looked alarmed.

"The men know more about her than you do."

And another spasm crossed the police sergeant's face. "I am her husband."

"Not by performance."

"She will leave me with no reputation."

"You never had any."

"I can't let her go on betraying me . . ."

"You can't stop her, either," and the Captain got up and laughed. "Remember the knitting needle." He looked at the police sergeant's suffused face, thinking: that is for driving a man over a cliff to his death. He felt better. He went back to the *Heinrich van Reyn.*

They would be lifting anchor before first light. He turned in early. But for the third time his sleep was disturbed. That troubling dream—the gull beating its wings against the port-hole, the forlorn cry, and the face of the man pleading through the glass—the Captain rose persecutedly and went on deck. It was that rather religious moment of intense silence: before the birds squawk, when the far rim of the sea is alive with light. Kanaka Tom was whispering with the helmsman. He beckoned. He pointed to a wet pool on the

69

deck and a darker patch by the galley—it was hard to tell the colour of blood in that mixed dazzle, but the Captain knew who had come on board in the night.

*     *     *

"Where is he?"

"In the wheelhouse."

"He will make a terrible mess there."

"Yes."

The Captain had a momentary pang. "He isn't . . . ?" but Kanaka Tom shrugged off his fears; no, he wasn't dead.

"He had that much consideration."

The Captain went into the wheelhouse. The man was asleep in a cramped position in the corner. He opened his eyes instantly: he was as vigilant as a cat. His arm was bound with a blotched strip of his shirt. Blood, the Captain thought with a grimace, makes the angriest of stains.

"What am I to do with you?" he asked.

"You could turn me in."

"What would *you* do?"

"If it were my ship? I'd turn you in."

He probably would. The Captain said angrily, "That's the difference between us. You're taking advantage of my compassion. You know that you are ruthless, and I am not."

The anchor chain rumbled. Lights blinked like eavesdroppers along the dark tongue of the wharf. A launch sputtered hastily across the water. It was only a customs official coming out to collect his *pourboire*. They won't even trust you until the next voyage, the Captain thought.

The man with the red hair said softly, "What will you do if he sees this?" He'd dripped on the steps.

"Tell him I had a nose-bleed." But already the helmsman was swabbing it up. "Stay here." The Captain felt jumpy.

**70**

He had to make a quick decision, irksome to a fat man of sluggish thoughts. "It won't take long to pay him off."

Four hundred new francs. Even in the Pacific, where coconuts fell freely and crabs waited to be roasted, petty bureaucrats had to live. The launch sped back in its phosphorescent foam. The Captain could make out the fringe of palms on the atoll; could hear the gulls rising hungrily with the first riffle of the breeze. It was almost day: it didn't promise to be a very good one. He went back to the wheelhouse.

"Red," he said haltingly—a man had to be called something: he felt impelled to call him Red—"what happened?"

"Does it matter?"

"You're supposed to be dead."

"I've been resurrected." The man listened to the thump of the ship as it turned in the lagoon. Then began in a curiously detached tone to speak. He'd had a good start. Worried because the jeep was low on fuel. Because he couldn't staunch the flow of blood. (He'd killed the dog that slashed him.) There was a bottle of whisky in the jeep and he drank a little and used the rest to douse the wound. He climbed fast on the gravel track that led to the hills. But it petered out to dirt— then to tangled creepers—and he could hear the dogs yapping distantly in the truck. He saw it reeling between the hairpin bends below.

They saw him, too. They released the two remaining dogs; they came belting straight up the slopes, cutting off the loops in the road. He swerved violently to confuse them. He needed speed to hold them off: and what speed could he maintain in those jungled hills? "I felt like one of Nero's Christian martyrs," he said.

"You weren't that innocent."

"Maybe not. Who is?"

"Well, Julie isn't, for instance . . ."

"Oh, her." He laughed. "I fell on velvet. It was nice while it lasted. That's a very healthy woman." He'd evidently been

**71**

able to satisfy her as a very healthy man. His eyes shone reminiscently. "That bastard of hers is no good to her. She needs a man to hold her down."

He was enraging the dogs with his wild jiggling; they couldn't close in. He heard their claws rasping on the open sides of the jeep. He kept the heavy jack-handle in readiness on his lap. They leapt windshield high—one clean over the hood—for a shockingly incongruous moment it reminded him of a well-trained circus act. The track was narrowing like a hardened artery. Of course, he'd been in bad predicaments before—in Algérie, for instance—and though it was a foolish question the Captain asked it: was he frightened?

"Good and sick and frightened," he said.

"I thought soldiers couldn't afford the luxury of fear."

Red said dryly, "Only civilians think that."

He couldn't swerve much longer in that restricted green tunnel: on the other hand he didn't dare stop. He'd have unwanted guests in the jeep. But stop he did, the bonnet ramming a dropped tree.

The Captain thought, poor Red. Maybe there'll always be someone on hand to say, poor Red.

The leading dog launched itself at him over the top. He struck at its hind leg with the jack-handle. It collapsed soddenly into the back of the jeep. He didn't have time to eject it; the other came sneaking in low at the side. Its teeth ripped the sleeve eagerly off his shirt. He saw—with rage—blood gush. Its weight took him right out of the jeep, over to the verge: with one eye he was appalled by the dog's frantic muzzle, with the other by the sheerness of the drop. He'd lost the jack-handle. He seized the bottle of whisky and smashed it on the animal's head. It went on worrying his leg like a zombie in its death-throes: so he jabbed the prongs of the broken bottle into its . . . this, the Captain shrank, is for someone less sensitive to horror to hear.

Red lay flurrying with it. He felt the vegetation yield; the

72

dog fell away from him; he went with it over the ridge, hearing it crash like a lost echo far down. Tumbling himself through undergrowth, slapped from bush to bush—even in pain he had the mercenary's instinct of self-preservation. He came to a stop, buried in greenery, a long way down.

"I don't want to hear any more," the Captain said.

There wasn't much more to hear. The truck arrived at the top. Red could hear the police sergeant's voice. Then the native gendarmes trampling cautiously all over the edge. It was getting dusk. He lay quite still, guessing that they wouldn't want to go too far down. He heard them shout up confidently to the police sergeant ". . . *il est fini*," but he wasn't finished, then ". . . *mort*."

He wasn't quite dead, either.

Presently he saw the truck's lights beam into the sky. Heard it roll off. He lay in his nest, cursing the animal kingdom and the unutterably heartless human race.

The Captain sighed, "You shouldn't have involved me."

"Well, there's still time."

"No." The Captain felt the ship's bow lift as it met the swell. They'd passed through the reef into the open sea.

The dawn flashed. They slid by the navy anchored silently like a sprawled sleeping giant; he was aware of a glimmer of white caps: look-outs on the bridge watching the *Heinrich* go. The Captain thought, good-bye. He tried to sort out the mixed flags of the armada. I'm not sorry to see the last of *you*.

The *Heinrich* rumbled away from the island; the navy faded like a dubious dream; soon there was only a thin forest of spindly masts. The island blurred and vanished. It, too, in its way, had been rather a peculiar dream.

"What am I to do with you?" the Captain asked.

"Drop me. Wherever you're going."

"Kermadec. Calling at Christ's Island on the way."

"Put me off there."

"Anywhere but Christ's Island," the Captain said. "That community is a little too holy for you." Then, not with much hope, "I suppose the idea of payment . . . ?"

"It'd be a bit academic."

"Yes." The Captain sighed again. Goodness always cost money. "Well, you'd better come down to my cabin and let me bind your arm."

❋      ❋      ❋

Four days later they raised Christ's Island at dusk. It was too dangerous to attempt the reef in that light. They anchored outside for the night. The Captain sat on deck, smoking a cigar. He'd had a good dinner. He heard the church bell toll on the island. It was an unexpected sound to come crawling across that dark lagoon. The night was perfect. It had the sensuous feel of a warm plump peach. One of the natives—who gave that bush-topped barbarian a talent for music?—began to play an accordion. Kanaka Tom sang to it in a furry resonant voice. Red listened, eyes shining, flat on his back. China Tom knitted. Knit one, purl two. The Captain nodded dreamily, the cigar dropping to the deck in a spatter of sparks, and his last waking thought was: why is God so good to a sinner like me?

# Part Two

For he on honey-dew hath fed,
And drunk the milk of Paradise.

S. T. COLERIDGE<br>*Kubla Khan*

# 4

The Captain felt his cabin begin to vibrate loosely. Kanaka Tom had just clanged hard on the deck to rouse him. It was very early. They were about to pass through the gap in the reef. Again Kanaka Tom whanged violently on the deck plates. It alarmed the Captain. They were septic with rust: one more like that, he thought, and he'll crack them like eggshell. Hitching his robe about his great belly he went above.

He recoiled from his first view of the *Heinrich:* how unlovely she is. She will not last another five voyages. I hope God sees to it I'm not on her when she falls apart. The lagoon gleamed like old pewter. The sky was about to go mad with the dawn. There was a flickering neon glitter over the horizon. This is the moment that fills me with awe. And as the Captain peered at the trembling palms on the beach the sun lifted its hot rim over them and flashed straight into his eyes.

It was a miraculously theatrical introduction to the island —instantly it lighted up the tall white spire of the church, the wooden school buildings, the hospital, the community hall with its very strange flag: the Captain focused his binoculars on it and saw the golden lamb and the Hebrew hieroglyphics

77

that formed the word "shalom." Peace. My peace I leave with you. Christ's Island. The Captain watched it in a state of mild spiritual excitement, thinking: I may be a foolish sentimental man, but this place refreshes my soul.

He said to Kanaka Tom, "You didn't have to call me to take her in."

"No, Captain."

"I need my eight hours' sleep."

"Of course, Captain." It was hard to separate malice from stupidity in the barbarian's mocking face. "I should have known."

The silence was terribly moving. The birds hadn't yet begun to squawk. Light radiated the island like a halo. The Captain scratched emotionally under his robe. It makes a man feel nearer to God. The ocean heaved frighteningly off into the gloaming; how lost we are in this great vastness, the Captain religiously thought.

China Tom came on deck, rubbing his eyes.

"Are you going ashore?" the Captain asked him.

"What for?" China Tom watched the beach as the ship slipped through the churning reef into the lagoon. "They are a very good people. I am fond of them. But I am not a Christian. I have only a heathen Chinese soul to be saved."

"What about you?" the Captain asked Kanaka Tom.

"I might as well stay here."

"No loose women," said the Captain, staring at him with contempt.

Kanaka Tom laughed. "That's right. Plenty of priests. But no loose women," he said.

Out of the corner of his eye the Captain saw a red head stir under a blanket on the deck and the idiotic thought struck him: it's rusted. But it hadn't rained for nights. Well, he should be grateful for the blanket. Nobody asked him on board. The man got up and filled a bucket from the sea. He washed. Stripped to the waist, as hairy as Esau, but redder.

Then he came over to the Captain and stared curiously at the island. The sun glinted on his coppery unshaven bristles. "What's that?" he asked.

"Christ's Island."

"Why the holy name?"

"It *is* holy."

"Yes?" He wasn't very interested. "It'll be nice to stretch my legs," he said.

"Stretch them here. That isn't the place for you," the Captain said.

Red watched him sidelong. "Why not?"

"Never mind." The Captain felt embarrassed and guilty. "Stay on board. You are not to go ashore," he said.

"I won't corrupt them."

"I don't want to be offensive," said the Captain, "but I wouldn't be too sure of that."

Red continued to watch him sardonically. Then he laughed and went back to his bucket to shave. The Captain drew his robe about his dropped belly (something will have to be done about it, a ship's master shouldn't look perpetually pregnant) and went below to dress.

When he came up Red had gone. He said to China Tom, "Where is he?"

China Tom pointed to the beach.

The Captain looked over the side. The dinghy was still there. He said angrily, "I ordered him not to go. How did he go?"

Kanaka Tom said, "He walked."

Meaning, he swam. The Captain thought, the police sergeant was probably right. This man is a natural rebel. He has lost his only authority: the army. He will be trouble. It was a mistake to let him aboard.

The dinghy deposited him on the warm plushy sand of the beach. There wasn't even a rudimentary wharf; the island was far off the trade routes; the Captain was the community's sole purchasing agent and no ship visited it but the *Heinrich*. Father Leon once told him that months could pass without seeing a blur of smoke on the horizon. They landed stores from the ship across the lagoon by raft. That's the way to keep paradise safe, thought the Captain—it's hard for sin to invade it by raft. Men were a different problem. As the Captain crossed the beach he saw Red lying under the palms. He was naked. His pants and shirt hung drying in the sun. The Captain said with agitation, "Cover yourself up. Somebody will see you."

Red looked at him with surprise. "This is the Pacific."

The Captain wanted to say, no, it isn't, it's more like Jerusalem—but it would have sounded absurd. "Get dressed. You don't understand this place. I don't want you wandering about alone." Red dressed. "You'd better stay with me." The Captain knew then that he was going to regret not having left the man on Safu-Tura. Next time I'll be deaf to the cry of the afflicted. Charity is an unrewarding thing.

They walked through the deep groves of cultivated breadfruit trees, and the long orderly rows of thatched huts came into sight. Beyond them the white steeple of the church. It was deceptive from the ship. It was just a tall shingled finger on four stilts: pointing encouragingly to heaven in the sky. (It *was* there, wasn't it?) The lawns (look at them, clipped as neatly as a Dutch garden!) flamed with vermilion poinciana. The Captain, who'd first brought them from Hawaii, watched them with pride. The sun swept goldenly through the conical sugar-cane-leaf plaited huts. Each with its private latrine: Dr. Edmond was mad about hygiene. Each with its decorative plot of tropical blossoms. To think that natives could be taught to adore order and beauty, the Captain thought. Perhaps that was the great wonder of Christ's Island. That and the miracle of human kindness. To think that these people used to ornament the roof-poles with smoked heads.

They passed the great open refectory: the girls were laying

breakfast. The whole community ate together. Secretly the Captain could never quite get used to such social closeness. A man needs more privacy than he can occasionally get in the latrine.

He watched Red's face. It was inscrutable. I will surprise him yet, the Captain thought.

The island hummed with life. Much of it came from the hospital. There was a bubbling queue of children along the veranda. Dr. Edmond sat at his table, with the kidney dishes and tools of his trade: a vaccination session. The Captain marvelled that the chirruping kids weren't afraid. He hated the sight of a scalpel. They passed the doctor, one by one, rewarded with a lump of sugar, Father Joseph and Belle-Marie, the doctor's daughter, holding them in line. Now *her* he will look at: the Captain saw Red watch her, the lucent half-coloured face, the slim nubile body. They are loveliest at seventeen, the Captain thought. She was the result of the union of Dr. Edmond and some forgotten native woman. Well, that was in the old days. There is more religious order now.

Then Father Joseph saw him and uttered a cry of pleasure. He started forward and Dr. Edmond said, "Stay where you are."

"The Captain is—"

"—here. I'm not blind. He won't stray. So you're back, Captain?" Dr. Edmond said.

"That's right. I'm back."

"It's been four months."

"Papeete isn't exactly round the corner."

"No. Well, it's nice to see you again. What have you fetched?"

"The X-ray gear—"

"Never mind that. What else?"

The Captain protested irritably. "What good is it? You don't have the right electric power."

"Next year we'll be able to afford the generator," Dr. Edmond said. His French accent was still heavy. And he hasn't seen his homeland for twenty-five years, the Captain thought. The doctor murmured, "A little scratch, *petite*," to a black morsel. The quick calm cut of the scalpel: a smear of vaccine. And the child ran off. Red stood diffidently back. He was as out of place as a bum at a shareholders' meeting of the First National Bank. Well, he was warned. He should have stayed aboard. The Captain saw Father Joseph staring at him. Bell-Marie, too. "What about my cigars?" Dr. Edmond asked.

The Captain, who watched the pennies of the community with great care, grumbled, "They're too expensive."

"Did you fetch them?"

"Yes," the Captain said.

"My medicinal supplies?"

Here it comes, thought the Captain. He didn't count brandy as a medicinal supply. He said reluctantly, "Yes."

"How many cases?"

Now he's counting them in cases, not bottles. It was lonely on the island. Brandy was a great comforter. "Twelve," the Captain said.

Dr. Edmond looked at him and grinned. He hadn't shaved. He'd probably slept in his clothes. He was as creased as a bride's forgotten trousseau. He looked like a tired *boulevardier* who hadn't had time to clean up after a dissipated night. It was the hospital that dissipated him: not sex. He looked at Red and said softly to the Captain, "You've brought a guest."

"A guest," the Captain said bitterly, lowering his voice. "On a rest-cruise. Travelling at my expense."

"Don't you want to introduce him?"

"No." Now the Captain didn't bother to soften his voice.

"What's the matter with his arm?"

"A dog did it."

"A *what?*" Father Joseph's mouth puckered.

"A police dog. Before he killed it." They all stared at him strangely and the Captain had to go on—annoyed because he was sure Red was listening—"He isn't a very safe character. I didn't want to let him ashore."

"That arm should be seen to."

"I've seen to it. He won't die." The Captain knew that Red could hear every word. Let him. Truth is truth. Sometimes it has to be proclaimed.

Father Joseph whispered, "Who is he?"

What am I? The devil's advocate? The Captain wearily explained. "He's run out of wars. Business is slow. So I'm stuck with him," he said. "I'm dropping him at Kermadec. He's a very belligerent man," and he saw Red look up, thought he saw him grin ironically, then look away. Well, he's no angel of gentleness. "Don't get involved with him. He isn't your kind," the Captain said.

"You're staying for breakfast?"

The Captain said huffily—guiltily—"I'm glad somebody's asked me," and walked on. Red came behind. He closed up.

He said in a soft voice, "That was a good character build-up you gave me," and the Captain felt slightly nervous. He isn't completely disarmed. He still has those personal weapons: his fists.

"I only told the truth. I'm not your press-agent."

"God help me if you were."

The Captain said, "God help you, anyway." He wouldn't. He had better things to do with His time than waste it on militant vagrants like this.

They'd stopped by the kindergarten; Red stared absently at the careering whirl-about, listening to the bedlam of the kids. What a lot of them there are. Plenty of sex still goes on in those communal huts, the Captain thought. The birds screeched back delightedly from the palms. See-saws rocked. They're the same all the world over, a little noisier perhaps

83

when they're black. The Captain said indulgently, "I'm very fond of children."

Red said to him dryly, "You made some of them?"

"I am not that kind of man."

"Everybody's that kind of man."

And I'm his benefactor. The Captain was offended. Why do I bother with him? The school was next door—but there were no doors, for the sun was the life-giver, only rolled-up rattan screens to let it in—it was Father Ho's class, and the Captain listened to the fluting sing-song voice, watching the warm crinkled dedicated Chinese face. It was the advanced class: civics: they never taught *me* civics, the Captain thought. Father Ho chanted something in French (he chants everything) and Red grinned—he understood French.

The Captain said, "What is it?"

"Voltaire."

"*You*'ve read it?"

"In my less ignorant moments."

"You're too prickly."

Red looked at the Captain's round bulk and said, "Nobody could say that about you."

Father Ho saw them. The peaked eyes were lost in a violent Oriental grin. He grabbed at the skirt of his heavy grey soutane and came hurrying across. He embraced the Captain.

"You're back."

"Does it feel like my ghost?"

"God forbid. It's good to see you."

"Good to see you, too. Father Ho, let go of me. Your class will think you are mad."

"Did you fetch the piano?"

"What do you want a piano for?"

"Did you—?"

"Yes, yes."

"Bless you." The Chinese eyes were in two places at once,

84

on the Captain's flushed face and on Red, hovering sardonically behind. He whispered, "Your friend . . ."

"Nobody said he's my friend."

"Will you not present him?"

"No."

"What is the matter with his arm?"

Not again. The Captain said shortly, "Ask Father Joseph," disengaging himself from the benevolent clutch. He walked on.

Then the old people's garden: the cackling senile crowd: they were playing *boules*, the steel balls thudding in the lava dust. Bones creaked. Hands as mummified as Pharaoh's waved. Provençal translated to the Pacific—the strangest thing of all. A coffee machine hissed under the casuarinas. Red now began to watch with great curiosity.

Say *something*, the Captain thought.

Then the sudden vast glare of the sun, and the coconut plantations. The bent black backs, shielded by straw hats, weeding: the ladders in the banana groves: the echoing chatter from the copra drying-sheds. Now he'll have to say something. The Captain looked at Red. The tidy fields of taro. And breadfruit. All temptations of the devil. They make me fat, the Captain thought. And behind, the beach with its emerald shallows, the fishing canoes sliding like pencils across the mirror of the lagoon; the sun burning out of that blue porcelain sky and the tossing palms; the white churned foam of the barrier reef and the . . . oh, it makes me drunk with beauty. What a great Dutch sentimentalist I am! the Captain thought.

There was a shout from the banana grove and Father Leon, clutching his pruning shears, waved from a ladder and nearly fell off his perch. The Captain caught the drift of his exuberant yell ". . . are you . . . ?" and he echoed back, "I'm fine. How are you?"

". . . something, something . . . God be thanked."

85

This is no way to carry on a conversation. The three fathers were in the queerest sense complementary: melted together, it struck the Captain, they'd just about make the perfect man. Father Joseph's dogged devotion. Father Ho's careful wrinkled wisdom, and Father Leon's firework-banging energy. He was Spanish. The ladder shook. The cry came "Did you fetch the . . . ?" it sounded like "rotary hoer" and the Captain, who hadn't been able to buy it in Tahiti, nodded his head. This isn't the time to tell him. He'll fall off and break his neck.

Father Leon was making inquiring gestures in Red's direction and the Captain thought fretfully, I'm not going to explain him again. Nor apologize for him, either. He pretended not to understand.

Red said, "Why don't you tell him I'm a very unsavoury character?"

"Let him find out for himself."

"Who owns all this?"

"Does somebody have to own it?"

Red said cryptically, "Somebody usually does." He waved back. "It all had to be paid for."

"It was. They have wonderful crops."

"Nigger lucky."

The Captain thought with a flash of temper, he's uneducatable. I give him up. They'd reached the church with the curiously wrought Christ-figure—the cross bowed in a graceful arc so that He seemed to lean down in benediction: there was simply no agony in it at all—and the Captain said sarcastically, "Sam Harakaya made that. Nigger smart." He began to froth up like hot milk. "Nothing will make you understand, will it?"

"Not if you shout."

"You want to know who's the boss here?"

Red said nothing.

86

"He is," up at the cross.

Still nothing.

The Captain felt his tongue running away with him. He said loudly, "They're trying something very old. Something so simple that it's been suspect for two thousand years. They've gone right back to the experiment of the antique Christ." Let him laugh. "Love one another. As simple as that." Red didn't laugh. "They've got behind the jewels and the vestments and the scenery of the religion, they've started off the way it all began." The Captain knew that he was being over-dramatic, that he didn't have the right shape for drama, and standing there in the scorch of the sun a drop of sweat ran ludicrously down his nose. Is God making fun of me, too? He got very excited, "Of course, we know it won't work—men have to have something in it for themselves—but they're a very stubborn people. They go on doing it. Working together, not for gain, healing the sick, caring for the old: for nothing but love." He wiped the sweat off his nose. "You know? There isn't a weapon on the island. The wild pigs come out of the forest and root up their crops and they just trap them in nets and send them back." He muttered, "It's crazy," then looked up at the cross. "Just the same. He'd feel more at home here than in all that Michelangelo stuff at St. Peter's. But I wouldn't expect a man like you to . . ."

"What kind of man?"

"Well, brutalized. Hard . . ."

"That isn't loving one another."

"Laugh if you want. To think that this quiet primitive people . . ."

"Maybe it's only good for quiet primitive people."

He was probably right. The Captain hated him for it. "It's still a wonderful dream."

They were all trooping out of the banana groves for breakfast. Black satin skin under the big straw hats, the white flash of toothy grins. Red said, "They didn't dream it up." You could hear the babble at two kilometres. "Who started it off?"

She sat there in the sun, in the wheel-chair she probably didn't need, waiting for him to come up, that old, old woman, as wrinkled as a dried nut, and the Captain felt, as he felt every time he saw her, the slight pricking of his skin, the goose-pimples of awe. She lifted her stick and beckoned. The Captain wouldn't have dreamed of disobeying. "She did," he said.

      ❀     ❀     ❀

Red sat on a stone by the wayside. The Captain went across. He always let her—like Queen Victoria—speak first. She said, "You're fatter," prodding his belly lightly with her stick.

"I wish everybody didn't tell me."

"You're a very dignified man," she lied blandly. "You can carry it off."

"How are you, Ma?"

She guffawed. "Immortal."

She was, too. There's more than ninety years there, the Captain thought. The eyes still glowed. It was the sun that was cruel to her face. Old Mother Hubbard. Who went to the cupboard to get her dog a bone and found it bare. It wasn't bare any more. The Captain tried to make a mental picture of the young Nurse Hubbard who'd come here—half a century back—gathering them in from the islands to start the leper colony that had become something bigger when the leprosy was wiped out. Maybe too big? It had been almost too big for Him.

Dr. Edmond had arrived later. The three fathers a lot later.

They were trudging up in their grey soutanes. They looked like medieval monks coming in from the fields.

88

The Captain said to her, "If you want to see the ship's tally . . ."

"What's the hurry? You're not going to swindle us, are you? Who is your friend?"

"He isn't."

"Why isn't he?"

"My friend? I choose my company from better circles, thank you."

"How wonderful for you. Who is he?"

The Captain told her. "Let him sit there. An out-of-work soldier. As cold-blooded as a thug. Don't get involved."

She said calmly, "But *you're* involved with him, aren't you?"

"Only as long as it takes to drop him at Kermadec." The three fathers and Dr. Edmond and Belle-Marie had approached. The refectory was filling up.

"Ask him over for breakfast."

"No. He'd probably accept."

"Belle-Marie, don't let this fat Dutch mammoth give us lessons in hospitality."

"Yes, Mother." Belle-Marie went across to Red. He looked at the Captain and grinned. He'd sensed the drift of the conversation. Just to spite me he'll accept, the Captain thought. He did. He got up and came back with Belle-Marie. He stared seriously at Mother Hubbard, and she stared at him, and for a long while neither spoke. Then she said, "You don't look so cold-blooded to me."

"It's one of my sweeter mornings."

"The Captain's insisted you join us for breakfast," she laughed.

"It'd be a pity to disappoint him, wouldn't it?"

"Don't, then."

"Thank you."

"Are you a Catholic?"

"No."

89

"I hope you're hungry," Mother Hubbard said. "Perhaps you would wheel me in."

The Captain thought, isn't that strange? She's never once asked me. Red wheeled the chair into the refectory and Father Leon whispered in the Captain's ear, "You surprise me. You are not usually as hard as that."

The Captain protested, "Hard? Me? I'm the kindest . . ."

"The unfortunate deserve compassion."

"He deserves the compassion you'd show to a wild dog."

"Hush." Father Joseph flinched.

"You don't know him."

"*You* should. He is your brother in God."

My brother. They're mad. The Captain sat at one of the long crowded tables. He was entirely surrounded by natives. He didn't quite like all this social freedom: if God had intended them to be equal He would have made them white. Father Ho said grace. The Captain watched Red listening without interest, the cool intractable eyes surveying his hosts. It means nothing to him: he regards kindness as a sentimental expression of weakness. Then he saw Red watching Belle-Marie. Eyes met. Somebody had better tell her. He has neither morals nor scruples, the Captain thought.

The food was austere. A very dark bread, fried bananas and rice. The Captain could never understand why the religious thought it an act of grace to neglect their bellies. Mine deserves better than this. He heard Dr. Edmond say to Red, "Look in at the hospital later. Let me dress your arm."

"It doesn't bother me."

"It was a dog. It could have been rabid."

"It wasn't." The Captain saw Belle-Marie look at Red. He hesitated noticeably. "All right," he said.

"You were in the *légion étrangère?*"

Red looked at him, ate on.

"I am French," Dr. Edmond said. "One never forgets one's

**90**

national symbols. I have been separated from them for twenty-five years."

Red said nothing. He's closer than an oyster, you'll get nothing out of him, the Captain thought. Mother Hubbard had been listening. She called out suddenly to Red, "Where do you sleep?"

"On deck."

"Every night? It cannot have been very comfortable."

"It hardly rained," Red said. The Captain felt that in an underhand way he was being attacked. He began in an aggrieved voice, "It isn't a pleasure ship. Nobody invited him. Anyway, there were no more bunks . . ."

Father Leon said seriously, "There was your own."

My *own?* I have wandered into a world of spiritual dizziness, the Captain thought. Mother Hubbard said to Red, "We have a guest-house. You are welcome to it while the ship is here."

"There's the beach."

"And there are flies. And hermit crabs . . ."

"The beach suits me better," he said.

They looked at him strangely. The man repels generosity, the Captain thought. After he'd eaten he went back to the ship for another breakfast. He needed more than that spartan diet to fill his natural void. And so he never quite got to know what happened in the hospital during the next hour: he got three confusing stories from Dr. Edmond and Father Joseph and Belle-Marie.

Dr. Edmond told him: "He looked in after the meal. I examined his arm. That dog was no poodle. What a dreadful wound it was. You didn't do a bad job on it . . ."

"For all the thanks I got," the Captain said.

"He had a slight temperature. He hasn't been eating too well, has he? I thought it'd do no harm to hospitalize him for a day or two. I told Father Joseph and Belle-Marie to

**91**

put him to bed. What is it about the man?" Dr. Edmond hesitated. "He is . . ."

"Bloody-minded."

"Averse to kindness. There must have been some psychological shock; when the *légion* abandoned him, no doubt. Then . . ."

Father Joseph picked up the story in an agitated voice: "I took him into the ward to help him undress. He went quite mad. He said, there's nothing wrong with me. Keep your hands to yourself. I said, it will do you good. A few days in bed. Perhaps I wasn't too tactful: I had that torn shirt half off and suddenly—it was terrible—ask Belle-Marie . . ."

"He evidently doesn't like to be touched," Bell-Marie said. "I am a nurse. I deal with children. And this was unfortunately no child. I tried to calm him, told him he'd be well looked after: and he said something about being well able to look after himself. He became violent. When Father Joseph began to remove his . . ."

"I heard the explosion next door," Dr. Edmond said. The Captain couldn't tell whether he was angry or secretly amused. "Shouting. A great cry. I ran in. Expecting to find him in bed, but he was leaving. He'd reversed the situation. He'd put Father Joseph to bed. Father," Dr. Edmond grinned, "if you'll forgive me, the sight of you in the cot . . ."

I see nothing funny in it, the Captain thought. "I warned you to leave him alone. Let him nurse his prickles to himself."

"Why do you blame him?"

"Don't you?"

Dr. Edmond said softly, "We can be very possessive. He's entitled to his privacy. He doesn't have to have goodness shoved down his throat." He surprised the Captain. "He isn't a bad man. I like him."

"Until he hits you, too."

Father Joseph hastened to say, "He didn't *strike* me . . ."

"You were lucky. I have seen him chop a ship's captain down like a tree."

The Captain spent the rest of the morning with Mother Hubbard checking the ship's tally: the crates of X-ray gear, the sacks of insecticide, the school desks. He wondered if she'd heard of the incident. He felt slightly malicious. As they ticked off "one piano, upright, Bechstein" he said, "Do you know what happened in the hospital?"

"I know everything that happens in Christ's Island." She looked at him gravely. "Aren't you a little old to bear tales?"

"What? Me? They only tried to help him . . ."

"I know what they tried to do. It was his privilege to reject it." But it had left a speck of anxiety to grate like sand in her mind. "Your friend . . ."

"How many times do I have to tell you he isn't?"

". . . is a little volcanic. Did you know?"

Did I *know!* The Captain said, "What did you expect with his trade? Meekness?" It blew out of him. "Shall I tell you where I first found him? Chained like a beast in the hold of a ship." She winced. "I pitied him. Now I'm not sure it oughtn't to be his natural condition."

"You should repent that."

It's a strange society, the Captain fretted, in which a man has to repent telling the truth. He went back to his dinghy on the beach. A red head burned under the shade of a distant palm. The body nestled nakedly in the warm pale sand, as if ready to receive a lover. A split coconut lay at hand.

The Captain went across. He said angrily, "Your conduct was shameful."

Red looked at him dreamily. "Was it?"

"They wanted to help you . . ."

"Who asked them to?"

Now I know who he is, the Captain thought. Ishmael. His hand against every man's, and every man's hand against his. "Did you have to respond like an animal?"

93

"Oh, we're all animals of one kind or another, aren't we?"
It shocked the Captain: the man regarded him as a corpulent
figure of fun. Red said, "You do dramatize yourself, Captain.
This is very pleasant. Why don't you relax?"

The long breakers creamed in across the lagoon. The swish
was soporific. The palms leaned languidly back from the
trade wind; rustled softly; the sun was fissionable and radiated the Captain with sweat. He thought in a mesmerized
kind of way, I am ten kilos too heavy. It would be nice to
lie down on that sensuous sand. No, it is too beautiful. And
treacherous. It can soften and corrupt a man.

He said sourly, "You despise kindness."

"If you say so."

"I don't know why I was so good to you. You even take
advantage of me."

The Captain heard Red chuckle. Heard him say, "There
are two kinds of people born into this world. The chickens
to be plucked, and the butchers who pluck them."

"And I'm one of the chickens?"

"A fine plump one. You're not offended, are you? I like
you."

I hate you, the Captain thought, going insultedly back to
the ship.

❊    ❊    ❊

The *Heinrich* would be at anchor ten days. There was a lot
to be done while the rafts unloaded the cargo. The hull was
crusted. The Captain organized a scraping gang under Kanaka Tom, who thought any labour on the ship a ludicrous
waste. The engine tubes needed repacking and China Tom—
with the same defeatist attitude—got to work on them. It
kept the Captain busy for two days and he didn't go ashore.
Then he got a touch of dysentery and that kept him aboard

another day. The symptoms were distressing. He got up on the fourth morning, feeling weak, and went on deck.

Kanaka Tom pointed. A pirogue was crawling across the quicksilver of the lagoon. The three fathers sat in it. Father Joseph paddling. Father Ho saw the Captain and waved. He'll overturn the thing. Three men in a tub. Rub-a-dub-dub.

They climbed up on deck and Father Leon said anxiously, embracing him, "Where have you been? We heard you were not well."

The Captain said, "My insides." Father Ho took his arm compassionately and Father Joseph squeezed his free hand. The Captain felt surrounded by God.

"You're so pale. You must come back and see Dr. Edmond," Father Leon said.

"Not in that." The Captain looked down at the pirogue. "I'd crack it in half."

"You will be in time for Mass." The church bell began to toll.

"What for? I don't belong to your religion. It wouldn't mean a thing."

"It might mean something to God. He will be there."

If they said so. "Well, how has everything been?" the Captain asked.

Father Joseph looked at him covertly. Father Leon rubbed his face. It occurred to the Captain that there was something they wanted to say and didn't know how.

Father Ho murmured, "Your friend . . ."

That word again. "Oh, him," said the Captain. He'd almost forgotten Red.

"He is unpredictable. He—" and the troubled Chinese face crinkled with the effort to find words. "You know the women's bathing pool." The Captain knew *of* it. It was very private under the cliffs: a waterfall fed it. "He plunged into it. It scared the women. They ran away."

95

"Did you expect delicacy out of him?"

"But Belle-Marie stayed."

"Ah." And the pieces of a rather worrying jig-saw puzzle fell into place in the Captain's mind. "Why did she do that?"

"They swam together."

"Have they been seeing each other?"

"Yes."

"Warn him off. You know the kind of women he's accustomed to."

No, they don't, thought the Captain, looking at the three unworldly faces. But there's one thing they *should* know: this is how Christian charity pays off. Well, I've learned a bitter lesson. There'll never be any more of that. He muttered, "I don't know what you can do with him. He's an—" He could only think of the word "anarchist." He got into his own dinghy and followed the priestly pirogue as it paddled back to the beach.

He looked in at the hospital. The dispensary smelled of brandy. It was a little early for the doctor to be indulging in his medicine. He said, "If you can spare an unhappy man a few minutes . . . ?" and Dr. Edmond lifted his grizzled head from the desk. "Come in," he said. He looked older than the Captain had seen him before. "Lie down on the couch."

"I know what it is."

"If you know what it is why come to me? Lie down," Dr. Edmond said.

After a while he said, "Dysentery."

"I could have told you."

"Could you have also told me that you overeat?"

"I enjoy it."

"We all enjoy the things that kill us. Would you like Father Joseph to wash out your bowels?"

"No."

"Neither would I. Aureomycin will clear it. Until that next

96

big dinner." Rubbing his tired eyes, "Are you in a hurry? Where are you going?"

"To watch Mass."

Dr. Edmond said curiously, "Are you interested?"

"Only as a spectator."

"Well, that's how we all begin. As spectators." Dr. Edmond grinned. "There's hope for an unbeliever yet. Listen. God will excuse you a few minutes. Sit down." He made a small nervous Gallic gesture. "Your red friend. Would it be wrong to suggest that you return him to the hospitality of the ship?"

"No," the Captain said, thinking: you can lead a mule to water, but you can't make him drink. "Do you want me to try?"

"I don't know. Does it sound terribly cruel?"

"I know how you feel."

"You do? About Belle-Marie? Who told you?" The Captain shrugged. Dr. Edmond scrubbed his raw cheek with a papery sound. "I have nothing against the man. I like him. But . . ."

"Have you asked Ma Hubbard?"

"No. It would shatter her. She wouldn't withdraw shelter from a fly." Dr. Edmond put the bottle back in a drawer. "The brandy doesn't help much, does it? I am not a very good father. There is no mother. There is so much to do in the hospital, and so little time." He hesitated, uneasy about saying it, but it had to be said. "You know how it is with men like Red. He is a bird of passage. Belle-Marie is without experience. I would not like him to leave his seed behind."

"Oh, no," cried the Captain.

"Maybe oh, no. And maybe yes. I hope I am wrong about him." The church bell had stopped tolling. "Now go to Mass."

The Captain went over to the great open courtyard of the church, with its whitewashed pillars, the thatched screens rolled up to let in sun and air. The altar was planted under rustling palms. It was all very queer to the Captain, who was

97

used to dark chilled chapels. Then he thought begrudgingly, perhaps this is the way He preached—on a stony Judean hillside, under the cedars, His voice carried by the wind. There were about six hundred people on the island and the whole congregation, down to the last puling infant, was there. Father Ho was preaching. The foreign sing-song voice reached out and they listened with an almost violent awareness—sitting and crouching, nursing babies at the breast— that isn't quite proper, either, the Captain felt. A Chinese priest handing a white God to a black mop-haired congregation: the old men still bore pagan tribal scars. He heard Father Ho talking about "the especial kindness of mercy . . ." which meant nothing to him, then heard him say something about "the eleventh commandment, which is love one another, but not in expectation of love in return. Love simply because love is a blessing . . ." and the Captain thought, that wouldn't do for me. Why should I love anybody for nothing? First of all they have to love me.

He saw Belle-Marie. She was watching Red. He stood well back from the pillars of the courtyard, listening inscrutably. The sun made a small hot halo of his vivid hair. The message isn't going to do him any good. And he'd better keep his eyes off Belle-Marie.

Mother Hubbard sat in her wheel-chair in the sunshine. The terribly bright eyes rested on Belle-Marie, then on Red, and after a long while on the Captain. It made him feel guilty of eavesdropping. He walked away.

I didn't walk far enough, he thought later, when Mother Hubbard sent for him. She said, "What was the matter with your face?"

He said stiffly, "I am no Valentino. But there was nothing the matter with my face."

"I saw who you were watching."

"I can use my eyes, can't I? You ought to know what is going on?"

98

"All right," she said scathingly. "So tell me. What *is* going on?"

The Captain cried, "Oh, you're all out of this world. You simply don't accept the existence of sin. Well, it's still there. You're not going to shut it out with love, and you're not going to shut it out with prayer . . ."

"Stop rattling," she cried. "And answer."

"Red and Belle-Marie. He's trying to"—what was the vernacular?—"make her."

She looked at him distastefully. "Is it possible that you are growing into a dirty old man?"

"That's the lot. Now I'm finished," the Captain said.

"No, you're not finished." She began to handle her silver-knobbed stick like a sceptre. No, more like a weapon. She banged it hard on the floor. "Go on."

"What is there to go on about? You would call it sin. Red would call it human nature. Throw him out."

"Belle-Marie is utterly innocent."

"It makes her more tempting. What does she know about men? She isn't coloured enough for the natives. And who else is there for her to look at? Only—" The Captain was going to say, "the three fathers," but he stopped himself in time.

"We have never refused anyone hospitality," she said.

"It's time you did."

"I will not believe it of him."

"Ma—"

Down banged the stick. "And you charged too much for the piano. You have added your commission twice." In the end, ninety years or not, she was just like any other woman.

This is *my* decision, the Captain thought. He returned to the beach. He knew who he would find there: and there he was. Savouring the tropical breeze, lost to responsibility, as naked as Adam, with the split coconuts, and that ineffable view of the great circlet of the reef, thumping with surf, tufted with palms, the birds wheeling, darting for fish, under that pellucid blue sky. Picture-postcard material. Well, *he's* finished with Paradise. The Captain said to him sharply, "Get your things on. We're going back to the ship."

"*We* are?" Red said after a while.

"I don't know where your hands have been straying. But your eyes have strayed too far." Red looked at him. "You're going to leave Belle-Marie alone," the Captain said.

"And supposing I . . . ?"

"There's no supposing about it. I am your benefactor. You need me. You will do as you are told."

Red said mockingly, "That's like twisting my arm."

"I know what it is about you I would like to twist."

"All right." Red laughed. He put on his shoes. "I suppose there are other islands."

"I don't envy the one that gets you."

It annoyed the Captain that because of Red's arm he had to row him back to the ship.

That night, on deck, Kanaka Tom said to the Captain, "What harm was he doing? Why did you fetch him back?"

"Mind your own business."

"You interfere with nature. These islands were made for love. You white men. You come here from your frozen climates with your frozen ——s." The word was very physical and offended the Captain. Kanaka Tom saw it and laughed. He said derisively, "Listen. Let me tell you how it was in the old days. Sex was no problem. *You* brought the problem. Five or six boys take five or six girls into the forest, we play a little at love. The fathers say happy hunting. Everybody have fun. None of this ridiculous *amour-toujours*—I love you for ever and ever. Nothing is for ever. Love is only while you are young and the blood jumps and the belly is nice and flat . . ."

The Captain said in a stifled voice, "Go down to your bunk."

100

"I am a healthy non-artificial man."

"I know what you are," the Captain said. In the end it was *he* who had to go down to his bunk.

❊      ❊      ❊

The sun molten. The days drowsy. The rafts crawling like sea-slugs from ship to shore, laden with stores. The Captain watched them riding the piano across the lagoon—he thought for an apprehensive moment that the slightly antique product of Herr Bechstein would end up at the bottom with the *bêches-de-mer.* He was relieved to see the natives run it with an unmusical jangle up the beach. At night the stars. The whine of the accordion on deck. It is the languor that is making me fat, the Captain thought. The dysentery had eased. He called at the hospital for some chlorodyne but Dr. Edmond was out. Belle-Marie was in the dispensary.

The Captain watched the dark, sweet, pure face, the nubile body. (Ah, did my blood once leap to the touch of a figure like that?) And it gave him a pang: he wondered if she resented what he had done. He said tentatively as she made up the chlorodyne, "You will no doubt be glad when we are gone."

She said in a puzzled voice, "Why should I be glad to see you go?"

"You know what I mean." She couldn't be that simple. He didn't want to have to spell it out. "He will no longer be here to pursue you."

"Red?" The name sounded queerly familiar on her lips. "Whoever told you he pursued me?"

How difficult she was. "He's an experienced man. And you are only a . . ."

"You don't know what I am. You don't know what he is, either."

101

"A girl dare not trust him."

"I trust him. Love is nothing but trust," she said. "Do you want me to write the directions on the bottle?"

It nettled him. "You must miss him."

She said serenely, "Do you think so?" And her face shone.

A tiny bell of warning rang in the Captain's mind. He wondered why.

It didn't bother him during the day, but it returned that night when he lay down in his bunk. Sleep eluded him. The shining guileless face, the soft laugh, and . . . and then he knew. He swelled with anger. It was after midnight. He tossed off the sheets and in his bare feet went hastily on deck. The blankets were warm: but Red was gone. The moon was a vast dazzle and the Captain, staring across the lagoon, thought he saw a phosphorescent trail, the flash of a swimmer's bare arm.

You *cannot* trust him. I am going to forget I saw that, he thought. Kanaka Tom lay curled up in the scuppers because of the heat. The dark mocking eyes gleamed, and the Captain said to him, "How long has he been doing that?"

"Doing what?"

"He is in the lagoon."

"He has a passion for cleanliness."

"Hypocrite."

"Go to bed," Kanaka Tom said dreamily. "It's a long time since you were young."

A ghostly pink figure crossing the beach, someone coming to meet it, both lost in the long moon-shadows of the palms . . . I didn't see that, either, the Captain thought. I am not going to be involved.

He slept uneasily, dreaming the fervent dreams that hadn't afflicted him since adolescence: of a dark arbour of palms, a concealed bed of sand, love murmurs scarcely heard above the surf, a sudden mutual strain of limbs . . . he woke to an appalling orgasm. Light filtered into the cabin. This isn't going to be a very good day.

He went ashore while everything was dawn-fresh and dewy; the island was hushed; the sun hadn't had time to lift itself above the edge of the sea. He walked to the hospital with that sense of foreboding . . . it exploded before he could reach it. He heard the shouting while he was still on the beach. Then an insupportable cry of rage. He burst into the dispensary through the children's wards. He saw Dr. Edmond beating his fists into Red's face; a smudge of blood; Red's head jumped, and his eyes closed momentarily with each hard thud. He took it without resistance, his back hard against the door as if there was someone on the other side of it and he did not want her to come in. The Captain heard Belle-Marie mewing like a trapped cat behind it. She was banging despairingly on the wood. Dr. Edmond, with a fixed glassy stare, went on punishing Red's face . . . he'd relapsed into gutter French, the Captain couldn't make out more than the grunted *"bête, bête"* . . . and Red accepted it martyredly, leaning on the door, licking his split lips.

The Captain saw the children's shocked faces in the ward. That was terrible. He was afraid to interfere. One of the black nurses ran in. Then Father Joseph. Dr. Edmond waved them back. He'd stopped. He peered at Red's mouth, then at his smeared knuckles, then said tiredly, "Sit down. I am sorry. We must do something about your face."

Then to the nurse, "Go out."

Then to Father Joseph, almost irritably. "You, too. Next time knock before you come in."

They went.

Belle-Marie had stopped crying on the other side of the door.

Dr. Edmond said to the Captain as he went to his cabinet for iodine and plaster, "He lay with her." It sounded very biblical. "I found them. I shouldn't have been there." He plastered the blotched face. Red got up before it was finished and went out.

"It was stupid of me," Dr. Edmond said.

"How can you say that?"

"It had to happen. Sooner or later. If it hadn't been him, it would have been some coloured boy on the island. He would have taken her—tested her—before marriage. We try to teach them Christian matrimonial practice, but the old tribal customs still go on."

The Captain didn't know what to say.

"And who am I to blame her?" Dr. Edmond said with a dry grin. "I did the same with her mother. History repeats itself. The chickens come home to roost. Is she still crying out there?"

"No."

"She's a healthy girl. He has probably impregnated her." Mother Hubbard wheeled herself in and Dr. Edmond looked at her, then again at his raw knuckles, and went next door. They heard him whispering with Belle-Marie.

"I told you," started the Captain. "Warned you . . ."

"Be quiet," Mother Hubbard said.

"Hospitality doesn't always pay off."

"*Will* you be quiet?" She sat nursing the silver knob of her stick, listening to the whispers next door.

"God's love is all right for gentlemen. Not for . . ."

"You're a fool," Mother Hubbard said. She looked old and tired. Wounded. "I wouldn't have thought it could happen." Then, "Take him back to the ship. I don't want him to come ashore again."

"I'll see to that."

"Tell him I'm sorry."

"You don't have to be sorry," the Captain said. "It wouldn't have happened if you'd listened to me." He had to have the last word.

He found Red back on the ship. He thought grimly: he knows what to expect from me. No mercy. He said to him, "Well, you'll make no more trips across the lagoon."

Red leaned over the side, watching the island.

"Stop looking," the Captain said. "They've decided to dispense with your company. They don't want you any more." Red gave him a quick startled look. The Captain said cruelly, "It's getting to be like Safu-Tura, isn't it? Nobody wants you."

Red said nothing. His shocked face was very pale. He still watched the island. Paradise gained for a few days: then Paradise lost. Look at him, the Captain thought. Ishmael. The rejected of God. Who the hell *would* want him? "Well," he said harshly, "you won't defy me any more. If you do I'll batten you under hatches and take you back to Safu-Tura. There's a police sergeant who'd like to get his hands on you."

"All right."

"So just remember."

"Captain," Kanaka Tom called out angrily. "Will you be quiet?"

"I am the master . . ."

"Leave him alone."

"How dare you address me . . ."

"Captain," China Tom complained in a high pained voice. "You're spoiling my breakfast." He was eating his queerly-concocted food on deck.

"Eat it below."

"My stomach isn't strong enough. Your ship stinks, Captain."

If only it weren't for this labour problem, the Captain thought . . . He went down to the galley for his own breakfast, and before he'd tasted his first sausage he sniffed curiously: it *does* stink. I never noticed it before. Now I will have to start eating on deck.

❊    ❊    ❊

It began before dusk with a few specks of light, like fireflies just beyond the horizon. Then a dark rash was formed there, and the rash became the spidery forest of ships' masts and superstructures, and a navy—*the* navy, the Captain thought with baffled recognition—came heaving over the rim of the sea. The armada approached the island in a curiously geometric pattern and formed a crisp arc about the gap in the reef, ready to enter the lagoon with the morning light. The Captain remembered, as one remembers a voice from an old dream, the police sergeant's relieved shrug at Safu-Tura, "They're going a long way south. The farther south the better . . ." and he thought, with terror almost: this is as far south as they are going.

Their target is *here.*

His hands sweated. It isn't possible. He heard China Tom's throat give a kind of condemned creak. Kanaka Tom watched the approach with his hard barbaric alertness. Red's face impassive. Suddenly the bright scythe of a searchlight from one of the ships split the evening and swept the island like a spy: travelling across the townlet, from white church spire to the hospital—holding finally, almost with surprise, on the great crowd of the islanders who had formed up on the beach. In the hard beam the Captain saw Mother Hubbard in her chair, Dr. Edmond, the three fathers, the curious, photographically sharp faces, watching the ships stilly, and a cold pit formed where his stomach should have been—it isn't fair; I am the one who will have to tell them, he thought agonizedly.

# 5

The Captain said tiredly, "Don't keep saying it can't happen. It has happened. They're here." For ten minutes Father Joseph had been murmuring in a kind of anaesthetic shock, "No, no, it can't," Father Leon coming in with confused jerks, "There has been some mistake," Father Ho saying nothing, the grave hurt eyes watching the Captain's face. Dr. Edmond huddled in his chair, smoking his pipe. Mother Hubbard quiet, too, asking the bad questions that had to be asked.

"Why here?"

"Why not? It's a fine anchorage. Off the trade routes. These things need a measure of privacy. Bases. What have you. Rockets. I only know what I *know:* they're here. And why."

"They told you in Safu-Tura . . . ?"

"Gossip. Don't pin me down. Nobody gave it to them in writing."

"But rockets?"

"So they said."

"It isn't possible."

The Captain started dully all over again, "I keep telling you . . ."

"I mean it isn't possible to permit it. They cannot stay."

The Captain felt a great sense of exhaustion. He looked at Dr. Edmond. Somebody has to be the sane one. Dr. Edmond watched him wryly, puffing at his pipe. The Captain said, "Ma. If we can discuss it realistically . . ."

"On Christ's Island?"

"Any island. I am trying to . . ."

"Don't. And stop addressing me as if I were senile. You are wasting your breath."

It was very dark now, the fleet's lights twinkling like a regatta beyond the atoll, and a still, very perplexed crowd of the islanders on the grass outside the huts. The Captain said, "Have you looked out there? Seen the vastness of it? This is a naval operation."

"Is it supposed to frighten me?"

"God forbid . . ."

"He will. Forbid it." She was suddenly quite cheerful. The life force pulsing in the old body again. She rattled the floor with her stick. The Captain thought, look at her. Marshalling God on her side. She said, "Is it necessary to spread alarm and despondency?"

He tried to form words. None of them made sense.

"All you have given me is tittle-tattle," she said.

A naval squadron isn't tittle-tattle, the Captain thought.

He muttered, "They haven't crossed the Pacific for the tropical sunshine."

"Do you know exactly why they have?"

"I can make a reasonable guess."

"And guess wrong. Nobody knows that they are not just passing on their way."

The Captain found himself admitting reluctantly, "Maybe so."

"They may be gone tomorrow."

Father Joseph looked brighter. The strain went out of Father Leon's face. Father Ho, reverting for an instant to the

Chinese, hissed his relief. The Captain felt hypnotized, too. "That's true," he said.

"That is what I propose to assume. And welcome them—for the little time they are here—as our guests."

The convention was over. The stick came down commandingly. "It's late," she said. "Now I am going to bed."

Not to *sleep?* The Captain looked at Dr. Edmond, who nodded and grinned.

Mother Hubbard went to the door to stare at the gathering of the community, the dark anxious faces, and she said to Dr. Edmond, "Tell them it will be all right. There is nothing to worry about. Everybody is to go to bed." He did so. They melted obediently. It struck the Captain later as a most remarkable thing: not a child had cried.

Dr. Edmond followed the Captain a little way out on the stoop. He murmured, "What do you *really* think?"

"Now I don't know. She confuses you. No, I don't mean that. She fills you with faith. And I have no faith in faith. You see what I mean? She mixes you up."

In this state of confusion the Captain went back to the ship.

China Tom asked as soon as he reached the deck, "What did they say?"

"We may be all wrong about it. After all, nobody knows they're not just passing on their way." You see? I'm repeating her words like a ventriloquist's dummy, the Captain thought.

Kanaka Tom gave him a quick strange look. "You really believe that?"

"Of course. They may be gone tomorrow."

The Captain saw Red's eyes shining ironically in the dark. You keep out of it. You're one of their kind, aren't you? The armed ones. You're the last person to comment on a situation like this.

He was awakened early in the morning by the stunning blasts of sirens and he went to the porthole to look out. The fleet was entering the lagoon. The Captain could see a small sliver of the beach, much movement there, too, an unexpected fluttering of colour, and he went hastily in his pyjamas on deck. Kanaka Tom and China Tom and the whole Papuan crew watched with awe. The ships marched in impeccable line through the gap in the reef, the light cruiser leading, the two destroyers behind, the supply ship next, then the assortment of landing-craft like sheep behind the burly watchdogs, and the wash raced on to the island and the foam lashed the beach. The *Heinrich van Reyn* rocked in this busy traffic. The grey aristocratic shapes towered by, and the great masts, the spidery radar bowls, made her feel very plebeian and antique. The crisp white uniforms on the decks, the bellowing from the loudhailers, semaphores flashing. This is power, the Captain thought. He was very impressed. Finally they all swung to their anchorage.

And the *Heinrich van Reyn* was now hemmed in.

The Captain put on his best uniform. We Dutch also have a great naval tradition, he thought. A Papuan rowed him ashore, sliding between the great grey shapes as if escaping a prison. The dinghy approached the beach at about the same time as the gig came roaring out from the ships. It was very new, very purposeful, and its brass gleamed as if fresh from the makers, and it flew five flags in an exact pentagonal pattern: American, British, Australian, Pakistani and Filipino. This is protocol gone mad, the Captain thought. A sailor in uncreased whites stood in the bow ready to pole her off, but the gig's bottom touched sand a little way out and stopped, the screw fouled mud, and the motor stopped, too. The long smart gig lay out in the surf, and the group of officers stood waiting, and presently, with a kind of annoyed reluctance, they dropped down, one by one, in their personal brass and pressed whites, and waded ashore. At about this time the *Heinrich's* dinghy, with its shallow draught, rowed past them and the Papuan ran it neatly on to the beach. The Captain

110

felt queerly proud that he didn't damp a foot as he went ashore.

He looked back. Five officers floundering through the surf, slopped to the crutch, shorn of naval dignity and importance, and he knew he would always remember the picture; this was how SPUD came to Christ's Island.

* * *

They came wetly up the beach, straggling as they approached the Captain, the Britisher smiling faintly to hide the intense displeasure he felt because his sense of propriety had been hurt, the American irritated with conveyances that couldn't finish a job, the Australian grinning because it was, after all, fun, the Filipino squelching as he turned to abuse the sailor, the young Pakistani treading delicately over the crabs like a high-spirited colt. The South Pacific Union for Defence. They didn't look very unified, the Captain thought. He could recognize the chain of authority at a glance. The American said, "Commander Preem," and put out a thick hard hand.

"Captain van Eyck. I am pleased to meet you," the Captain said.

"That your ship? The *Heinrich von Rhine* . . ."

". . . *van Reyn*," corrected the Captain. There was a subtle difference. He added for no particular reason, "He was born there."

"Who? Heinrich?"

"Rembrandt."

The Australian laughed. The Commander searched the Captain's face with astonishment as if suspecting some slight. He presented his associates, glancing back at the gig with renewed annoyance, unpeeling his wet pants from his calves. "Lieutenant Darling." The Britisher first.

"Do you do?"

This dinner-jacket-in-the-jungle thing is no myth, the Captain thought. They all have the aroma of the best clubs.

Then the Australian. "Lieutenant Welch." He showed the Captain friendlily that his fingers were wet with sand and didn't offer to shake hands.

The Filipino. "Lieutenant dos Vargas." He said, *"Buenos días."* Then, "I am happy to find you." Bilingual. Well, just. He was the most decorated of the five. The Captain couldn't remember the Filipino navy being seriously involved in any war.

Then the Pakistani. "Lieutenant Ayub-Ahmed." He was a slim dark young man. He smiled at the Captain with a wonderful set of teeth and his tender feminine face opened up like a flower.

The sailors had waded in from the gig with heavy tubs, and they buried them in the beach and planted the five flags. The Commander watched them with ceremonious attention. It outraged the Captain. Which of them is taking possession?

Commander Preem said to him, "We'll need a fairly wide anchorage. You'll have to move way across the lagoon."

The Captain began to protest, "According to mercantile practice the first in . . ." and Commander Preem looked at him impatiently and said, "Hell. What's the difference? There's no wharf." There was a slight bulge under his belt as if he had spent most of his naval career in an office chair. The Captain thought, this is a protocol man. He probably sleeps with Navy Regulations under his pillow. Everything will be done according to the rules. He had an earnest, seriously tense face. The Captain gave him another sharp look. There's something terribly dutiful here. The pale blue eyes were never quite still, flicking about restlessly as if someone might take advantage of him. He will always look up Navy Regulations to see what he can do about it. The Captain mused, we have a word in Dutch for that condition: "itchy."

112

This man takes his Service seriously. You must be careful not to irritate him.

Then his mind repeated what the Commander had said. A fairly wide anchorage. Does that mean a fairly long stay? Please God not.

The Commander was staring at the church spire projecting above the palms. It seemed to puzzle him. He murmured to the Britisher, "What do you make of that?"

"Odd."

"I don't figure it out."

The Captain had seen through the *Heinrich*'s porthole a bustle of movement on the beach, a flutter of colour—it had reminded him of the massed gay pennants of a bull-ring—and now he was able to determine what it was. The whole community had turned out to greet the ships; strips of bunting ran along the palms, and the Captain could hear the vivid chatter, the high excited cries of the children, could see Mother Hubbard and Dr. Edmond and the three fathers grouped up beyond the beach in a formal deputation of welcome—he thought tetchily, there's no need to overdo it. But visiting ships were as rare as space-pilots to Christ's Island. A little emotional extravagance could be excused. Commander Preem and his officers watched the gala array with a perplexity that in turn perplexed the Captain, whispering amongst themselves, but though he stretched his ears to eavesdrop he couldn't hear a word.

Then Commander Preem turned and saw that the gig's crew—they were Filipinos—were planting the flags below the highwater mark and he said painfully to Lieutenant dos Vargas, "For Joe's sake. Tell them to get their minds out of neutral. Those flags'll float clear back to Papeete."

Lieutenant dos Vargas said with a shrug, "They are moronic. I despair of them," and went over to a rock and sat on it to shake the sand out of his wet shoes. The Captain saw Lieutenant Ayub-Ahmed's dark petal-like face go entranced

113

and he was sure he was trying to make out the slang, "Get their minds out of neutral." Lieutenant Darling glanced with a dry grimace at Lieutenant dos Vargas: this couldn't happen in Nelson's navy. And Lieutenant Welch, the Australian, just laughed. What a mixed bag this is, the Captain thought. How do they communicate?

Commander Preem went down the beach to harangue the Filipinos—they listened with courtesy and a stupefying lack of understanding—and the Captain walked over to Lieutenant dos Vargas. He was a plump man with a brown glistening face. This one enjoys the good lusts of life, the Captain thought: food and women. He said, "I sympathize."

"Why?"

"For a man of sensitivity to have to command such human material. How hard it must be."

"You can have no idea." Can't I, the Captain thought. You should try the mental level of my Papuan crew. "It can break the heart. They are dragged into the navy from the farms and the plantations and they do not know a compass from a cow's arse," Lieutenant dos Vargas said. "But I will make a crew of them yet."

Not in my lifetime, the Captain thought, looking back at the Filipinos: they were listening to Commander Preem with humble futility. Surely, at least, their uniforms could fit? He said friendlily, "I was at Safu-Tura when your fleet called in."

"Indeed."

"There was a lot of gossip."

"There usually is."

"Still. You must be very near your destination now."

Lieutenant dos Vargas put on his shoes and began, "For reasons of security I cannot . . ."

"Oh, come. I commanded a Dutch minelayer during the war. We are natural allies. It is absurd to think there are spies hidden up in the palm trees to listen in."

"True."

114

"Where is it you are going?"

"Matsutura," Lieutenant dos Vargas said.

The Captain said, wrinkling, "I do not know it. Where is it? In the Marquesas?" and Lieutenant dos Vargas gave him a peculiar look.

"When will you arrive?" the Captain asked.

And again Lieutenant dos Vargas gave him a slanted baffled look. He trod water out of his shoes, swearing softly in Spanish at the unpleasant feel, and went back to his associates.

Matsutura. I must look it up on the charts.

The Captain walked on ahead up the beach. They were all crowded outside the church and he said to Mother Hubbard, "Did you have to make all this fuss?"

"Is this a fuss?"

"You never put out bunting for me."

She chuckled, "You would only be embarrassed." Then, watching him intently, "What did they say?"

"You can set your mind at rest. This isn't the place. They are going somewhere else."

Dr. Edmond said quickly, "You're sure?"

"I am sure."

"God be thanked," Father Leon said.

"Now will you take my advice? Stop all this nonsense. They haven't exactly dropped in from Mars. Treat them with a natural reserve . . ."

"We are reserved. And they are still our guests."

"It isn't necessary."

"Hospitality is always a necessity. Now," Mother Hubbard said briskly, "which is the one in authority to address?" The five officers were approaching.

"The American. Unless you are multilingual. And say as little as possible . . ."

She said, "I do not have a clapper for a tongue," looking slyly at the Captain. "Like some people."

115

"Ma . . ."

"I can be trusted to control myself." She sat in her wheel-chair, watching them, waiting for one of them to speak. The Commander searched the crowd with his complicated eyes, those restless butterfly-flutters, beginning with a flicked arm-chair salute, "Commander Preem," addressing Dr. Edmond, who pointed to Mother Hubbard. "Good morning," she said.

He looked at her. She was so small. The silver-knobbed stick propped in her hands. He said, "Good morning," then added uncertainly, "ma'am." She has a natural presence, the Captain thought. After all, they addressed Queen Victoria as ma'am.

She said gravely, "You are very welcome." Precisely what Queen Victoria would have said.

"Thank you." The Commander looked a little lost. The Captain had the feeling that there was something on the tip of his tongue—saw him glance strangely at Lieutenant Dar-ling—but he said nothing.

"Present your friends," she said.

Commander Preem brought forward his hybrid assortment. The Lieutenants Darling, Welch, dos Vargas, Ayub-Ahmed. They sound like a splinter of the United Nations, the Captain thought. Lieutenant Ayub-Ahmed gave her a soft filial smile, and Lieutenant dos Vargas—bolder—touched the back of her hand with his lips. She said amusedly, "It is a long time since anybody did that." She liked it.

"They have been neglectful."

"It is nice to hear a gallant fib," she laughed. "Now you will want some refreshment."

The Captain was still puzzled by Commander Preem's ex-pression. He came out with a troubled flurry, "The Navy Records say this island isn't inhabited."

"But it is, isn't it?"

"You shouldn't be here."

"But we are here, aren't we? We have been here for forty-two years."

The Captain thought he heard Lieutenant Darling murmur dryly, "Squatters," but he couldn't be sure. "It doesn't make it legal," Commander Preem said. He sounded like a counsellor who'd got hold of a bad brief. He will worry at this like a mongrel, the Captain thought. Why the hell should anybody care? "The international position's plain," Commander Preem said. "The French had the island in the eighteen-twenties, and they yielded the rights to the Dutch, but there was some argument with the British who . . ."

"It doesn't seem so plain to me," Mother Hubbard said. "When I arrived half a century ago there was nothing but the birds and six lepers who'd been banished from the islands. So here we are." Adding, "And here we remain." Remembering to say as a pleasant afterthought, "With God's grace. You'll stay to lunch, of course."

The audience was almost over. She made a half turn in the wheel-chair.

"Perhaps you will like to see what we have here. Dr. Edmond will show you round," she said.

"You mentioned refreshments," reminded the Captain. He was thirsty.

"Father Ho."

Father Ho's face glowed like polished ivory. "Come with me, please," he said.

Commander Preem's mouth opened—he stared obscurely down the beach where the gig's crew had finished planting the flags, then up at the palms with the decorative bunting. Father Ho had led on, and the Commander went after him automatically. All the rest followed. The ships in the lagoon were as active as factories. They see life, at least, the Captain thought.

Before they had gone ten steps Dr. Edmond whispered to

**117**

him with a grimace, pointing to the gig's crew on the beach, "Why are they doing that?"

"You know what navies are. They like to show the flag."

"*Five* of them?"

"It saves jealousy."

"It offends me."

"Hush," said the Captain. "They'll all be gone soon. Then they won't offend you any more."

They walked round the church. Lieutenant dos Vargas stopped to look at the altar under the palms; he peered with wonderment up at the arched Christ-figure. Then crossed himself devoutly. The Captain found Commander Preem nudging up to his side. He thought, this is a very confused man. What is he so excited about? The Commander said in a stringent whisper, "They have no right here."

"What do you mean, right? They were here before I was born. Who has a better right?"

"It isn't legal . . ."

"What is legal in the Pacific? Only the Polynesians and the Papuans are legal."

"The old lady . . ."

"Mother Hubbard."

"*What?*" Commander Preem stared at the Captain as if he'd perpetrated a bad joke.

"Her name is Hubbard. She is the mother of this island. Don't get so hot over nothing. This climate is bad for the nerves."

And in this mentally-crossed state they reached the refectory. It had been laid with plates of the little hearts of palm-salad called *cœur de coco* and tiny fried breadfruit cakes and glasses of squeezed lime. There was ice in them. The long oak tables gleamed. The officers sat, silently impressed, and the native girls in their best gingham dresses bustled about to serve them. The Captain, who was next to the Australian, Lieutenant Welch, saw him watching them. It's always the same. Those vital-statistics-searching eyes. Lieutenant Welch leaned over and murmured cordially, "No tits?"

The Captain swallowed.

"This isn't Bali. It isn't that kind of island."

"More's the pity."

"Please. You will offend them terribly. You must keep your sexual impulses to yourself."

Father Joseph was handing round warm damp towels. Commander Preem, on the other side of the Captain, watched him and said, "What is he? A mish?"

"A what?"

"They all are, aren't they? Missionaries."

"No. I wouldn't call them that. Servants of God."

The Commander's pale unsure eyes worried this out. "Comes to the same."

"No, it doesn't. It isn't just religion that moves them. Not organized religion. It's"—here it comes—"love." Watch him look at me as if I were mad.

The Commander looked at him corner-wise in just that fashion. He ate a cake. It crackled between his teeth. "Who's there to love? The nigs?"

"While you are here you must never use that word."

"Who, then?"

The Captain—irritated at having to explain it, first to that irredeemable cynic, Red, now to these uniformed sceptics, for Lieutenant Darling was listening, too—said, "You. Me. Everybody. Love isn't selective. It's the Christ story. They live it. Well, it *is* Christ's Island." The Captain found himself getting flurried and involved, and he said, "Of course, it doesn't make sense. It's a spiritual dream-world. But it moves you, doesn't it?"

He wasn't sure about Lieutenant Darling. And the Commander watched him broodingly and crackled at the crisp cakes.

Then Lieutenant dos Vargas bent forward earnestly and said, "It moves me."

"You're a Catholic," Commander Preem said.

"A Christian."

"I'm a Baptist."

"Same thing."

It's no use, the Captain thought. He wiped his hot face with the damp towel. It isn't explainable. Dr. Edmond leaned over sympathetically with his Gallic grin and patted his hand.

Father Leon said, "Now if you are ready?"

"It's hot outside," Lieutenant Welch said.

Lieutenant Ayub-Ahmed said, "*I* would like to see." The petals of his dark face glistened. What Kashmir garden did he come from? wondered the Captain.

Commander Preem rose without enthusiasm, and all the rest got up and followed the three fathers out. Dr. Edmond said softly to Father Leon, "Let me take them." Then to the officers, "I don't know what you expect to see. A hospital? It's just a place for the sick. This is it." They'd stopped on the veranda. Lieutenant Welch sniffed reluctantly at the dispensary. Then momentarily lost his inhibitions. He'd seen Belle-Marie inside. Dr. Edmond said in a dry voice, "My daughter," and Lieutenant Welch sighed. They went through the three wards. There were a lot of old people in the first. They grinned widely at the visitors. The black splayed features shone like stove-enamel against the starchy whiteness of the sheets. They were playing with jig-saw puzzles, and reading (yes, they *can* read, the Captain thought, watching Lieutenant Darling's impassive face). Some of them dreamily smoked their pipes in bed. The children in the next ward made all the din. The third—for operative cases—was quiet: it smelled of ether and medicaments and the heavy bandages and the sad looks of pain and anxiety troubled the Captain, and he didn't go through this.

Then the banana groves: the taro plantations. Fathers Ho

120

and Leon and Joseph hopped excitedly ahead like museum guides. And the soutanes swished. The old folk's garden, the inmates lounging like retired executives, with black bare feet and frayed straw hats. Then the school. The whole conducted tour. I'll sweat down to a grease-spot, the Captain thought. But he saw Lieutenant Welch beginning to look pensive. You see? They *can* be moved, he said to himself.

Commander Preem stood for a long while outside the kindergarten watching the kids. He said in a nostalgic voice to the Captain, "I have three like that."

"Black?"

"Jesus God, no." The Commander recoiled.

Never mind. He's thawing fast, too, the Captain thought.

And at last—long long last, his tunic clinging to him like a wet stocking, persecuted by flies they came back to the church and the great communal clearing under the trees. The breeze rustled the palm fronds; the shade was tempting; and the Captain saw with an almost hopeless exasperation that it was being prepared for an arboreal banquet. Lunch for six hundred. This is for an army. No, he corrected himself dully, for a *fleet*. What can you do with them? It is absurd. The girls were laying the pandanus leaves that substituted for plates, the sitting mats, row upon row, the drinking shells for *kava*, and in the centre of the clearing the chefs—six muscular, sweat-shining young bucks—were stoking the traditional Papuan earth-oven. Angry as he was, the delectable smell of suckling pig stirred the Captain's taste-buds. The rich stench of charred wood, the layers of taro and fish and breadfruit and sweet potatoes, buried under earth and flavoursome green leaves. The Captain saw Mother Hubbard supervising from the shade of a palm. He looked at Dr. Edmond.

Dr. Edmond said, "It's a *fête*," and grinned. "We don't often have guests in such numbers. It's a long time since we indulged ourselves." And the church bell began suddenly to

121

toll; the plantations emptied; the Captain saw the villagers expectantly streaming in.

Commander Preem flushed, looking faintly embarrassed. He glanced at his fellow-officers and said, "Well, now. This is good of you. We wouldn't have expected this."

"You would honour us."

He walked across to Mother Hubbard and said to her sharply, "There's no need to spoon-feed them. You can overdo this hospitality thing."

"They are our friends."

"They're nobody's friends."

"Then let us make them so. We live an austere life, it will do us good to pleasure them. Now go away, Captain. You're growing fat and stuffy. Try to enjoy yourself."

She wheeled herself over to Commander Preem and called out to him, "Will you send across to your ships and invite as many of your crews as you can spare?"

"Be glad to."

"Thank you."

"Thank *you*," Commander Preem said.

The Captain felt his sticky creased uniform. He went back to the *Heinrich* to change. In for a pfennig, in for a pound. But I still think it's wrong, he thought.

❀       ❀       ❀

He said hastily to Kanaka Tom as he got on board, "There's some kind of banquet. Lunch for the ships. See to things while I'm gone," and saw Kanaka Tom glance thoughtfully at China Tom as he went down to his cabin to change. Red sat silently under the wheelhouse watching the shore.

When the Captain came up, refreshed, a pirogue had approached the ship. Belle-Marie sat in it. The Captain was surprised to hear her call up gaily to Red, "My father asks, are you a drinking man?"

He leaned over and laughed softly, "I've indulged. Why?"

"He says, will you join him in a small one? And will you please come to lunch?"

"Delighted."

"Come then."

"Swim?"

"No need. I will take you across."

"Black tie or . . . ?"

"Come," she said. "You are wasting time."

Red looked demurely at the Captain, who bristled; he went over the rail and lowered himself delicately into the pirogue. Belle-Marie paddled back across the lagoon. It left the Captain feeling vaguely cheated.

Kanaka Tom mused, "I wonder if some island houri will come across and collect *me*? I feel in a party mood, too."

"You will stay here and . . ."

"One more to lunch won't make much difference."

"Two," China Tom said.

❀     ❀     ❀

. . . it isn't so bad, after all, the Captain thought dreamily. He was belly-heavy with succulent pig, reclining like a pasha on his eating mat. And just the *kleinest* bit drunk: the kava had been carefully watered down, but it was still pretty potent. The open earth-oven glowed, filling the grassy clearing with an ineffable smell. They were playing baseball out beyond the church, selected teams of the native boys and the ships' crews, and the excited voices rang out like a school at play. The Captain glanced at Commander Preem, the stubborn, terribly earnest, terribly dutiful face flushed and relaxed—he isn't so bad, either. He cannot help doing what he has to. You have to take them as they come.

And the Captain's eyes travelled dimly along the gorged faces of the crews. They had come streaming ashore in gigs and whaleboats: finally one of the landing craft had butted across the lagoon, laden like a holiday ferry, the boom in the bow dropping to deposit a great surge of them in the surf. Aryan and not-so-Aryan faces, swarthy Filipinos, dark tragically tender Pakistanis—they're really the same all the world over. Before the racial prejudices get grown in.

The Captain felt warm and full of charity. He raised his drinking shell in a toast. He wanted to say something nice to Commander Preem.

"To the Pentagon," he said.

"I'll drink to that," Commander Preem said.

"It's a very good kava."

"Nothing wrong with it. Except that it's not bourbon," the Commander said.

For no obvious reason it made both of them laugh.

China Tom in his off-duty whites eating with passionate concentration, as if the food might not last. Kanaka Tom, who'd bothered only to change his soiled shorts, drinking with the same single-minded urgency. This is a wonderful party. It was a wonderful thought of Mother Hubbard's. It makes the whole world kin.

And there she sat, the *patronne*, smiling faintly, watching the great concourse with her puckered, wise, old eyes. She met the Captain's eyes. Nodded. He bowed to her and raised his shell.

He thought lazily, I would go over and watch the baseball, but this swag-belly of food is holding me down. The crack of the bat. A ball soaring. Yells of derision—the islanders and the crews seemed to have different rules—and a black half-naked boy ran like a maniac to slither over the base. Lovely. To be young. Any colour. Just to be young.

Suddenly Lieutenant dos Vargas nudged him. His sensually-expert eyes shone. He said, "*Quién es esa bella muchacha?*"

"You speak Dutch?"

124

"No."

"English, then."

"Who is that beautiful girl?"

Belle-Marie. She sat across the ring, turned sideways to Red, her face consuming his. They held hands loosely. The Captain thought, this is too naked. In company. They shouldn't look at each other like that. He muttered, "It's the doctor's daughter. Watch your tongue."

"*Que péna!*"

"What?"

"A pity. I might have . . ."

"The girls of this island are not for sleeping with."

Lieutenant dos Vargas said simply, "Somebody has to." The kava had made him lustful. "Sleep with them. The red-top does, doesn't he?"

"Be careful."

"How ravishing she is."

The Captain looked uneasily at Dr. Edmond. He heard him say in a sudden reckless voice, "I would like to donate my brandy to the party," but Mother Hubbard also heard it and shook her head.

Dr. Edmond made with his mouth to her: "Please?"

She puckered her lips back and made: "No."

He looked very sad. The Captain could see why. He glanced across the clearing and saw that Red and Belle-Marie were no longer there.

He made an agitated start but Dr. Edmond gripped his arm and said in his ear, "It's all right. Let's pretend that they have gone to watch the birds."

"Somebody ought to . . ."

"No. There's nothing we can do about it. I am not going to make her hate me." The drums began to rattle. The girls had seated themselves in a widely-spaced circle. "Let us enjoy the party," Dr. Edmond said.

The Captain had seen the sitting-dance before. He thought

it, in its demure way, rather sexual: even in those fresh gingham dresses. The *apirima,* which is the "dance of the hands,"
the ring of the girls sitting tailor-fashion in the grass, undulating to the unobtrusive rhythm that was getting louder
and more insistent all the time. The miming of the fingers and
the dreamy swing of the eyes. The drummer, part showman,
part virtuoso, caressed the shark-skin of the gourds, using el-
bows, chin, fist, nose even, grinning with pride. It became
very gay, the drums wilder, and the Captain, looking at Lieutenant Darling, saw that the detached Britisher had flushed.
They wouldn't recognize him in those high-class clubs of his,
he thought. Lieutenant Darling said in an excited voice,
"This is really very good," and the Captain, with surprise,
saw him following the ritualistic movements with fascinated
jerks of his head. He felt a little excited, too.

Lieutenant dos Vargas, bobbing beside him, said, "*Es una
cosa maravillosa* . . . it is wonderful." He shone like a lamp.

Mother Hubbard watched it very carefully for abandon.
The girls rose statuesquely, forming two parallel lines, the
young backs undulating, the bosoms modestly controlled,
the drums hammering *boom-boom-de-boom,* and the Captain thought: it's a kind of hypnosis. You find yourself not
quite in control. They'd come streaming in from the baseball
to watch.

It acted on Kanaka Tom—that edgy barbarian—like alco-
hol. He leapt impetuously in between the trim files of the
girls. His beehive-mop bristling; a totally unsuited flower
stuck behind his ear. Capering like a Holy-Roller. Both Dr.
Edmond and the Captain watched the black-flesh rippling
movements strangely. They knew a fertility dance when they
saw one. The Captain looked up at the spire of the church,
thinking: it's wasted on them. And then everything became
electrically charged. Lieutenant Welch crowed. He went forward irresistibly to join in. This infected Lieutenant dos Vargas. He uttered a hoarse cry of pleasure and went forward,

too. Kava and drums. It was a great mistake to mix them, the Captain thought.

He saw Mother Mubbard stiffen anxiously. The Lieutenants Welch and dos Vargas, childlike, had put themselves at the head of the girls to lead them in the snake-line which is the beginning of all dancing: *boom-de-boom* went the drums. The half of Lieutenant Darling that was human swayed happily, cheekbones flushed, and the half of him that was a respected member of the Athenaeum said, very precisely and controlledly, "Oh, damn good." The Captain, looking at him curiously, thought: now I know why so much of the world speaks English and not Dutch.

Commander Preem was over at the drums. The Captain had heard him say excitably, "I used to be a dab with them," and suddenly he was over there, slapping amateurishly at the gourds.

The Captain began to get alarmed. He watched the human snake winding this way, that way, about the grass. He could feel heat and intimacy being generated. There was a lot of giggling amongst the girls. He didn't like the sound of it. He muttered to Dr. Edmond, "Better do something," and Dr. Edmond said, "Hush, they mean no harm," but he wasn't very sure about it. *Boom-boom-de-le-boom.* It's making me jumpy, too, the Captain thought.

Red and Belle-Marie had returned. They stood watching with surprise. The Captain thought spitefully, they probably didn't mean any harm, either, but you can guess just what they have been doing under the palms.

He knew what would happen next. He saw some of the sailors tugging the giggling girls out across to the trees. We're going back a hundred years in a few minutes. The three fathers went flurrying after them. A whistle blasted suddenly in the Captain's ear and Lieutenant Darling leaned over and said reassuringly, "Not to worry." Petty-officers with truncheons and more blasting whistles appeared out of the fringe

**127**

of the trees and waved them back. "The navy anticipates everything," Lieutenant Darling said.

Thank God. This could have become a love-nest. The Captain sweated. Kanaka Tom was in a convulsive trance. The din was frightful. And then . . .

. . . she will always be in command, the Captain thought. Mother Hubbard pointed with her stick and the drums tailed off; the impetus of the thing ended: the snake-line stopped. The school's four-piece string ensemble had gathered on the dais, and she nodded, and in the suspended silence the strains of "The Blue Danube" stole across the grass. It was as if the corseted generation of Franz Josef had come waltzing ghostlily across the clearing. Mother Hubbard rose delicately. She went across to Commander Preem. He looked at her with stupefaction; then at the wheel-chair; she said gently, "It is not always needed. You know how it is. The doctor insists. At my age the bones get a little soft." And then, "If you will oblige me?" inviting him to dance. He took hold of her as if she were glass. They waltzed featherily across the grass.

Lieutenant dos Vargas guffawed breathlessly beside the Captain, "The old lady is a wonder."

"By God," Lieutenant Darling said.

The four-piece ensemble sawing strenuously at the strings, the sailors and the girls floating demurely to Strauss. Dr. Edmond murmured to the Captain, "You see, there was nothing to worry about."

But it was a very near thing, the Captain thought.

He'd had too much kava, and the outlines of the palms began to shimmer: he didn't know when he fell asleep. He woke to the cool of the dusk. A single star shone with the brilliance of a lamp out of the darkling sky. He was astonished to see them all squatting raptly, the white uniforms glimmering in the shadows—doubly astonished to hear the choir on the dais singing to them softly, "The Lord is my shepherd"—the voices coming out of the grass, "He leadeth me beside the still waters . . ." It had an odd Polynesian lilt that the psalmist couldn't have anticipated. And the waters of the Pacific weren't very still. But it moved the Captain sentimentally. Red sat silently near him. Does it move that hardened mercenary, too?

There was a religious shine, a wetness, in Lieutenant dos Vargas's eyes. The Captain said to him with feeling, "It's good."

"Yes."

"And all out of a handful of lepers and great faith and loving belief."

"Yes," Lieutenant dos Vargas said.

"This place is like a seed. It will germinate. You will see." The Captain peered up. "It reminds me of that lonely little star. You say, oh, that tiny spark, it cannot last. But people have been looking at it since the beginning of eternity and it is still there." The Captain knew that he was being rather theatrical. And he went on in the same overdone fashion, "You will only be here a few days. But you will remember us when you are gone."

He wondered why Lieutenant dos Vargas should give him a long hard-to-make-him-out stare.

Had he offended him? He said apologetically, "No hard feelings. We have grown quite fond of you. But everybody will be glad to see your ships go."

Now Lieutenant dos Vargas shifted a complete right angle and stared peculiarly right into his face.

Dr. Edmond had joined Mother Hubbard. Fathers Ho and Leon and Joseph sat with them peacefully on the grass. They looked like a group of the apostles uplifted by the Sermon. The Captain went across.

He beckoned to the choir—the soft Polynesian voices, the up-and-down rhythm, somehow not completely religious—

"Surely goodness and mercy shall follow me all the days of
    my life,

And I will dwell in the house of the Lord . . ."
—and said to Mother Hubbard, "What a beautiful thought."

She looked at him tranquilly. "I am glad you approve."

"Look." He nodded to Red, listening stilly. "Even he's affected. That roving butcher . . ."

"*What* did you call him?"

"All right. I'm sorry."

She reminded him sternly, "Though I speak with the tongues of men and angels, and have not charity . . ."

"Yes, yes, I take it back." The Captain shrugged, pointing to Lieutenant dos Vargas. "I seem to have offended our friend, too."

"You should be careful with your tongue."

"Well, I don't take *that* back. Nobody'll be sorry to see them off to Matsutura . . ." and the silence became almost splinterable: as cold as a frosty November wind. The Captain felt as if he had spat in church.

Father Leon got up. He pushed his face close to the Captain's and said with a kind of paroxysm, "Where did you say?"

"Matsutura."

"That is where they are going?"

"Yes."

Dr. Edmond made an exhausted sound. "Then they're not going. They are staying," he said.

The Captain looked at Mother Hubbard. His bowels twitched for no apparent reason. She said very faintly, "When I came here forty-two years ago this island was called Matsutura. Perhaps it is still so on their charts." Her face looked quite wasted. She said to Father Ho, "Ask the Commander to come across."

He came over, flushed, maybe a little "kava happy," those anxious, terribly jumpy eyes for once relaxed. Mother Hubbard said to him with brutal urgency, "Where is your destination?" and Commander Preem's eyes stopped being relaxed. All the happiness went out of his face.

He looked at her.

She asked, "Is this it?"

He said nothing.

"Christ's Island?" she insisted in an appalled voice.

He wouldn't even accept the name. His mouth began to form the word "Matsutura" obstinately, but she wouldn't let him use it—trembling, banging hard down with her stick. Dr. Edmond grew anxious. He pressed her hand quickly. He seemed a little ill himself.

"You must see. It isn't possible," she said.

Then Father Leon, the excitable one, got up. Relapsing in his great agitation into Spanish, he said, *"No entiendo,"* then again, violently, *"No entiendo!"* but Father Ho (he was yellower than the Captain thought even a Chinese could be) took hold of him and said, "Hush." The Captain thought Father Joseph would weep.

And Commander Preem's eyes started their nervous this-way-that-way business again. The Captain knew suddenly what was the matter with him. He is unused to the burden of command. This is his first seaborne assignment. They have lifted him out of some office arm-chair.

The Captain saw him freezing up, his mouth tightening primly, and thought: he isn't going to say a word.

Mother Hubbard said to him painfully—she wasn't capable of bitterness— "You were our guests."

The Commander made an empty sort of gesture down to the beach where the flags were. As if to say: you have eyes. You should have known.

"We thought it the merest whim. An act of naval pride," she said.

Well, it wasn't, his eyes said. It was an act of possession. We're here: and here to stay.

She said loudly, "No."

The Commander grimaced at the Captain and his eyes appealed: will you tell them? These are operational orders.

131

"What was it you intended here?" she asked.

And the Commander's eyes corrected her stubbornly: *intend*. Not intended. He stared again at the Captain. I'm not going to be your interpreter, the Captain thought.

"Something naval? A base?"

He shrugged it off with a wave. You wouldn't expect me to say. Even if I knew. Security had hold of his tongue.

"Rockets? Things like that?"

He mumbled something. Watching her colourlessly. And shrugged again.

She said with sudden fear, "Perhaps . . ." making with her frail hands the familiar mushroom nuclear shape. He peered at her uselessly with an impossible gesture. Don't ask me.

"Here? On Christ's Island?" She was breathless. Something will happen to those old arteries, the Captain thought. "It would be an act of defilement," she cried.

The Commander just looked at her.

Then looked back. The Captain—in his anxiety—hadn't noticed how quiet it had grown. They were all aware of the raised voices, the stretched emotion, and the whole community had crept near. The Captain felt the shared tension. How silent they were. The Commander's officers had come up behind him. He stared at them. He didn't know what to say.

Dr. Edmond spoke for the first time. He said, "You have no right here."

And speaking for the first time, too, Commander Preem said, "You have no right here, either." The Navy Records had this place uninhabited. It belongs to the birds. The birds won't object to what we have to do.

The Captain saw Red listening aloofly on the fringe of the crowd. Nobody is going to get that rootless vagrant involved.

Then Mother Hubbard said to the Commander with paralyzing simplicity, "Now you must go. All of you. With your ships."

132

That finished it. Lieutenant Darling's mouth opened with incredulity. As if he were about to say, "Well, really"—and ten seconds later that was what he actually did say. It must be an all-time classic understatement, the Captain thought. He'll have something to tell them in those very high-toned clubs. Lieutenant dos Vargas froze with pure distress. Lieutenant Ayub-Ahmed looked beautifully tragic. And Mother Hubbard, leaning forward unexpectedly, took Commander Preem's hands between hers, saying, "Forgive me. I would not want to wound you. How painful it must be for you," with such intense sincerity that he refused to believe it. He made a frustrated gesture to his officers and they all walked off.

The party was over. The great mob of the sailors went streaming rather sorrowfully down to the beach.

The Captain gave Mother Hubbard a shocked glance as if to say, "It's bad enough, don't make it worse," and ran hastily after them. He caught up with Lieutenant dos Vargas before he reached the surf.

He said breathlessly, "Please. Tell me . . ."

"No, no, I mustn't talk to you."

"What is it you are going to do here?"

"There are reasons of great security . . ."

"What difference can it make now? For their sakes." The Captain stabbed the Lieutenant at his weakest point, "After all, you're a good son of the church."

"God knows I am in need of grace." Lieutenant dos Vargas crossed himself fervently. He was watching the Commander's back. He muttered, "We are nothing. We are just a holding force. We are going to build an airstrip for the transports to fly in. The big stuff will come later."

"Big stuff?"

"The construction units. The battleships. The cruisers."

"And then—?"

"Even God wouldn't expect me to tell you that." Commander Preem turned sharply. "Please go," Lieutenant dos Vargas said.

The Captain walked back slowly. He thought: I suppose I'd better tell them. They'll find out soon enough. He could hear the passionate clamour of voices around Mother Hubbard. They broke off expectantly as he approached.

He told them.

"It still can't make much difference," Mother Hubbard said.

The Captain said with alarm, "What are you talking about?" He felt that he was listening to something as unreal as a spiritualist meeting. "This is SPUD."

"You don't make it sound very menacing, do you?"

"The South Pacific Union for . . ."

"I know what it means," she said.

"You cannot defy a fleet. There are *navies*. Five of them."

She reminded him softly, "When the Assyrians came down like wolves on the fold . . ." and he had to stop her: this is the sort of thing that makes a man grow old.

"Stop quoting the Bible."

"It was Byron."

"God or Byron. Neither can help you. There aren't any more miracles. Only the ones made by the Chiefs of Staff." He appealed to Dr. Edmond, "Tell them. You're a practical man."

"Not over this."

"They have operational orders . . ."

"So have we," Father Leon said. He fingered his soutane. "Holier orders."

The Captain thought with pity: they simply don't belong to this modern world. He turned to go. Someone murmured cynically in his ear, "Well, it's the way the story has to go." It was Red. "They crucified Him, didn't they? They'll crucify this island, too," but Mother Hubbard heard it. She cried out with great violence, "No. Once was enough. Never again," and Red looked at her and shrugged and went back to the beach with the Captain and Kanaka Tom and China Tom.

The landing craft and the gigs were streaming back to the ships. Kanaka Tom rowed the dinghy across the lagoon.

China Tom sighed, "It's a pity. There's no more room for the good in this world."

"They could be sensible at least."

"What makes sense, Captain?"

"You have to live with the facts of life."

"Or die. Trying to make them better."

"Shut up! What do you know about it? You're only a—" The Captain was going to say, "Chinee," but managed to bite it back in time. He relapsed into sullen silence.

❉　　❉　　❉

He came up half an hour later. He'd just heard Kanaka Tom stamp for him on deck. He found them all at the rail. Listening. He started to say, "What's going on . . ." but China Tom quelled him with a hiss. It was the evening service. The Captain could hear the psalm, the soft passionate voices singing out of the darkness, "For though I walk through the valley of the shadow . . ." and suddenly— as if there were a great many other listeners, too—the searchlight from the cruiser, then the destroyers, split the night: focusing for a dazzling instant on the white spire of the church. And on the island the chant rose, as if magnified by an amplifier, and after a while the searchlights on the ships went out. Red looked enigmatically at the Captain. His face never betrays anything, the Captain told himself. The massed voices stole across the lagoon ". . . I will fear no evil, for thou art with me . . ."

I wouldn't be too sure of that, the Captain thought.

# 6

The night was hot and ominously still: as if great electric strains were building up. The Captain knew he wasn't going to sleep. He was as tense as an expectant bridegroom. He spent the wakeful hours listening to the everlasting sound of the Pacific, the gritty thump of surf on the reef. He was exhausted by the time the luminous blue of the night started to turn into the grey ghostliness of the dawn. And then other sounds came to the Captain's pricked ears. A vast bustle in the lagoon—the crackle of loud-hailers, voices upon voices: the beat of innumerable engines. This is the time to stay where I am and mind my own business. And he got effortfully out of his bunk and went up above.

The *Heinrich* had moved away from the armada over to the far side of the lagoon. Lights flashed about the secretive huddle of ships. Chains clanked. There was still no glow in the sky—just a red lick down under the rim of the world—and though the Captain strained his eyes he couldn't really see what was going on. He could guess, though. D-Day is here. He sighed to himself, if I were sensible I'd go back to my bunk and plug my ears with cotton wool. But my heart is too soft.

136

Something moved on the island, no bigger than a candle-gleam, in the vicinity of the church. They were up, too. Heaven help them.

He put on some clothes and rowed himself over to the dark shore.

He went up the beach, threading blindly through the alley-way of the palms: stiffening with sudden shock at the near-ness of human sounds. He saw them locked in rapturous ani-mal combat. The Captain had never witnessd so blatantly the sexual act. Its first impact was to freeze him fastidiously, mouth open—staring at Red's bowed possessive head and the black stream of Belle-Marie's hair. They hadn't heard him. His tongue clove to the roof of his mouth. There's a time and a place for everything. You can overdo this South Seas idyll thing. He could just make out Belle-Marie's dewy face in the darkness. Closed tightly like a flower, then opening exultantly in the sacrifice and delirium of love. It moved him extraordi-narily; she caressed Red as tenderly as if he were her child. The lover-mother. He'll never escape her, the Captain thought. His lungs began to work again. He crept back through the soft sand and made a wide circuit round the palms.

And then round by the hospital, still physically shaken, making for the candle-glow by the church. They *were* can-dles. On the altar. The open nave was packed—he would never have guessed from the great silence how many of them were there: rapt, earnest, prayerful. There was no movement but the tiny butter-yellow flames jumping in the between-night-and-dawn breeze. And feeling as awkward as a Roman centurion who'd blundered on something appallingly intimate —say, a secret Christian service in the catacombs—the Cap-tain shrank back against the trunk of a palm. How long had it been going on? The stillness transfixed him. That queerly religious steel-blue sky: with its furnace glitter of stars. He was relieved when the soft patter of responses began—a

137

woman's impulsive sob starting a baby crying. That shocked him. *Everybody* was there.

And as if he hadn't had enough shocks to begin a day with . . . my God, what he saw coming out of the shadows literally froze his heart. A bowed figure moving laboriously from the side of the church, bearing a heavy cross. The Captain caught the scrape of the butt. And his first wild thought was: is this Him? The second coming? He actually heard over his own heart-beats his breath sawing like steel through wood. And then Father Leon went by, shouldering the cross, two islanders walking silently beside him, and the Captain uttered a stricken whisper:

"*What are you doing?*"

Father Leon peered into the gloom under the T of the cross. "Oh, it's you," he said.

"What are you . . . ?"

Father Leon, changing the cross from shoulder to shoulder, wiping the sweat from his face, pointed down to the flags on the beach and said, "They have come to take possession. This is to tell them that God had taken possession first."

"You mustn't," the Captain cried agitatedly. "It'll only make them mad."

Father Leon stared at him bewilderedly. "Why should it make them mad?"

"It can't do any good."

"It must. It will. How heavy it is."

"Will nothing make you understand . . . ?"

"We understand what we have to." One of the islanders tried to help Father Leon with the cross, and he said in an exalted voice, "No, no. It is my joy and privilege. Let me," and went on, a staggering step at a time. The Captain watched him, dry-mouthed, go down to the shadows of the beach. It must have been terrible watching it go up to Calvary. Presently he heard the clump of spades in the sand.

And he jumped—what a state I'm in—as someone brushed

**138**

by him out of that strange blue light. How I wish the sun would come up, the Captain thought. He seized Dr. Edmond's arm and whispered, "Tell them not to. It'll only make trouble."

"As if there isn't already enough trouble," Dr. Edmond said in a mocking voice.

"Do you have to make it worse?"

"Could it be worse?"

Not much, the Captain thought. Looking back, he saw that the flag standards had gone. He made a useless gesture, "What's the use?" Father Leon and the islanders were heaving up the cross—its butt sank with a soft thud into the pit they'd dug.

"What use was it before?" Dr. Edmond asked.

"That was two thousand years ago. . . ."

"No, it's now. Here and now."

"It won't make any difference."

"What will?"

"Well, nothing. You can't resist them. . . ."

"We have to." The Captain started to speak and Dr. Edmond bore down over his voice loudly, "*Have to.*" And because the Captain still tried to get a word in he repeated with a shout what Mother Hubbard had said, "Once was enough."

The Captain smelled his breath. Brandy isn't going to cure the toothache of *that* sorrow, he thought.

He stared at the church and muttered, "How long have they been there?"

"All night."

All night! It shocked the Captain. Couldn't God hear them in the first five minutes? Dr. Edmond said with a harsh laugh, "You're getting old and fat and defeatist, Captain," and shook his hand off and went on towards the church.

I'm the only sensible voice in the wilderness. The prophet has no honour in his own country, mourned the Captain. He was getting the religious metaphors a little mixed.

139

The noise out in the lagoon was now very loud. It still wasn't possible to see anything—just the dazzle of spotlights, dark shapes fussing busily about the water—but the clank of chains, the snorting huff of engines went on: as if factories, working overtime, had forgotten that it was almost dawn. The mast lights of the cruiser and the destroyers glittered like false stars. The sky had the very pale sheen of the belly of a fish. Any minute now the sun will come shoving up.

And then—just behind the Captain—voices. He was hidden by the trunk of the palm. Belle-Marie saying to Red, "You have to help them."

And him answering her softly—lover fashion—"Don't be silly. Nobody can."

The first wise words anybody's uttered, the Captain thought sourly. And they had to come from *him*.

"What are they to do?" Belle-Marie asked.

"They're doing it. Praying," Red said.

And wasting their breath, the Captain thought. Let them pray to the joint naval chiefs of staff of SPUD. He remembered rather irreverently that three of them were Protestant, one Catholic, one Moslem—the prayers were liable to get crossed.

He heard Belle-Marie say again stubbornly, "You have to help them."

"No, I don't. And I can't."

"Red."

And heard Red laugh, "You're not going to turn into one of those nagging women, are you?"

"I will be whatever you want me to be."

"You know what I want you to be. I just showed you."

"Red, help them."

"It isn't my business."

"It's everybody's business."

Red said—the Captain thought rather sensibly—"I'm not concerned with everybody. Just with myself."

140

"Nobody can live quite like that."

"Can't they?"

There was some muttering in the darkness. Then Belle-Marie's voice appealing painfully, "Red, in God's name . . ." and the Captain thought angrily: just listen to her. Straight from a lover's embrace. God might have something strong to say about that. More muttering. Then she misquoted something rather astonishingly. "No man is an island sufficient unto himself."

There was a small silence. Red said to her wonderingly, "What did you say?"

"No man is an island . . ."

"That's what I thought you said. Who taught you that?"

"My father read it to me. It is by . . ."

"I know who it's by. You didn't get it quite right. And you don't have to believe it, either. Whoever the bell tolls for, it isn't for me."

"For you," she said. "For me. For all of us."

The Captain, listening irritably, thought: but not for *me*.

The sanctus bell in the church struck them to silence. The Captain's nerves tingled. The cross—silhouetted starkly against the pale flat shine of the sky—made him feel very cold. The banging and the clanking out in the lagoon was getting louder: it was as if the frantic factory activity were now reaching its peak. A little rim of fire burned where the sea met the sky. But there was still nothing to be seen. Only the thick shapes of the ships, and what looked like a dark ant-crawl about them—some kind of collectivization, an orderly assembly of vessels, seemed to be going on. If only the sun would end the suspense, the Captain thought.

He must have made some noise. Red was suddenly aware of him. The Captain saw his eyes shining ironically in the dark.

Father Ho had begun to address his flock. The Captain

141

found himself listening with enormous concentration to every word.

". . . we will greet them as friends," he heard Father Ho say, the strange up-and-down Chinese voice that the Captain could never quite connect with a Western religion, rustling like palm fronds, yet suddenly urgent, suddenly forceful, reaching out across the silent congregation, "because we are involved lovingly in all mankind. Because it is the word of our Lord, and it admits of no various interpretations, no other meanings. Just that one precept: love your neighbours as yourselves. It is a fragile message, battered by cynicism for two thousand years, yet endures, and it lies here in our hands, a still small voice that reaches deeper than the dagger of enmity into every human heart." Mother Hubbard's head bent as if she were asleep, though the Captain saw her hands twitching. Dr. Edmond crouched by her, leaning forward intently as if to make sure he didn't miss a word. "There is my brother," Father Ho said. "Love him. There is my enemy. Love him also. Cherish him all the more because his fury is his pain and his private shame."

This sort of thing is dangerous: it can mesmerize you, the Captain thought.

And Father Ho's voice rose, as if seeking to reach beyond the congregation, beyond that dreadful din in the lagoon, "Out there, toiling so busily and reluctantly and painfully, are our friends. Greet them so. Receive them as brothers because they do what they have to, with sadness, with personal sorrow, under orders they may not resist, and because of their distress we will receive them with a very special brotherly love. No man will lift a hand against them . . ."

The Captain saw Red look at him. He shrugged.

". . . no man will raise his voice to abuse them. They are terribly vulnerable to our reproach. No man will shame them, no man will cry out, cursed be your . . ."

And a streak of fire ran right up the sky. The sun. It was

as if a darkened stage had suddenly been lighted: dressed and ready for the impending performance, the curtain up, the actors moving into position for the opening lines—the Captain, blinking in the dazzle, saw the cruiser and the destroyers thronged with auxiliary vessels, all marshalled in line, the lagoon soapy with foam, semaphores winking, like runners waiting for the starting pistol. He thought with awe, so this is what D-Day looks like. A concentration of power. It cramped his stomach.

He glanced nervously back at Red and saw him watching with a flat professional stare. He has seen that sort of thing before. I never want to see it again.

The sun rushed up as if eager to get the operation started. The shadows of the ships' masts lay like prison bars across the lagoon. The Captain saw in the pink chocolate-box glow a tall mobile crane squatting on two linked barges. It reminded him grotesquely of a knight in armour resting on two horses with his lance down. He saw tractors on the landing craft. Earth-shifting machinery. The blunt snouts of jeeps. A totally mechanical invasion. Men wouldn't come rushing ashore with bopping guns—just bulldozers grinding and clanking up the beach like a science-horror film. Shades of Wellington. Up, guards, and at 'em! The construction unit is here.

The cross looked solitary and meaningless down there.

The voice in the church had faltered. It grew loud:

"*Them* we will receive as brothers. *Them* we will greet as friends. But their engines of power," Father Ho cried with passion, "we will *not* greet with friendship. Their machinery of brutalization we will *not* love. Them we will—and must—with sorrow and agony resist. For the machine has neither memory nor the recollection of past sacrifice, neither hope of eternity nor knowledge of God, neither charity nor kindness, and its final appetite is for the souls of men." The Captain heard it with a kind of insane detachment—as if it were a cry

143

from an old lost century. He wiped the sweat from his fingers. He wished Father Ho would stop. But the thin earnest voice went on, "These things we will *not* welcome. This island is to us as a temple. To them we will say, you may not come here amongst us. That the Lord's still small voice shall not be drowned in the roar of the . . ." but it was a klaxon blaring in the lagoon that drowned it. The Captain thought: it's beginning. Phase one of the operation. He saw the tall crane move imperceptibly. It was as if a skyscraper had started sliding past Manhattan Island.

He saw Kanaka Tom and China Tom just behind him, and thought with a sweat of anger: did they have to come to gloat?

Belle-Marie had started again on Red. I wish she would stop, too. The Captain heard her say, "You have to . . ."

"Hush."

". . . help them."

Father Ho had begun to bless the congregation. It sounded very old and biblical. Hebrew. *"The Lord bless thee, and keep thee . . ."*

"I'm not involved," the Captain heard Red say.

"You were involved when you became involved with my body."

Red looked at her sidelong.

*"The Lord make his face shine upon thee, and be gracious unto thee . . ."*

Would she never be quiet? "You used to be a soldier," she said. "You could tell them what to do . . ."

"A soldier knows when he's defeated. He knows when to run away."

She burst out, "Are we already defeated?"

"Before you even lift a finger."

*"The Lord lift up his countenance upon thee, and give thee peace . . ."*

And suddenly Belle-Marie began to cry.

144

The lagoon boiled with foam. The Captain watched the ironmongery of invasion approaching. He could hear the loud-hailers calling between the landing craft, see the crane nodding in the swell—at the sight of it the birds rose from the atoll with nervous squawks. I wish I weren't here to see it happen. I'll never be able to forget it. A hand gripped his arm—he almost jumped out of his skin—it was Father Leon returning from the beach with sand on his boots. He said staunchly, "Be of good courage. He will not forsake us," and the Captain—wondering, what's he encouraging *me* for?—looked at him with alarm.

It was over. They came in a dark mass out of the church. The Captain—not sure of their intentions for a few moments —watched them move blockily down towards the beach. Dr. Edmond wheeling Mother Hubbard, Father Leon aligning himself with Fathers Ho and Joseph, the islanders in their precise social order—the elders first, the men, then the women, the children last. The Captain twitched with panic. He moved in front of them and said loudly, "What's this? What do you think you're going to do?" He saw Belle-Marie leave Red to join the crowd.

"Object," Mother Hubbard said.

"What with? Your bodies?"

"Why not?" Father Joseph said.

"Why not?" the Captain repeated. It enraged him: he began to have difficulty with his breath. He said, "It's mad. Go back. You mustn't," searching about for a reasonably sane face. Dr. Edmond just stared at him. They're not arguable with, the Captain thought. "You *have* to let them in." He started to shout ridiculously, "Where are your beach obstacles? Your underwater defences?" He looked at Red. At least, *he's* an ally. He said furiously, "Tell them. You were once a soldier. You can't stop a landing operation with faith."

Red gave it a little thought and nodded. "You can't stop a landing operation with faith," he said.

145

The professional voice. Thank God for a little wisdom. "Go on," the Captain urged. "Tell them. Someone can get hurt."

"Someone can get hurt," Red said.

"Tell them they're beaten before they even lift a finger . . ."

"Your ears are too long," Red said.

The Captain stiffened.

"I heard you myself. A soldier knows when he's defeated. He knows when to run away . . ."

"They're not soldiers. They're people. People sometimes stay to fight when soldiers run away."

The Captain cried out cheatedly, "Don't listen to him," but nobody was paying him any attenion. They were all watching Red.

Mother Hubbard said to him softly, "We are listening."

"It won't make any difference in the end," Red said.

"Leave the end to God," she said.

"You can't even hold them up for long."

"Every hour," Father Leon said, "gives Him time to come to our aid."

Red looked at him ironically. "He needs time to think it over?"

"He needs perhaps a demonstration of our faith."

Red said, "All right. Let's give Him a chance," and laughed.

He's a monstrous cynic, the Captain thought. Now I know what makes him tick. Like all soldiers of fortune he enjoys applying his trade. Look at him. Fulfilling himself. And something else. He doesn't fool me. They threw him out. The rejected. Now suddenly they need him. How he must enjoy it. Appealing to him for salvation. God help us from his kind of salvation. The Captain began to be very frightened of Red.

"Tell us what to do," Mother Hubbard said to Red.

"They're a mixed bunch," he said. "They can't be very

146

happy about the situation. Their morale won't be high. So let's start eating at their morale . . ."

The Captain interrupted, "Don't trust him. He'll lead you into trouble," but nobody wanted to listen. He took off his cap to wipe the sweat-band. Looking back across the lagoon at the nearness of the armada—how can they *not* be frightened? He saw Red beckon to Kanaka Tom.

"I am ready and able," Kanaka Tom said.

The Captain ordered him violently, "You're not to get involved . . ."

Kanaka Tom said softly, "How can you forbid me? I am a pagan trying to help your God."

"This heathen Chinee, too," China Tom said.

Mother Hubbard watched Red intently. She isn't sure of him, either, the Captain thought. She said to him, "Do you understand? There is to be no violence."

No violence? With *him?* I've seen him in action, the Captain thought.

Red said nothing.

Mother Hubbard said again insistently, voice higher, "Is that understood? Not a finger is to be lifted in violence . . ."

"No violence," Red said. But it'll come in the end, the Captain thought. He heard Mother Hubbard sigh. She looked at Dr. Edmond. He nodded.

And they all went down to the beach.

❁       ❁       ❁

The Captain ran ahead of them. They'd seen the gathering of the crowd from the landing craft: they slowed down by the shallows, the iron stalk of the crane dipping on its twin barges like a stork peering for fish, the tractors bouncing—a pinnace went ahead and Commander Preem waded out into the surf. Lieutenant Darling came with him.

Commander Preem stood in the pool of his soaked pants

and said to the Captain, "What's happening here?" He got worried very easily. "I don't want them crowding the beach. We'll need all the landing space we can get."

The Captain said, "If you'd wait just a little."

"Wait? Why?"

"Time to make them understand . . ."

"Understand what? There's a lot of gear to come ashore. We mustn't have them cluttering the approach." The Captain looked back. The mass of the community had paused on the beach in the narrow avenue they'd cleared of palms. He thought, it *does* make it awkward: on the other hand, you might say it's a godsend to them. He recognized the voice of Lieutenant Welch from the landing craft, tossing in the surf just off the beach. The Captain watched the mass of machinery fascinatedly—how simple it would all be if they were only frightened like me.

Commander Preem said to him, "Stand them well back. Get them clear of the approach."

"I can't give them orders."

"It *is* an order."

"You must give it yourself."

Lieutenant Darling murmured cautioningly in Commander Preem's ear and the pale obstinate eyes flicked. The Commander cried, "What in the name of sweet Jesus . . ."

"Hush," the Captain said. "You mustn't talk like that here."

The Commander looked at him curiously for a long time, collecting himself. He looked again at Lieutenant Darling. Then sighed. He said, "We've a tight schedule. I can't keep that load offshore for long. We have to come in."

"Talk to them."

"Nobody can talk to them." And the Commander used a very descriptive—and reasonable—expression, "They're obsessed."

"It's a special community."

"Only one thing special about them. They've no right here."

148

"After forty-two years?"

"Forty-two years don't make it legal." That office-chair mind. "I have a directive from the chiefs of staff to occupy and prepare for constructional purposes . . ."

"They will not let you."

"Not *let* us?" Lieutenant Darling's mouth half-opened to speak—he thought better of it—and Commander Preem said with the faintest bewilderment, "How can they not let us?"

"I don't know."

"Don't talk such damned nonsense."

The Captain thought, I'm trying to be a mediator and this is my reward. He said stiffly, "Do it your way."

"That's why I'm in command."

Lieutenant Darling whispered to the Commander, "The general directive says something about observing the local rights of native inhabitants . . ."

"It isn't inhabited. Or shouldn't be," Commander Preem corrected himself.

The Captain thought, this isn't a very real conversation. Lieutenant Darling went on murmuring, "With public opinion so sensitive. One walks carefully these days. Nobody'd want a squawk to . . ."

"This is a speck in the Pacific. Christ. It'd have to be a long powerful squawk."

Lieutenant Darling looked vacant. The British, with three hundred years of keen colonial instinct, had made a point. He said, "Too true," and sucked his teeth.

The Commander said painfully, "What do you expect me to do? Hold off while I cry like a scalded rabbit to the chiefs of staff: there's a mad religious bunch in illegal occupation who don't want to let us come in? My God. They'd have a collective haemorrhage."

"No doubt."

"That's the dirty business of command. Somebody has to make the rough decisions. Regardless. That's why they

149

dropped the responsibility into my lap. I'm not going to look silly, chucking every petty burp back at higher authority . . ." and then Lieutenant dos Vargas came trudging ashore through the surf.

He cried, "What is holding us up? We cannot stand off-shore for ever," and then saw the population gathered on the beach and his soft Spanish eyes grew wry. He said in a shocked voice, "What is this?"

"Local objection. Now let's get in. Act. Talk afterwards." The Commander grinned palely and said, "Couple of bottles to the tribal dignitaries and everything'll be all right."

Lieutenant Darling glanced thoughtfully at the Captain. Still sucking his teeth.

The Commander waved back to Lieutenant Welch and the engines of the landing craft ground and they moved inshore. The blunt bows dropped. A brisk practised activity began with a rumble. Men poured thigh-deep into the sea. They've come to take Troy, thought the Captain, aghast—these mechanics and artificers and boiler-room fitters second class: not with the glittering spears of the Greeks, but with crowbars and towing hawsers and chocks. The tractors rolled down off the landing craft into the spume, and the bulldozer, skidding in the surf, arrived with the clank of a dinosaur. The barges bearing the crane struck soft sand: a tractor backed into the swirl of muddy water and took it in tow, and the great iron stalk, banging and nodding precariously, was dragged through the shallows. The officers, megaphoned like film directors, yelled, and the Captain wondered who could hear their voices above the din. His heart banged. He shrank, as one shrinks in anticipation of the thunderclap after the flash. And the thunder sounded. I knew it, he thought. Now God help us.

He saw an echelon of the islanders, maybe sixty of them, all men, move as if on a signal down the beach, blocking the approach through the palms: saw them lie in a silent carpet under the treads of the bulldozer and that dreadful iron-panting crane: saw the Commander watch with the stony stupefaction of a director seeing unwanted extras walk into the crucial scene of the film.

And the engines died and the clanking ceased; for the first time the Captain could hear the agitated screeching of the birds. They lay—it seemed to him—in a curiously religious pattern. Flat on their faces in the sand, the surf wetting their outstretched fingers, the way nuns lie on acceptance, arms out in dramatic representation of the cross, symbolizing the act of sacrifice. The ships' crews watched them. Far up on the beach the rest of the community watched them. And way up by the church—in her wheel-chair, like a fragile empress removed from the scene of battle, Dr. Edmond beside her—Mother Hubbard watched them, too.

Commander Preem, wetting his lips, trying to form words, made a husky sound and then said to the Captain, "My first active assignment. And Jesus. They had to give me this."

So he *is* an office-chair commander, the Captain thought. He never met anything like this in those filing cabinets. He felt queerly sorry for him.

"All right, for God's sake, let's shift them," the Commander said.

Lieutenant Darling still looked vacant. The Commander said to him in a high voice, "Will someone get his mind out of neutral? I said shift them." The Lieutenant sighed and shouted to the men. There was no rush to come forward. A petty-officer yelled and a crew, dropping hawsers, went into uneasy action, lifting the bodies, hauling them feet first—then with whatever part of the anatomy came to their hands—out of the way. This isn't what they signed up in the navy for, the Captain thought.

Then the approach was clear and the tractors began to roar again, and above the row the Captain heard the clear blast of a whistle, and another detachment of the islanders

moved automatically down the beach and stretched themselves in a living carpet in the sand. The Captain thought
with a tremor of alarm: who's organizing this? He needn't
have asked himself the question. He saw Red on a spit of
coral, directing operations, China Tom gathering together the
next replacement echelon. (He saw something else that might
give the Commander paralysis: Kanaka Tom forming up for
a return engagement the islanders who'd just been shifted.)

The tractors stopped churning, and again the clanking died
down. This battle is going to go like St. Vitus's dance, the
Captain thought. He wanted to get away from it before
nerves frayed. The sailors looked woodenly at the officers.
Lieutenant Darling's face crinkled and went pink—a sign of
great emotion in an Englishman. Commander Preem, peering wildly over the heads of the crowd, said to the Captain,
"Who the hell's that?"

This isn't my business. The Captain said obtusely, "Who?"

"That bastard with the red hair. What's he up to . . ." but
again the question was answered by events. The sailors
shifted the second wave of islanders, recoiling with dismay
as the third advanced on the blast of the whistle—the human
carpet was formed again. "Who is that man?"

"I don't know." My lie will find me out, the Captain
thought. He muttered, "He's your own kind." The Commander looked at him strangely. "The military, I mean. Not
the navy. He used to be a legionnaire."

"Who put him up to this?"

"Nobody put anybody up to anything."

"A trouble-maker."

The Captain said resentfully, "He isn't making any more
trouble than you are."

"How did he get here?"

"I fetched him."

"*You . . .*"

You see how I'm getting dragged into it? The Captain

152

said, "I've had enough aggravation out of him," and stalked six paces off.

It was getting to be like a carousel. The sailors shifting the men, Kanaka Tom returning them round the beach like manufacturer's rejects—a vigilant blast of the whistle, and China Tom sent them back in another wave.

The sailors began to look disgusted. "This can go on for ever," Lieutenant dos Vargas said in a horrified voice.

"No, it won't," Commander Preem said. His eyes looked mad. One of them fluttered as if grit had burrowed under the lid. He isn't the one for this, the Captain thought—it needs the cold detachment of a surgeon, and this man's nerves are as raw as scraped flesh. The Commander went back to the sea, shouting as he went. The Captain saw one of the Pakistani crews, unloading stores, drag fat snakes of barbed wire to form a kind of corral. The Commander returned. He said, "That'll stop the merry-go-round," planting himself by the Captain. He seemed to want him as an audience—maybe as a witness for the defence.

The Captain said, "You've no right to do that. They are people, not cattle."

The Commander said stubbornly, "We have to come in."

"With a little consideration . . ."

"You can see what he's doing."

"They're entitled to ask him to help them."

"He isn't helping them. He's inciting them to defy a lawfully-organized defence operation."

It took them forty-two years to organize it, the Captain thought.

The sailors were depositing the islanders behind the wire. Now there was no return. Kanaka Tom was one of the last to go. The Captain saw him lying with a kind of luxurious abandon in the arms of two sweating Filipinos, a look of false martyrdom on his face.

Now the women advancing indomitably, singing. I never

want to hear that hymn again, the Captain thought. Red's whistle shrilled. The Commander watched him with a slanted frustrated squint. He said to a pair of red-banded naval policemen, "Take him in."

They were Australians. They hesitated.

Lieutenant Darling said anxiously, "You don't have powers to make civilian arrests . . ."

"He isn't a civilian."

"The directive exempts . . ."

"It doesn't exempt mischief-makers. He isn't going to make a laughing-stock of me. Take him in," the Commander said.

Red saw the policemen coming. He made a tentative movement of escape—he darted sideways and they fell on him. The sand churned in a brief struggle. They took him down to the sea's edge. He squatted behind the wire, under guard, eyes gleaming. He's probably enjoyed every minute of it, the Captain thought.

The island women tended to fat and the loose dark flesh slipped in the sailors' sweaty hands. The Captain saw a group of Pakistanis walk with revulsion back to the ships.

Then China Tom borne off with a sad yellow secretive smile. It made the Captain feel ashamed.

And the children last. "It should never have happened like this," Lieutenant Darling said in a harassed voice. They came down, chanting, to lie under the tractors like midget sacrifices—they scarcely understood what it was all about. The sailors, cursing audibly, rode them off piggy-back.

Now the beach was empty but for the three priests in their coarse grey soutanes standing in the approach. Father Ho quite still, Father Leon's mouth taut and angry, Father Joseph's hands up like a traffic policeman to ward the tractors off. The dark intent crowd behind the wire, watching, relieved by that solitary red head. This is one of those pregnant scenes I will remember with horror for years to come, the Captain thought. The bulldozer went first. A Filipino drove it.

154

It stopped. He looked back with a grimace of appeal. Lieutenant dos Vargas cried unendurably, "They are priests of God. I cannot ask him to do it." He shouted to the man, "*Vamos,*" and the Filipino got down with sickly relief and walked off.

Commander Preem said, "I don't ask any man to do what I wouldn't do myself." His face glistened with sweat. The Captain thought, it's terrible. They've no right to make him suffer like that. He mounted the bulldozer. It clanked slowly forward. The ram scooping up the priests, trundling them softly aside like dolls in the sand; Father Joseph sprawling as demeaned as an outraged housewife with the skirts of his soutane over his head, Father Leon rising belligerently, but Father Ho held him back. The bulldozer went on and the tractors came behind. Then the crane rattling like a bag of nails. There was nothing to stop them but Dr. Edmond and the figure in the wheel-chair—as still as waxworks—and the bulldozer went round them, leading its monstrous iron regiment by the church. Over to the communal clearing by the school. The Jeeps following like an occupation army, swarming with men. The Captain watched them setting up bivouac.

His mouth tasted of lime. I suppose they won a battle. But they aren't going to enjoy it. It was that totally undeserving vagrant—looking at Red—who really had the victory, he thought.

✿ ✿ ✿

The island rang with their din. The Captain didn't want to go near the camp. He didn't want to go near Mother Hubbard and the community, either. What can I do but help them mourn? Then, in the middle of the morning, Lieutenant Ayub-Ahmed came looking for him. "The Commander would like to see you in his office," he said.

"Since when did he have an office?"

"Please."

"I'm very upset."

Lieutenant Ayub-Ahmed's face moved with distress. "It is a matter of sorrow to us all."

"I don't have to come and see him. I'm not under his orders."

The lieutenant's liquid eyes flashed a warning and the Captain decided: I can take a hint. He let himself be led over to the camp.

And he walked straight out of the languor of the Pacific—out of the timeless idyll of palms and lagoon-glitter—into the frantic industry of a building site. It deafened him. Air compressors whining, pneumatic drills ripping up coral. They'd put up whole rows of prefabricated huts. Sailors sweating in dungarees and soiled white caps. The landing craft ferrying stores over from the ships as on an endless belt. They'd even laid a road of metal plates up the shifting sand of the beach. Jeeps rode it like a Californian highway. And in a green clearing under the banana trees, where the children had once played, the earth-shifting machinery—the bulldozer and the tractors—not to mention that *affrighting* crane—stood waiting silently for the word of action. It's here. The big boot of civilization. Already the PX, the commissariat, was operating —Coca-Cola has finally come to Christ's Island, the Captain thought.

Out of the corner of his eye he saw Red in the care of naval police outside the guard-hut. It gave him a guilty pang and he averted his eyes.

He heard raised voices as he entered Commander Preem's wooden office. Dr. Edmond was there with Mother Hubbard; the shocked worn face moved the Captain. Dr. Edmond saying passionately, "He did what he did for us. At our request. We ask you to release him," and the Commander, looking pale and truculent and haunted, sighed. They've

156

given him a terrible job to do. I don't envy him, the Captain thought.

"No," he said. "I can't do that."

"He mustn't be the scapegoat . . ."

"Scapegoat nothing. The man's dangerous. He likes trouble. I'd never know what he's up to," Commander Preem said.

The Captain wondered: why am I wanted?

The Commander looked at him squarely. "But I'll tell you what I can do." The Captain got suddenly nervous. He means, what *I* can do. Whatever it is, I won't do it if it gets me involved. "When are you leaving?" the Commander asked.

"In five days."

"All right. You fetched him. You take him away. Keep him secure under locked hatches until you're gone."

The Captain cried, "But that's exactly where I found him. Under locked hatches."

And Commander Preem, shining with sour triumph, said, "There's your answer, isn't it? You see what I mean."

"I'm nobody's jailer."

"Please yourself."

"I won't do it."

"Take it or leave it. That's my last word," Commander Preem said.

Mother Hubbard said faintly, "What will you do with him?"

"Toss him into the cruiser's brig. Turn him over to the nearest French dependency when it goes."

"That would be cruel."

"Why? What in hell"—the Captain wondered what Mother Hubbard had said to ignite him: he went up like a petrol blaze—"makes him so sensitive? Cruel," the Commander shouted. "My assignment's cruel. You think I'm getting joy out of it? I have orders. I have to carry them out." Dr. Edmond began to stare curiously at the Commander in a medical way. He was mumbling, "You saw what he did. Made *me* do what I did. Right there in front of my ship's crews. Made me into Captain Bligh." He'd gone ashen, his eyes twitching with a terrible sense of outrage. "I saw what his game was." And suddenly it occurred to the Captain that Red was even smarter than he'd thought. So far everybody, himself included—the gendarme at Safu-Tura, his wife, Julie—had danced like puppets to his strings. The army disengaged you from nice human feelings. You belonged to nobody. And for the second time the Captain began to be frightened of him. "Well, that's the last cute trick he'll play here," the Commander said.

Mother Hubbard watched him with bewilderment. He wiped the twitch out of his face.

The Captain said, "My ship is not a prison. I will not be responsible for him. And that's *my* last word," and he walked off.

He heard the voices rising again in the office, and presently Dr. Edmond wheeled Mother Hubbard out. They went through the camp. Mother Hubbard watching the bedlam of construction as if creatures from Venus—over-developed electronic zombies—had taken command. Dr. Edmond looked grim. The Captain said to him sympathetically, "Well, that's that." They saw Red by the guard-hut. "Maybe everybody'll be happier when he's gone."

"He hasn't gone yet."

"Now, look. Don't let's get notions. The Commander could be right about him . . ."

"He suffered for us."

"He never suffered for anybody. A few bangs? He's a soldier. He accepts them as part of his trade. You know what I think? He enjoys a good battle . . ."

"It was to help us."

"Where did his help get you? Be shut of him. Good riddance." I know it's the policy of despair, the Captain thought, but somebody has to get this sense of persecution—these dreadful dreams of religious resistance—out of their minds. "The Commander has the final say . . ."

"God has that," Mother Hubbard said, and before the Captain had a reasonable answer Dr. Edmond wheeled her off.

The sun climbed high and the clatter in the camp never ceased. The Captain found a niche for himself under the palms far along the beach. He had a bottle of beer. He took off his shoes and prepared himself for sleep. The lagoon glared like a mirror. He watched the natives rush a couple of outrigger canoes through the surf, saw them paddle out and begin to fish peacefully by the ships. The sight tickled his fancy. The contrast between twentieth-century stark naval power and the primitive and the picturesque. And as his eyes drooped he saw Red, with his police escort, go down the beach. Exit the trouble-maker. I hope he finds his prison accommodation better than Captain Malaise's ship.

A gig, its motor puttering like a lawn-mower, two white-capped sailors yawning in the blaze of the sun, waited for them in the shallows. Escort and prisoner waded out to it and got aboard. A whoosh of foam and the gig turned and made for the ships.

The Captain watched drowsily. I wonder if I shall ever see him again. The gig rocked by one of the canoes; the natives, fish spears poised, still and black and statuesque, reeled, and the outrigger cracked and they fell in. The Captain, sitting up, startled, saw their heads bobbing in the water. Heard them cry out. The gig slowed down automatically and came back in a skidding circle of foam to pick them up. The other canoe paddled over to help. And something—a needle of perplexity—pricked the Captain's mind. It said: there's something here that isn't quite right. It was probably his subconscious that anticipated what happened next. The gig hauled in the dripping natives, the second canoe assisting alongside.

159

And then, in a quick flurry—because of the wild flail of arms the Captain couldn't see anything too clearly, distracted by the shouts—the gig overturned, spilling them all, satin-skinned natives, white sailors' hats, police escort and the red head, into the sea. The natives swam like eels. The outrigger canoe raced frantically towards the shore.

The Captain couldn't see who was in it: but he could guess. His mouth foolishly wide, the sweat of consternation trickling down his face. They had seen from the destroyers and klaxons began to bray. Ratings working on the shore ran along the beach to intercept the canoe. It entered the surf, and the natives and the red-headed passenger sped up the sand and vanished into the palms.

Scarlet Pimpernel could scarcely have done it better. And what for? What chivalrous purpose did it serve? I don't seem to be able to escape it—just being a *spectator* can get me implicated, the Captain thought. He put on his shoes quickly, leaving the beer to fizz itself flat in the sun, and hurried unobtrusively away from the beach.

❋        ❋        ❋

Dusk. The bedlam of construction hadn't ceased in the camp. Arc lights blazed, dimming the stars. The Captain looked in at the hospital: it was a sanctuary, cool and white and sterile. Dr. Edmond and Belle-Marie were in the surgery, dressing the arm of a small black girl. Father Leon was working in the dispensary. The Captain waited for one of them to speak. He said at length, "I suppose you know what happened down on the beach this afternoon?"

"The spirit," Dr. Edmond said to Belle-Marie. She handed him the bottle and he cleansed the child's arm.

"You're not going to pretend that . . ."

"It will hardly hurt at all, *petite*," Dr. Edmond said to the child.

"It was such a foolishly quixotic thing to do," the Captain said. "You owe him nothing. You shouldn't have interfered."

Dr. Edmond dusted the arm with powder. He made no reply.

"Where do you think you can hide him?"

Dr. Edmond looked emptily at the Captain and strapped the child's arm. The din of pneumatic drills suddenly rattled the surgical cabinet. He said angrily to Belle-Marie, "Tell them to be quiet. There are sick children and they cannot sleep."

She went out. The Captain stared blankly at the black mite. "What's the matter with her?"

"Tore her arm on the barbed wire," Dr. Edmond said. Smiling wryly, "The Belsen touch."

"Please."

"You were there."

"What else could they do? You mustn't be bitter. You're still a Christian . . ."

"It wears thin under pressure," Dr. Edmond said. "I'm evidently not as good a Christian as I thought."

The child made noises sucking a piece of sugar-cane. One day she would be a buxom native woman—would she remember that like a concentration camp inmate she'd once sat behind wire? The Captain went into the dispensary. He said nervously to Father Leon, "Shouldn't you speak to him?"

"To say what?"

"It's all over."

"How can that be?" Father Leon looked at him wonderingly. "It will not be over until they are gone."

"They're here."

"But not to stay. Not to *stay*," Father Leon insisted as the Captain opened his mouth. He pointed to the church—the pneumatic drills split the night again and for a moment his words were lost—"How could we accept the blessed sacrament with those monstrous things of concrete and iron about

161

us," and the Captain knew what he meant. Everybody has them. They're about us all. "They are another cross on which to hang the children of Man." Father Leon's dark Spanish face worked. He said sternly—the Testament burning his tongue—"Render unto Caesar the things which are Caesar's, and unto God the things that are God's." Unfortunately Caesar had a very large fleet out in the lagoon and a lot of fearsome machinery. And God, when all was said and done, was only a still small voice. It's too much for me, the Captain sighed. I'm too fat to get involved.

Belle-Marie had just returned. The Captain murmured to her, "Where is he?"

She studied his face in the dusk. She laughed softly, "He isn't very far."

Who did she think she was fooling? They were hiding him up in the hills. He wished he could tell her: let him go. He's just a liability. He had made the Commander lose face and they would soon ferret him out.

He had to walk by the camp to get back to his ship. The hissing glare of the arc lamps made him blink. He heard a strange language—it was the Pakistani section. They were stacking crates in piles, sweating garrulously, like ants working against time. He didn't know what it was that had jerked his mind—he'd gone six paces past and his steps dragged irresolutely: it was too ludicrous, he didn't want to look back. He turned. His eyes sought the man he'd briefly glanced at: it was something familiar in his stance. But where was the red hair? They'd dyed it black. The man shouldered a crate and the arcs shone on his face. The Captain's stomach somersaulted lightly. There was no better place in which he could—temporarily—hide. They were a multilingual bunch: nobody would query a man who'd wandered in from another section. Red (the name was suddenly absurd) caught the Captain's eyes. Nothing moved in his face. As he turned the Captain

162

saw on the back of his working dungarees SIGNALMAN P. ROKOSOFFSKI.

He walked off unsteadily, wondering if Signalman Rokosoffski had yet missed his clothes.

❈　　　❈　　　❈

He couldn't sleep. It had grown quiet in the camp; sooner or later even they had to rest. But his mind swirled. I shall be glad when we lift anchor and get away from here, he thought. He twisted corpulently, sweating, in his bunk. It was odd to hear, for a little while, at least, the surf in the stillness of the night: the island breathing: the restless birds calling again. He must have dropped off into a doze. But it had no depth. And when he heard the three detonations—then a fourth and a fifth—he was almost automatically out of his bunk. He looked out of the porthole. It was quite dark. But suddenly a spreading pink glow. And instantly the destroyers' searchlights gashed the night.

He was frightened. He went to rouse Kanaka Tom and China Tom. And grew twice as frightened. They were not in their bunks.

# 7

The Captain would look back on them as moments of pure horror. He stood in the gangway in his pyjamas, chilled, though the night was humid, feet bare: watching the ragged fringe of fire creep somewhere along the base of the hills behind the town. Hearing the sixth detonation—it was more of an iron crunch, as if a great foot had trodden on a heap of discarded cans—and before the echoes bounced back from the hills a tall billowing cloud poked hotly into the sky. And now all the cruiser's searchlights came on.

I warned them. Mother Hubbard had said, "There is to be no violence," and now the violence was here. He dressed scantily, determined not to go ashore—nobody is going to connect me with this. What had happened?

He got the story eventually—a little at a time—from Dr. Edmond and Father Leon and Kanaka Tom. He said furiously to Kanaka Tom, "I should have been told. I am your master. Why *wasn't* I informed?"

Kanaka Tom grinned insolently. "You cannot hold a secret."

The Captain cried, "As if I would betray you . . ." and yet inadvertently he might. It would have terrified him. I am a

164

man of peace: somebody might have had to raise the voice of sanity.

"Who promoted this? Not Father Leon. Whose idea was it?" he asked.

Kanaka Tom looked at him obliquely.

Red. Of course.

"He organized it, too?" the Captain demanded.

"It's his line of business, isn't it?"

"War. That is his line of business. . . ."

"There comes a time when a man has to strike a blow for his conviction."

"Convictions?" The Captain's voice rose, "When did you ever have a *conviction?* You hypocrite. It thrilled you." May that false halo slip and choke him, he thought.

Kanaka Tom told him: "There had to be six of us. No more, no less. And all able to drive. This is not a very advanced island. There wasn't much choice. Dr. Edmond and Father Leon. China and myself. Red and . . ."

"How familiar you are."

"He is my friend."

"He is nobody's friend. Red and who else?"

Kanaka Tom said carelessly, "Some nigger." It transpired that he was referring to one of the islanders who'd done a collegiate training course in Papeete. "We each knew what we had to do. We had to do it quickly, in darkness, without confusion. I'll tell you something." Kanaka Tom laughed. "Privately I didn't think it would ever get to be done at all. There are limits to effrontery, and this was mad." The Captain vehemently agreed. "None of us slept. We waited for the moon to go behind the hills. About two hours off dawn."

The lamps going out in the camp. The pneumatic drills silenced for the night—even those arch-fiends of noise had to rest sometime. Here and there a tent glowing, a hastily thrown-up bamboo shelter leaking candle-light, where a few card-games were sputtering out. The last Coca-Colas being consumed. Now sleep. It had been an emotionally exhausting day. The voices died away. Kanaka Tom said, "We lay in the banana plantation, stiff as boards—God in heaven, what a long time those matelots took to shut up shop." The moon, that violently lambent moon of the Pacific, slipped across the island. Fell finally behind the hills.

They'd posted guards round the store-pile against pilfering: a totally unjustified slur on that very moral community. Two men to patrol the vehicle park. Who was going to steal a bulldozer? They all did what men do who aren't at war and have nothing to fear—they went instantly to sleep. This was the midnight watch. At three in the morning the dog-watch replaced them. This was the worst watch of all. The relieved guards had hardly gone before the replacements found themselves cosy niches amongst the crates. The men who should have patrolled the vehicle park curled up in a couple of Jeeps. The sound of the surf was as potent as sleeping-pills. Within thirty seconds they, too, were asleep.

One of the guards, a Filipino, told the Captain later, "There are bad dreams and *very* bad dreams. This was a nightmare. A hand over my mouth, firm but not cruel, a voice pleading in my ear, 'My poor friend, do not resist. In God's name do not make me hurt you . . .' It felt like a large man. And the voice was Spanish. Who else would talk like that but a priest?" Father Leon, the Captain guessed. "Then somebody else, grunting like a native, trussing me up." Probably Kanaka Tom. "They gagged and blindfolded me. How considerate they were. They put me very gently into the grass."

The other guard said harassedly, "Jesus on a rocking-horse—"

"I can understand your feelings. Never mind the profanity," the Captain said.

"I thought I'd drop a litter of kittens with fright. Hardly

**166**

scrubbed the sleep out of my eyes. And there I was, all trussed up like a chicken. Never saw a face. Hardly heard a sound. Just someone laughing. Then out on my face in the grass. Man, if this is what they call *peace*, I surely do not relish the prospect of war."

The starting of the motors suddenly ripped the night. The tractors belched. A chief petty-officer came out of one of the huts, stupefied with sleep. He thought at first it was the beginning of a thunderstorm. And while he turned the idea over in his mind precious seconds were lost. He stood there, knuckling his eyes, yawning, and saw the dark shapes of the tractors leaving the park. Recognized the frightful din of the bulldozer. There was just the reflected glimmer of the moon behind the crests and, as his eyes grew accustomed to the gloom, he saw what looked like an obelisk—it was the crane—crawling laboriously up the dirt-track towards the hills. It banged and rattled like a foundry. He saw the headlamps suddenly come on and cut brilliant swathes in the dark. He thought next that it was a night manoeuvre, which was absurd. Then that the Commander had given orders to get the machinery ready for a dawn start. But the dawn seemed to be a long way off. And while he thought all these things out, too, more time was lost.

The racket was ear-splitting. He told the Captain—anybody else who would listen—that a rocket leaving its launching-pad couldn't have made more row. Now men were pouring dazedly out of the tents. Asking questions. The petty-officer found the Commander at his side. He wore the bottom half of his pyjamas. His feet were bare.

The Commander said, "Who the devil gave orders to shift them?"

"Sir—"

"Who's driving those things?"

"Sir—"

"Did you ask them?"

"Sir, I just came out," the petty-officer said.

He'd come out two minutes earlier and by now the whole earth-shaking convoy was quite a long way off. It seemed, for some inexplicable reason, to be climbing up into the hills. The Commander and the petty-officer began to run. The vehicle park looked as naked as an open-air concert auditorium in the rain. Nothing was left in it but the Jeeps. The Commander stumbled over somebody in the grass. It was the Filipino. They loosened the gag: they might have saved themselves the time, for the man—in a highly emotional state —couldn't tell them a thing. He spoke only Spanish. And wept. The petty-officer found the other trussed guard and he told them a defensive garbled story about being attacked—being bound—he was frightened and his story got tortuous, and while he told it more precious time was lost.

The headlamps were now thin bobbing shimmers up in the hills.

Lieutenant Darling appeared. He wore a Sulka robe—the best of the St. James's haberdashers—wherever he went. Lieutenant Welch was nude—he slept in nothing at all. He said with comical incredulity, "Is somebody *stealing* those things?" and Lieutenant dos Vargas, who had been trying to console his Filipino, said simply, "What else?"

"Stealing," Father Leon admitted to the Captain. "One can split moral hairs: one can seek refuge in Plato. But stealing is the only word. It *was* theft. Between greater and lesser evils one chooses the lesser. I have prayed God to forgive me my sin."

"To manhandle men . . ."

"No, no. It was, oh, so gentle . . ."

"How could you?"

"Perhaps because I was frightened? Fear is a great anaesthetic," Father Leon said.

168

"Why not Father Joseph? And Father Ho?"

"They are very holy men," Father Leon said reproachfully. "I am of coarser clay. It was not for them."

The Commander and his officers made for the Jeeps. They revved the motors. But some essential parts had been removed from beneath the hoods and they wouldn't start. And while they were doing this the last few minutes that might have been useful to them were lost.

The Commander was capable of one sick enraged word. "Follow." He began to run. And the rest—a long trail of officers and men, fifty or sixty of them, barefooted, pyjama'd—went fruitlessly after the convoy. Lieutenant Darling remembered something very clearly about this. He said severely, "Lieutenant Welch. He didn't wear a stitch."

Now Kanaka Tom took up the thread: "No knowing how far back they were. We figured on a five- to ten-minute start. We'd disengaged the Jeeps. That would waste more of their time. We could see the camp ablaze with light, men running, but it was too dark to tell if they'd closed up. Dr. Edmond led in the truck. He knew the way. China Tom and Father Leon and the nigger with the college degree had the three tractors. I had the bulldozer. And Red last of all with the crane. That terrible crane. You couldn't hear a locomotive whistle above the noise we were making, but I heard it crashing behind like kettles raining. I'd look round now and then and see it rocking, thinking for sure it'd overturn. It was a bad track, overgrown and pitch-dark, and getting steeper, and we whined up it, the fire-flies hopping in the headlamps —I thought if machines had souls, this is how they'd ride to hell.

"Then Dr. Edmond flashed the truck light three times and we knew we'd arrived.

"The track was just the verge of the gorge. It gave me diarrhoea. I wouldn't have gone that far if I'd known it was there. We did it quickly: what had to be done. Dr. Edmond set the truck moving and jumped out. It just vanished into the gorge: hardly a whisper to begin with, then a crump like a bomb far down in the trees. The tractors following, one after the other, crunching over the side, China Tom and Father Leon and the educated nigger jumping out—Father Leon was two seconds late and I thought, good-bye, but Red dragged him clear in time. I let the bulldozer go. It hit what was already down there and exploded. Half the valley seemed to be on fire.

"And last—wobbling and grunting—the crane. Red eased it over the side, dropping out of the cab, and the thing stuck for a second or two on the edge, teetering like a drunk: it seemed to take a week to go over, another week to land. And then like a hydrogen bomb. The island jumping. Flames rushing up.

"We'd been told to scatter and make our own way back. I wouldn't have stayed with that ringside view of hell if you'd made me a gift of the *Heinrich van Reyn*. I was down on the beach inside thirty minutes. I nested up in the sand with China Tom." Kanaka Tom said piously, "I'd fought the good fight." The Captain looked at him with revulsion. "I remember thinking before I went to sleep, I deserve my heavenly harp for this."

Dr. Edmond told the Captain the rest. "Red didn't leave. He went into the undergrowth. And waited. He waved to me to go, but I lay at his side trembling—arms, eyelids, nostrils, as if I'd been electrically shocked. We realize our limitations. I am not a violent man. Presently they all came running up breathlessly, half dressed, one of them quite naked—it wasn't at all funny—and they stood staring with dismay down into the gorge. We were so close that I could see their eyes gleaming like red pebbles in the flames. The bracken had caught: it was as if an entire car-breaker's yard were burning below." Dr. Edmond said guiltily to the Captain, "One hates

**170**

insensate destruction: even of machines. In some evil way, perhaps, they have a life of their own. I saw the Commander's face. Wild with grief—it was the face of a man bereft of his senses. I felt strangely sorry for him.

"Then I happened to look at Red. He was studying the Commander's face coolly—like a tailor measuring a customer for a suit. In fact, he was measuring a man for his doom. He'd become professionally engaged . . ."

The Captain had to burst out, "Of course he's a professional. You asked him to do a job. He did it. What did you expect?"

Dr. Edmond sighed, "It made me suddenly anxious. I crept back alone down the hill."

One last footnote from China Tom. He told the Captain that Red decided to go back to his "unit"—he mingled with the men streaming back to the camp. He figured that he was safe there for perhaps another day. There was an alarming little incident. As he went through the camp in the dark someone saw the SIGNALMAN P. ROKOSOFFSKI on the back of his dungarees and hailed him, "Hi Rocko," and Red, not looking round, lost himself agilely in the huts. He rejoined his Pakistanis. They'd begun to look at him rather curiously. But they were good-mannered people and asked no questions. Red said that he'd grown to like them very much.

✾　　　✾　　　✾

The Captain didn't return to the ship. The sky was getting light. Bands of islanders were climbing the hills like pilgrims to whom some unexpected miracle had been granted, to stare at the smouldering wreckage at the bottom of the gorge. The Captain passed the church. The solitary wheel-chair in the shadows. A shaft of the rising sun struck Mother Hubbard's shocked, bewildered face. Father Ho knelt at the altar. An-

171

other troubled heart. The Captain thought with pity, they're learning the hard way: when you sup with the devil you need a long spoon.

\*       \*       \*

They'd searched the huts, the school, the old people's home, before the sun was fully up. The Captain was outside the hospital when Lieutenant Darling and a police squad arrived. Dr. Edmond was making his round of the wards with Belle-Marie. The Captain wanted to hear what was being said. He edged a little way into the ward. He caught the tail-end of Lieutenant Darling's harsh demand ". . . where is he?" and Dr. Edmond's disdainful reply, "Do you think I would tell you if I knew?"

"We have to find him."

"I do not have him," Dr. Edmond said.

He clipped his stethoscope to his ears and sounded the chest of a child.

Lieutenant Darling watched him. Unshaven. He looked faintly wolfish. Not so much of the gentleman this morning, the Captain thought. He could begin to appreciate the calamity that had struck them: they must be reeling from it. He grew nervous. Suppose they start asking me questions? I should have stayed outside. He heard Lieutenant Darling say angrily to Dr. Edmond, "I don't have to tell you, of course, what he did in the night."

Dr. Edmond seemed interested only in the flutter beneath the ribs of the child.

"You're playing with forces too big for you. We have a tightly-organized mission," Lieutenant Darling said. "There are large sea movements beginning. Air transports waiting. Units ready to be flown in." He sounded like a naval instructor trying to make a difficult class understand. "The man's destroyed the earth-shifting machinery. It could take weeks

172

to assemble and fetch fresh plant. These things are planned rather like railway time-tables—the joint chiefs of staff expect their trains to run on time. We have an eight-day schedule to lay an airstrip."

"Then you will not be able to lay it," Dr. Edmond said.

"There are other ways," Lieutenant Darling said cryptically. "And you may like them less. By the way," he added suddenly, "were you there?"

Dr. Edmond said nothing.

"Let me see your hands." Dr. Edmond showed them. "They're scratched," Lieutenant Darling said.

Belle-Marie's eyes flitted from her father's to Lieutenant Darling's face.

"Doctoring is a hazardous profession," Dr. Edmond said.

"But you know where he is, don't you?"

"Yes. Since you ask me. What are you going to do to make me tell you? Twist my arm?"

"No." But somebody's arm is going to be twisted. So long as it isn't mine, the Captain thought. He'd made himself unobtrusive on the edge of a cot, playing with a furry toy, and he handed it back to the child and got ready to go. Lieutenant Darling had just said coldly to Dr. Edmond, "May I make a suggestion?"

"You're going to make it, anyway, aren't you?"

"Turn him in. He'll bring you a lot of grief."

"We already have the grief. And it arrived with you, not with him."

Lieutenant Darling said to Belle-Marie, "I suppose you wouldn't tell me?"

"No."

"What makes you think he's worth the loyalty?"

"Probably nothing," she said.

"How obdurate you are. It can't make any difference in the end." Lieutenant Darling glanced thoughtfully at the Captain, who made an ambiguous gesture—don't look at me.

173

How could I possibly know? "We'll find him. If we have to turn over every leaf in the island," Lieutenant Darling said.

As he went Dr. Edmond called after him angrily, "Have you searched the church?"

"No."

"Why not? There are no bars about God's house."

"You mustn't be harsh." Lieutenant Darling turned with a sigh. "You have a nice hospital."

"How long will you permit it to remain?" Dr. Edmond had returned to examining the child.

Lieutenant Darling asked softly, "What's the matter with her?"

"*Leptospirosis.*"

"Is that bad?"

"Anything that strikes at a child of seven is bad. I have a lot of work to do. Will you please go now?"

And Lieutenant Darling went.

The Captain came across. He said uneasily to Dr. Edmond, "I don't want to interfere . . ."

"Then don't."

". . . but if you'd take my advice you'd hand him over."

Dr. Edmond looked at him sardonically. "Why don't *you* hand him over? You know where he is."

"I?" The Captain grew flurried. "I'm neutral."

"Nobody's neutral. You were born into this world. Everybody carries a little responsibility for its sins." Dr. Edmond readjusted his stethoscope. "Can't you see I'm busy?"

"I know when I'm not wanted . . ."

"You're not. Good-bye."

The Captain left. Sailors had just finished searching the kindergarten. They now began to examine the plantation sheds. That isn't the place to look for him: you'll find nothing but bananas there. He watched them secretively in the sunshine—again with that awful fear of involvement—then went away and spent the rest of the morning like a city rub-

174

bernecker outside the perimeter of the camp. It was in the last stages of construction. They were wiring up the vehicle park. Bolting the stable door after the horse had flown. Pneumatic drills ripping up coral for drains. It numbed his ears. The island had known the thunder of stormy surf, the whine of high winds—never anything as frightful as that gritty artificial roar. It's a pity. They won't let paradise live for long. Somebody tapped his back.

"I've been looking all over for you," Lieutenant dos Vargas said humorously. "Where have you been hiding? Anybody would think you had a woman tucked away. The Commander is waiting to see you."

"Let him wait."

"Come."

"He has no right to order me . . ."

"Come," Lieutenant dos Vargas said, leading him off gently by the arm.

"What does he want to see me about?"

"This terrible dilemma. What else? There is an airstrip to be laid. And all the machinery is gone." The Captain couldn't tell if it was shock or begrudging admiration in Lieutenant dos Vargas's voice. "Do you think the man is a Spaniard?"

"With that red head?"

"There are red Spaniards. Only a man of Latin blood would have the audacity to do a thing like that. Do not anger the Commander." Why, the Captain wondered furtively. What have I done to . . . ? "He is under great strain," Lieutenant dos Vargas said.

What looked like a Court of Inquiry had been assembled in the Commander's office. He sat, pale and sleepless, sweat-patched under the armpits though the day's heat had hardly begun, that curiously unstable face bent to his desk. The Captain could hear his hard breathing. The Americans—second to the Dutch, of course—had some of the finest naval human material on earth. How did this man come to have a command? And why do I feel so terribly sorry for him? He means well: he's trying compassionately to do his duty. But he just doesn't have Nelson's trick. His officers were lined up behind him. The sword of justice—well, maybe revenge—was about to fall. Red's neck should have been there to catch it. The Captain was appalled to see Fathers Ho and Leon and Joseph huddled like a hastily convened church council before the desk. Dr. Edmond, stethoscope sticking out of his pocket, his white jacket blood-specked, sat impatiently in the corner—he looked like a dentist who'd just left a patient in the chair. The Commander pointed to Father Leon. He took a long time to word the sentence. He said bitterly to the Captain, "He was there."

"Where?"

"You know damned well where. Don't ask me to spell the alphabet. He's admitted it."

The Captain glanced painfully at Father Leon. Did he have to . . . ?

"I could not tell a lie," Father Leon said. "What I have done I have done. I do not deny that I . . ."

"Hush. You have confessed enough," Father Ho said.

"The sin is mine, nobody else's . . ."

"And I'm carrying the can for it," the Commander said. His eyes began the twitch that so disconcerted the Captain. I know the expression for him. Hag-ridden. And it's Red who is riding his back. The Commander said to Father Leon, "Do you know what I can do to you for this?"

"As you wish," Father Leon said bravely. "I am prepared for it."

"The bastard." And Father Ho winced. "That red . . ." the Commander choked on the word. "He's behind it. He's the one I want." He burst out with tragic violence, "Why's he doing it?"

The Captain thought he knew why. He just shrugged.

"For money?"

176

Dr. Edmond said scornfully, "Nobody uses money on this island."

"Then why?"

"Perhaps because he sympathizes with us."

"When did that kind of man ever sympathize with anybody but himself?" The Commander cried, "I'll tell you why he's doing it. For the hell of it."

Dr. Edmond said, "You are nearer to hell than he is." Lieutenant dos Vargas began to look unwell.

"All right," the Commander said. He stared at the sweat on his blotter as if wondering how it had got there. There was more on his face. "Now I want to talk to him."

Nobody spoke for a moment. Is he serious? the Captain wondered. He was.

"Why?" Dr. Edmond asked curiously.

"I want to know what he's up to. Once and for all. Face to face across this table. He's got to be stopped. *Bought* off, maybe," the Commander said cunningly, and then he was aware of Lieutenant Darling's odd expression and shrugged. "Well. Warned off. One or the other. He's got to be told."

Lieutenant Darling murmured, "It wouldn't be proper . . ."

"Don't tell me what's proper. The hell with protocol. I want to talk to him."

"He'd be mad to come," Dr. Edmond said.

"You just pass him the message."

"To put his head in the lion's mouth . . ."

"He's free to come and go. He has my word on it. Just this once."

Father Ho rubbed his hairless cheek. He looked thoughtfully at the other fathers. "Very well," he said. "He will come."

"You know where he is, do you?"

"Yes."

"Give him the deadline. I want him here inside two hours or . . ."

"Why two hours? Two minutes will do," Father Ho said.

Something rather terrible began to happen to the Commander's face. The Captain didn't want to look at it. He sensed rather than caught the dry whisper, "Two . . ."

"Why waste time?"

"Get him."

"If Father Joseph may . . ."

The Commander's gullet moved almost inaudibly. He said again, "Get him." And Father Joseph went out of the room.

It grew unnaturally quiet. The Captain looked at his watch. The first minute ticked away. He glanced at Dr. Edmond. His eyes were hooded. Now I know what they mean by time being relative: it can stretch like elastic. Lieutenant dos Vargas stared fixedly ahead. Lieutenant Darling looked as if he had bitten on a sour plum. The second minute was almost gone. He's no fool. He isn't coming, the Captain thought. The fifty-fifth second . . . and Father Joseph entered with an apologetic flourish. Red walked into the room.

And again the black hair jolted the Captain. It belonged to a different, less militantly ironic face. He looked well and relaxed. He's been eating better rations than he's used to, the Captain thought. Red said pleasantly to the assembled officers, "You've kept me busy. You've no idea how much of that electronic equipment there is to unpack." The Commander was watching him sufferingly like a bull stuck with the picador's barbs.

Then he stared for a long—very long—time at his service dungarees. He said to Father Joseph, "Where was he?"

Father Joseph pointed generously to Lieutenant Ayub-Ahmed. "With that officer's gentlemen." If the lieutenant could have grown wings he would have flown straight out of the room.

"If he attempts to . . ."

"I won't go back. I knew it couldn't last for ever," Red said.

"I could have you shot for what you did last night."

178

"How do you know what I did last night?"

"If you're going to deny . . ."

"I'm not denying anything. I'm not telling you anything, either," Red said. "And you wouldn't shoot me."

"I have powers under my directive . . ."

"You're all hedged about with rules. Geneva Convention. Red Cross. But if it was the other way round I'd shoot *you*. I don't fight with gentleman's weapons," Red said.

"If I were you I'd watch my tongue," Lieutenant dos Vargas said. "You have obviously seen combat. What was your rank?"

"You mean, was I an officer? I wasn't *Sergent porte-dra-peau*."

Colour-sergeant. The Captain wondered: what sort of regiment trusts its battle emblems to a man like that? No, that's a shameful thought. He has the scars of service. I've seen them. Ruffians like that *do* fight.

"You should still watch that tongue."

"It's a little late to improve my social graces," Red said.

"You have no business on this island."

"Have you?"

And Lieutenant dos Vargas dabbed his glistening face and with the same exasperated flourish waved the handkerchief like a flag at Red. Its colour—white—was unfortunate. They are afraid of him, the Captain thought. So am I. Jesus God, one man with his mind made up can push a whole mountain of power and authority around. Lieutenant dos Vargas's voice rose, "This sort of talk is crazy. It makes no sense." He had been watching the Commander's eyes all the time: his own had begun to copy that mesmeric twitch. "This is to be an important base. Whole navies are involved." He began excitably to tick them off on his fingers. "The Republic of the Filipino Peoples. Pakistan. The United States." In order of importance. "Great Britain." Did they figure that low down?

"Our sister nation of the Pacific, Australia." At least they rated a place. "You cannot defy them all . . ."

Commander Preem interrupted him, "Don't let him make you mad." His whole face seemed to be built on little quivering wires.

"He is insufferable . . ."

"That's his only weapon. He wants to make us all mad." Flick, flick, went the embittered eyes.

"He knows that resistance is hopeless."

"No," Red said.

"He actually thinks . . ."

"Not hopeless. Very nearly. But not quite," Red said. "We're locked away on this speck in the ocean, but the world has sensitive ears. It'll hear. Until then we'll do everything we can to hamper and delay you."

The Captain looked at Dr. Edmond. He was watching Red strangely. He isn't convinced, the Captain thought. But the faces of the three fathers had lighted up. This is the revelation of hope to them.

What a messiah to choose. An expatriate with Signalman P. Rokosoffski's name on his back.

Lieutenant Darling said sharply to Red, "You've done a great deal of wanton damage."

"No more, no less, than I meant."

"What do you think it can get you?"

"Time."

And Lieutenant dos Vargas said softly, "You would not get it from me. If it were my decision you would not walk out of this room . . ."

"But it isn't. I have his word." Red glanced securely at Commander Preem. "Isn't it lucky I'm dealing with him?"

In Manila, perhaps, Lieutenant dos Vargas would have slapped his face. The Commander stopped him peremptorily, "Be quiet now. Let me talk to him." He fidgeted with the desk implements. It shocked the Captain to see how his blotter was patched with sweat. He isn't a well man. Red knows it. *That's* his weapon. He'll play on his instability and try to drive him mad. Lieutenant Darling looked down at his superior's head, and the Captain thought—was quite sure—that he heard his anxious sigh. Who chose him for the responsibility of SPUD? Did someone in the office of the joint chiefs go down the Navy Lists with a pin? "What's in it for you?" the Commander asked Red. "I'm trying to figure what makes you tick."

"Would you believe me if I told you?"

"I doubt it."

"I'm not a liar."

"I have a very clear opinion of you," Commander Preem said.

"I've served all my life. Armies aren't proverbially grateful. But there's a kind of *esprit de corps.* One develops military honour. Even mercenaries like me." (Hypocrite, the Captain thought, catching Red's eye.) "And to be disbanded —dropped with your wound stripes and your pride of service in the gutter as if you'd been all used up—*honneur* gets to be a dirty word. The legion was my father. Orphans yearn for new homes. I've found one here. If I can help these people I will. They've more right here than you have. Or *am* I a liar?"

"Yes," the Commander said.

"No, he isn't," Dr. Edmond said. He isn't going to swallow it? the Captain thought with alarm. "I believe him. We've given him something better to serve."

Red looked at Dr. Edmond and laughed, "You could have overlooked a reason. For instance, that I've fathered a son on the island . . ."

"It's a little early to determine the sex."

"I'm a very virile man."

"I hope there won't be too much of you in him," Dr. Edmond said.

181

The three fathers stared at them wanly. Suddenly all the fine clear ideals had become fuzzed.

The Commander said to Red, "Get out." Red moved. "Wait." Red stopped. "It won't be for long. There isn't a hut in the island that'll hold you. Not a hole in the ground. I'll ferret you out if I have to . . ." but the Captain never found out what the Commander might have to do for his voice failed him. The jumpy eyes had begun to affect the mouth.

Red measured him shrewdly—appraisingly—he'll drive him to do something terrible, the Captain thought. As he turned to go the Commander saw the SIGNALMAN P. ROKOSOFFSKI on his back. It was as if he'd been diabolically slapped.

"That's service issue," he cried. "He isn't going to walk off with that." And to Lieutenant Welch, "Strip him."

"Sir." Lieutenant Welch flinched and went after Red.

Father Joseph said poignantly, "No, no," and ran out.

They listened to the scuffling beyond the door. The Captain couldn't see what was happening. He went to the window. Father Joseph, in a state of clerical undress, stood in his vest and gabardine skirt. Red was walking off swiftly in his soutane. Nobody was ever less fitted to wear it. He'd left the dungarees on the ground.

The Commander said to Dr. Edmond, "Are you going to co-operate or not?"

"Who co-operates with his executioner?" Absently Dr. Edmond fingered a surgical spatula in his pocket—as if he'd suddenly remembered the patient in the chair he went out.

The Captain wondered why he'd been called. The Commander said to him, "Were those two men of yours involved last night?"

How can I do without them? the Captain sweated. "Never," he lied.

"They were in that business on the beach."

"They're very gullible men. They are easily led astray," the Captain said.

182

"Warn them. There'll be no more soft-play. Whoever wants it the hard way can have it."

"What are you going to do?"

"Do? Clear the ground for the airstrip."

"But you have no . . ."

"There's human labour. They destroyed the machinery. They can clear it for me," the Commander said.

＊　　　＊　　　＊

The Captain heard the bugle in the afternoon. The camp had grown strangely still. He left the hospital veranda—and his beer—and went with Dr. Edmond to the communal clearing by the church. The ships' crews were marshalled smartly, uniforms crisply starched and dazzling in the sun. It looked like a naval review. White, not so white, and brown Asiatic faces stiffly watching the Commander. Lieutenant Welch saluted and announced to him, "Ships' companies at quarters, Commander," and the Commander, in his number-one uniform, accompanied formally by his officers, returned the crews' mass salute and the five flags rose and fluttered ceremoniously in the breeze. The cruiser's band began brassily and interminably to play the national anthems. What *is* this in aid of? the Captain wondered. He was very impressed.

The whole population of the island, from the senile to the babes in arms, watched—perhaps not voluntarily, it now struck the Captain uneasily, for he saw a detail of quartermasters busily rounding up stragglers behind the crowd. A forced audience. Mother Hubbard's wheel-chair in the foreground. The three fathers very perplexed.

The Captain tried to guess what Dr. Edmond was thinking. For some reason—probably because it wasn't in the repertoire —he'd begun tunelessly to hum the Marseillaise.

Kanaka Tom and China Tom had come up softly to watch. The Captain gave them a warning glance. Only Red—

where can he be? the Captain wondered: he couldn't even think of him without a flush of sweat—was absent. And maybe he *wasn't?* The Captain found his eyes anxiously searching the crowd, the fronds of the palms, the whitewashed pillars of the church. He's like the mosquito. You never know where it is until it's stung you. Keep away from *my* neck. He reached up with an unthinking gesture to brush it off.

The squads of the sailors wheeled on a roared order and began a flank march round the perimeter of the clearing. Navy Day in Christ's Island. What's it for? A show of strength? Lieutenant Welch led the parade, hand snapping to the salute as he passed the flags. The band crashed on. The Commander stood, strangely solitary, at the review point. He just somehow didn't look violently naval in his crisp whites and decorative brass. Those years in the office chair had given him the wrong shape.

Dr. Edmond was watching him intently. He murmured in the Captain's ear, "He's going to do something very foolish."

"What?"

"Wait and see. What's that they're playing? Bizet?"

"The Filipino national anthem." Dr. Edmond's remark had made the Captain nervous. "What do you mean, he's going to do something . . ."

"Press-gang tactics."

"Oh, no!"

"Oh, yes. It isn't so long since Captain Bligh left the Pacific."

"He wouldn't dare . . ."

"He would. He *must*. Poor man." Dr. Edmond said compassionately, "That uniform makes such terrible demands. Be resolute. Be strong." He grinned wryly, " 'You shall faithfully carry out such orders as the Navy Department and my lords of the Admiralty shall lay upon you . . .'" and the Captain stared at him with astonishment. Whose side was he supposed to be on? "He isn't really a bad man," Dr. Edmond

184

sighed. "He just wants to be congenial. And we won't let him. He'd like to do the job peacefully, and we insist on carrying on a holy war. Christians are the most *awful* people to deal with. They won't bend. In the end you have to burn them or hang them on the cross."

The sailors had formed up into compact squads all round the clearing, and the Commander—lonely in his responsibility—stood watching them centrally, the sun flashing goldenly on his braid.

Again Dr. Edmond sighed. "It's like Shakespeare." He seemed to be in the mood for quotations. He happened to have this one the wrong way round. " 'Stiffen the sinews. Imitate the action of the tiger . . .' " and for the last time, very sadly, Dr. Edmond grinned. "Only it isn't much of a tiger under that uniform. Poor, poor man. They *should* have sent someone like Captain Bligh to do the job. After all, legally we *are* squatters, aren't we?"

The Captain said in an appalled voice, "Don't talk like that . . ."

"He'd take us all by the scruff of the neck and pitch us out."

"If you so much as suggest that to Mother Hubbard . . ."

"Oh, I wouldn't. She's too old. Do you know, when she came to the Pacific real aeroplanes had hardly begun to fly? Now the world's crept up on us with its problems." Commander Preem had taken the final salute. The massed sailors stood at ease. Dr. Edmond said, "He's only trying to defend peace. And we're trying to defend God."

What, the Captain wondered, is going to happen now? A table had been brought into the centre of the clearing. And the Commander sat. His officers standing well back, as if cut off from him by the loneliness and sacredness of command. Nothing, for some terrible over-extended minutes, *did* happen. The Commander stared sombrely at the crowd. And with great seriousness, without hostility, with sadness even, the islanders stared back. The sun burned. The breeze hissed

185

in the palms. While this mutual scrutiny lasted the Captain could hear uncannily the mocking call of the birds swooping over the lagoon, the swish of the Pacific on the strand. The Commander began to speak. "Well, all right," he said. "Now hear this." The clearing should have been wired for sound. His voice was almost lost. He started again, louder, "Now hear this. We know what happened last night. We know what you *did*. Oh, not many of you had a personal hand in it, not physically I mean—maybe only a bunch of you. So far I've put my finger on a couple of the malcontents."

No names, no pack drill. Father Leon and Red. The Commander slanted a sudden bitter look at Dr. Edmond. That made three. For some reason the Captain (why *me?* I wasn't there) felt himself included in the sin.

"But you all sanctioned it," the Commander said. "And every man jack of you bears a piece of the guilt." This is where he starts to do something foolish, the Captain thought. And yet he has to do it. We're all caught up in this like a Greek tragedy. I'd do it, too, if I were in his shoes. "Well, now," the Commander said. "I have a job to do. SPUD, the chiefs of staff that is, happen to think it's important. And I can't do it over the backs of a hostile people. I've tried to be reasonable, and maybe it won't work, but I'll go on trying, trying to be civilized and reasonable, and until *you* see reason and start being civilized I have to discipline you. Keep you under some kind of control. All right. If you want it that way. You have to have it." The Commander waited a few moments, staring with bitterness at the islanders, letting the silence, like butter on hot toast, sink in.

And then he announced, "You're under permanent curfew. Nothing and *nobody* moves in this island betwen dusk and dawn. You're confined to your huts. The island will be patrolled, and any man, any woman, any *child*, moves out after dark will discover that the patrols have authority to make the order stick."

The Captain said agitatedly in Dr. Edmond's ear, "He can't do that . . ."

"He's doing it."

"This is a free community. What right has he to crack the whip . . ."

"There's his right." Dr. Edmond looked across the lagoon at the ships. "It's quite some whip."

The Commander was still speaking. He said, "But you're going to have the chance to purge your guilt." He sounded like a travelling evangelist offering redemption. "We're going to start clearing the ground for an airstrip. I need every strong back on the island. Every man, every woman, who can hoist a spade or tamp coral, and make a little money on the side while you're working off the sin." He gave a persuasive laugh. It must have stuck in his throat. The Captain now saw something strange begin to happen. He could hardly believe his eyes. Two paymaster sergeants—he guessed what they were—came forward with two large steel boxes and dumped them with a banker's clang on the table. They unlocked them formally. They piled neat heaps of silver dollars, the sun flashing on them, the heaps growing until there was no more room for them—the table began to look like Midas's desk.

The Commander rang one of the coins for sound. The Captain hadn't known they still minted silver dollars. He thought they'd last used them in the Montana mining towns for setting in the floors of barber's shops. The Commander said softly, "Two dollars a day for men. Dollar and a half for women. And a nice bonus for extra work."

The islanders stared seriously but bewilderedly at the silver heaps. There wasn't even a medium of barter on the island; they produced nature's liberal gifts and shared them. What was money for?

One of the sergeants sat with a register at the Commander's side. "Come forward and give the sergeant your names. He'll enrol you," the Commander said.

The Captain whispered disbelievingly to Dr. Edmond, "I wonder whose bright idea that was?"

"Strings of beads for the natives. Public relations," Dr. Edmond said.

Nobody had moved. The Commander said with more force, "Sooner we get rid of the curfew the better." Was he pleading with them? "This is your chance."

And still that great quietness. The sergeant with the register looked embarrassed. He squinted with anxiety at the islanders in the sun.

"I need three hundred men," the Commander said. "I must have them."

"No," Father Ho said.

"Fair day's pay for a fair day's work. I'm offering . . ."

"Spiritual death. You offer us bribes to connive at it," Father Ho said.

The Commander looked sad. Or worried? The Captain was sure he heard him sigh. "You leave me no option, do you?"

"None. But go. And leave us in peace," Father Ho said.

"At least I gave you the chance." Father Ho glanced sharply at the Commander. He began to be worried, too. "If your people won't give me the labour I'll have to indenture it in the Joshua Islands," the Commander said.

"No. You must not do that," Father Ho said with dismay. "They are barren soil . . ."

The Commander peered at him obliquely as if he didn't comprehend.

"They are pagans," Father Ho cried. "We have had so much trouble with them . . ."

"I don't need Christians. I need broad backs," the Commander said. "I can have them here by tomorrow night. Please yourselves." He was trying desperately to be reasonable. "I'll leave the sergeant here. You've got four hours to enrol." And he rose. In his distress he jerked the table, tipping silver coins in a flashing stream on to the grass.

188

The Commander stared at them as the sergeant bent to scoop them up. "I'll double the pay," he said. "I don't have the authority, but I'll take the risk on my head. One way or the other. I'm sorry. Enrol your people or I'll have to hire the labour elsewhere." He was sweating for some reason. Again that twinge of anxiety. A premonition, the Captain thought. I have one myself. The Commander walked off, and Father Ho—it was hardly possible for that parchment face to go pale—hurried back to consult with Mother Hubbard. Orders crashed out; there was a bedlam of formation movements; and with some corrective bellowing—the Filipinos and the Pakistanis appeared to have Asiatically different conceptions of direction—the sailors marched off.

The sergeant sat solitarily with his register in the middle of the clearing.

Dr. Edmond had vanished. The Captain hurried round the perimeter and plucked Lieutenant Darling by the arm. He beckoned over at the departing Commander, "Does he *have* to?"

"Yes, he has to," Lieutenant Darling said coldly. "He's been more considerate than I would. He's given them all the latitude they deserve."

"He really mustn't. Fetch them in from the Joshua Islands. Couldn't you use your sailors instead?"

The lieutenant stared at him with revulsion. "Radar specialists? Engine-room technicians? The navy doesn't train its men to be shovel fodder. What's wrong with the Joshua Islanders?"

"They're not very good men . . ."

The lieutenant said exasperatedly, "You're as mad as they are. They don't have to be good. Just strong." He looked back at the apostolic huddle round Mother Hubbard's chair, Father Leon and Father Joseph waving, Father Ho quite still, looking stricken, the elders gathered like anxious disciples about them. "Do you think they'll ever accept the situation?"

189

He read it in the Captain's face: no. "They think they have the moral right to be obdurate. So do we. Nobody does what we're doing for personal gain. We believe there are things in life—including their scales of morality—that are worth defending. It's a perilous world we live in, and they have to be defended. It's what we're here to do. And that's that."

The Captain went despondently back to his ship. He wondered if Red had been there to hear the palaver. Perhaps—it wasn't so impossible, either—buried in the crowd. He found Kanaka Tom eating on deck. He said to him brusquely, "Where is he?"

"Who?"

"You know who."

"Hidden in your bunk," Kanaka Tom said.

"*What* . . ."

"Under my plate."

"If you think it's funny."

"Look in my pocket. He may be there," Kanaka Tom said.

I hate him more and more: the day I fire him will be happier than any wedding day, the Captain thought.

He didn't wait for the four hours' grace to pass. Before the third hour was up he went on to the bridge and focused his binoculars on the clearing. He could see the sergeant still sitting there, looking incomparably lonely. Nobody had been near him. The fourth hour passed. This, the Captain thought, is the moment of truth. About twenty minutes later he saw one of the Australian destroyers begin to make smoke. It turned about its anchorage, made for the gap in the reef; slipped through; the Captain stood uneasily on the bridge until it vanished over the horizon. "Peace, peace; when there is no peace." Jeremiah—in much the same turmoil—had said that.

*　　　*　　　*

190

The destroyer returned late the following afternoon. It approached the island slowly, making scarcely ten knots; and behind it—in the low shimmer of the sun it was difficult for the Captain to discern it clearly—came what seemed to be a haze of midges on the surface of the sea. The binoculars resolved it into a fleet of canoes. The destroyer entered the lagoon. The canoes followed, riding the thumping swell about the gap in the reef. Some of them very long, with the rudimentary crab-claw sail and lashed outrigger, manned like galleys. The Captain counted perhaps forty of them. He saw that they had brought their possessions wrapped in pandanus leaves, their cooking pots and totems. They have come for an extended stay, he thought.

This was the area of the Pacific in which the ancient Melanesian-Negritos rubbed shoulders with the Polynesians. The Captain stared at the coarse, black, primeval faces with the heavy brow ridges. He looked at the cruiser and the destroyer flotilla, thinking, we already have the twentieth century: then he looked at the canoes and thought, now the Stone Age has arrived. Kanaka Tom had come up to watch. The Captain could detect a family relationship. The canoes slid by the *Heinrich van Reyn*, putting on speed triumphantly, paddling with sharp digging thrusts for the shore.

Kanaka Tom leaned over the side. "That isn't so good," he said after a while.

The Captain didn't think so, either. But he had a feeling that he and Kanaka Tom didn't mean quite the same thing. "What isn't so good?"

"You're not using your eyes, Captain."

"All I see is men. Not very pretty . . ."

"But healthy. They have brought no women with them. They will expect to find them here," Kanaka Tom said.

# 8

Night came dramatically to the Pacific. The palm fronds fluttered like paper fans: a single diamond-like star glowed: and suddenly it was dusk. They managed it almost as theatrically on the island. The arc-lamps blazed on. The Captain, watching through his binoculars from the wheelhouse, had what amounted to a front seat in the stalls.

He wanted to see what was going on. They had divided the Joshua Islanders into two parties. One was putting up its own temporary village of grass-roof shelters: the other had already begun to work. No time was being wasted. Naval ratings, guiding them like foremen, were staking out the perimeter of the airstrip with painted posts and ropes. In the shine of the arcs, from the vantage point of the bridge, the Captain could distinctly see the diagonally crossed runways, the servicing pads, the hangar areas, all marked out with white ropes as one outlines a picture for children to colour in. The new arrivals, perhaps, weren't very bright. There must have been three hundred of them. Labour in the Pacific was cheap: one could buy it by the job lot. The navy offered every modern factory incentive; a juke-box blared out for them as they worked.

192

The Captain could see the immigrants listening fascinatedly. He thought cynically, soon they will be asking for Sinatra. The Coca-Colas will follow. And finally—in the full flush of civilization—they will be asking to be taught the Twist.

It was now quite dark and the Captain turned his binoculars on the street. It was deserted. A ghost-town. He could see a faint gleam in the hospital. Another in the church—one of the fathers, perhaps, in this moment of anguish, seeking spiritual guidance: but what could God say to him? This is man's final tyranny. The curfew is here.

The family huts glimmered, but nothing—nothing but a passing white-uniformed naval patrol—moved in the street.

The Captain went down on deck, saying involuntarily to himself in an angry voice, "It's cruel," and China Tom, who was also watching, looked at him understandingly and hissed. "Well, isn't it?" demanded the Captain.

China Tom nodded. "All is vanity and vexation of spirit," he said.

"Eh? Where did you get that from?"

"Ecclesiastes."

"I didn't know Chinamen read the Bible."

"There are many things about Chinamen that you do not know," China Tom said.

"You're right, though. That's all it is. Vanity and vexation of spirit. It's terrible. I'm vexed. I've had enough of it. I'm going to bed."

"Sleep well," China Tom said.

❊　　❊　　❊

The Captain woke in the morning with the curious sensation that a warm furry animal was resting on his chest. The heat was stifling. He looked at the barometer. Tapped it disbelievingly. Then went above to peer at the sky. It had a flat, leaden glare. There wasn't the faintest breath of wind; the mere act of climbing on deck had fetched him out in a prickly rush of sweat. He took another look at the barometer—staring at it as if it were playing tricks on him—his face creased pinkly and babyishly from the pillow, thinking: isn't it a bit early for the hurricane season? We are in for a little blow.

Why was Kanaka Tom sleeping? He went to the gangway and shouted for him to come up.

"Look."

Kanaka Tom peered scientifically at the very still palms, at the dull opalescent sky. "Just a small puff. It won't be very bad."

"The barometer says different. It has dropped seven points."

"This is better than a barometer." Kanaka Tom, sniffing at the air, wetted the tips of all ten fingers and held them up. "My people have been using it for five hundred years."

"You're a primitive. You'd better secure the anchors."

"If you want to."

"I want *you* to want to. If it gets worse you can start battening down."

He spent the rest of the morning in a fuss of anxiety. He liked the languor of the Pacific; when occasionally it boiled up into some natural convulsion he took it as a personal affront. The *Heinrich* was no chicken. He suspected—was quite sure—that nothing kept her senile bones together but their arthritic rust. He'd ridden out storms in her, convinced each time that it would be the last. And there was always damage. And it cost money. And he was at heart a timid man.

By midday the sky was spread with a yellowish haze. It turned yellower: as if it had been sprayed with sulphur. Down on the rim of the sea it looked glutinous. And still no wind. The air blanketed the ship like warm glycerine; the little smoke from the stack drifted smuttily down on to the deck. The Captain's skin felt electric. I am very nervous. I have

194

never seen—felt—anything like it. I wish I could look over the horizon and see what is coming up.

He ordered Kanaka Tom to lay on double anchor watches and, late in the afternoon, went ashore. Again he was amazed by the glacial stillness of the palms. The island was normally one vast crackle of swaying fronds. And the birds: so silent. Incidentally, where were they? You could expect to see them perched in vast colonies along the atoll—had they emigrated? There was nothing along the great line of the reef but the oily sea and the saffron glare of the sun and heat indescribable. The Captain ripped open his collar. This will give me a thrombosis. It is possible for a very fat man to burst like a balloon.

The camp was busy. He heard the tap of typewriters inside the huts. (The bureaucrats are here, you know when a navy or army has finally won a battle: the typewriters arrive.) He looked through the window of Commander Preem's office and saw him dictating sweatily to a sailor. Nelson didn't spend the aftermath of his victories dictating to sailors. The Commander fanned himself dully. Don't worry, the Captain thought: the air-conditioning plant will soon be here.

He went beyond the banana plantations where the Joshua Islanders were hard at work. They were ripping up the grass with mattocks between the guide ropes—they were bright enough to use tools without knowing what it was all about; they couldn't comprehend even remotely what an airstrip was. Lieutenant dos Vargas and a crew of sailors were directing them. The thick, curiously obtuse faces peered back naïvely, the sailors yelling at them as one yells impatiently at backward children—they *are* children, the Captain thought. Very ugly ones. They filled him with unease. They chanted as they sweated in the blistering sun, carting coral, tamping it down, listening to the distant blare of the juke-box in the px. They didn't clearly understand what that was, either. Was it a man inside the box?—if so, how did his voice

195

become suddenly female? For many years, back on Joshua Island, they would still be trying to work that out.

The Captain didn't care to go near them. One bushy-mopped buck, stripped to a rudimentary G-string, looked at him and grinned. The teeth were filed. The Captain felt as if something indescribably menacing had smiled at him. He went over to Lieutenant dos Vargas and said symphetically, "They haven't exactly given you the easiest job on earth."

"Holy Mary. They will drive me mad."

"How long will they be here?"

"Long enough to put me in my box. Aborigines." The lieutenant stared at them strangely. "You have only to look at them to realize how old the world is."

"Nothing can be as old as they are. They belong to the dinosaurs. I'd be careful with them."

"I wouldn't go near enough to one to *have* to be careful. Why?"

"They are unpredictable. They laugh, they shout, they play with you one minute, then brain you the next."

"Jesus God. Prehistoric." The lieutenant whispered, "Do you know? Some of them even came with stone axes?"

"I hope you didn't leave them around."

"We stripped them of everything. We are not mad." The lieutenant looked up at the sky and wiped his face. "This heat doesn't make it any easier, either."

"Something is blowing up somewhere."

"It's going to miss us. By at least a hundred miles. It's Carlotta." The Captain opened his mouth bewilderedly and the lieutenant said, "Hurricane Carlotta." It made it suddenly very personal. "We've had the storm warnings from Honolulu. It's moving down by the Gilberts. Let *them* have it. Better still, let the Joshua Islands have it. We will have a few squalls by tonight."

"If it's nothing worse."

"They're watching it on radar. We have the course plotted. Not to worry. It won't come within a hundred miles."

The Captain did not know—would not know for several months—that the trackers in the Honolulu airbase were seeing the trajectory of the storm shift slightly as it met a buffer of cold air from the Antarctic. Even if he had known it, it wouldn't have occurred to him that it could change the course of his entire life. They saw Hurricane Carlotta in their luminescent radar bowls as a kind of spinning galaxy, moving down longitude 170—she had been heading approximately for the Gilberts, but the shoulder of Antarctic air shoved her east a little: and now Christ's Island lay directly in her path.

Happily unaware of this, and slightly reassured by Lieutenant dos Vargas, the Captain went back to his ship. The Honolulu Weather Bureau now sent out radio warnings of the hurricane's changed course. In those peaceful radar shacks Carlotta—spinning and glowing like a nebula in an astronomer's telescope—gave no inkling of her power. She had just passed over a few uninhabited islands in the Pacific and mashed them as one mashes a turnip in a press. The "eye" of the hurricane, that area of comparative calm, was perhaps twelve hours from Christ's Island, but the outer whirl of the storm was much nearer than that.

The Captain perhaps sensed it—sensed *something*—as he set foot on the *Heinrich*. The haze was shredding into long striae, black as Tophet, very low down. It was hard to breathe the sticky air. The hell with their radar tracks, he thought. I feel it in my bones. A hundred miles off be damned. This is just over my shoulder. And he ordered the hatches battened down. Kanaka Tom didn't argue. Even he looked thoughtful now.

It was getting dark now, and a glaring ochreous moon—what a weird colour—seemed to fly across the sky, getting the illusion of speed from the wisps of cloud pacing it like missiles. The Captain took another look at the barometer. It stood at 27.19. He'd never seen it that low. He gave it a vindictive tap—as if sure of its malice—and in revenge it dropped a further half-point. We are in for it all right.

197

It occurred to him that this might be the moment to get away: cross and clear the path of the storm. He'd almost finished loading cargo. There wasn't much to keep him at Christ's Island, and he debated the various dangers, wondering whether to ask Kanaka Tom—but that barbarian would just wet his fingers and hold them up in the air. The Captain always had the decision. He would wait two hours and see how it went. There would still be time.

He'd *had* time: but already he'd lost it. Only he didn't know it as he told Kanaka Tom to get up steam in readiness and went down to his cabin for a rest. "Call me if it gets worse," he said.

❀ ❀ ❀

He heard Kanaka Tom stamp on the deck, heard him shout, "Come," and he went up. It was still stickily calm, the air highly charged, and he wondered why he'd been called. Kanaka Tom pointed to the shore. "Listen," he said.

There was a great deal of thick shouting and laughter, and it seemed to come from the vicinity of the church, perhaps from the huts in the street. Our aboriginal friends are out for a little fun, the Captain thought. The laughter rolled across the lagoon and stirred a buried memory. He'd once heard something like it: the crowds pouring out of the public houses, taking over Glasgow on a Saturday night. It was the least pleasant sound he had ever heard. He now heard something else of sharper significance. The lagoon had been oilily still, and he caught a splash, then a rumble, and he was aware of the sea beating with a sudden surge on the reef. It was as if a disturbance, started way out in the wastes of the Pacific, had finally arrived.

He looked up. He disliked the colour of the moon.

"You know what?" he said softly to Kanaka Tom. "I think we'd better pull out while there's time. We'll steer due east and maybe miss the worst." It was a relief to have at last made up his mind. "Tell China Tom. Let's get the anchor . . ."

"Just like that?" Kanaka Tom looked at him sidelong. "You're not even going to say good-bye to your friends?"

The Captain resented the contempt in his voice. "They'd understand."

"They are sweet and good people. I am only a low-class nigger and *I* would not understand."

It made the Captain angry. "If you want this ship to stay afloat . . ."

"She isn't going to stay afloat much longer, anyway," Kanaka Tom said.

"Don't say that."

Kanaka Tom said disdainfully, "She's insured, isn't she?"

The Captain began to shout, "You're talking about a living thing . . ."

"A dying thing. A hulk of rust and misery. If you had a grain of pity for her you'd let her go to the breaker's yard." The Captain's mouth opened with outrage and Kanaka Tom interrupted him rudely, "All right, finish your order. I'm supposed to be here to carry it out."

The Captain felt a sharp warm puff of wind. As if something had momentarily been spat out of an oven. "Very well." Who is giving *who* orders? "I'll be back in twenty minutes," he said.

"Give them my love," Kanaka Tom said.

The beach was deserted. Again the total absence of birds worried the Captain. Not even the cry of a solitary gannet, he thought. All the noise was concentrated in the area between the hospital and the church: where the huts were. Where the Joshua Islanders were roistering. The Captain didn't want to go too near them. What enormous primitive black feet they have. Just like Kanaka Tom. The borrowed pants and vests somehow debased them. He stood watching them in the darkness, hidden by the palms.

199

They were swaggering by the huts, peering inside, laughing at the families kept in by the curfew. Making rather free sexual gestures: they do the same things with their fingers all the world over, the Captain sighed. He could guess how demeaned the imprisoned inmates of the huts felt. There were groups of watchful sailors, Pakistanis and Australians, patrolling the street with sticks. They made the Captain think of policemen in a red-light district. And the Joshua Islanders passed up and down, keeping just this side of trouble, booming chestily, like seamen off a ship, looking for what all seamen on leave look for. The Captain remembered what Kanaka Tom had said about them not having brought their women. Christ's Island, he thought with revulsion, is the last place to find *that* . . .

. . . his skin freezing with a shock as someone came out of the shadows and touched his arm. Commander Preem. He said rather fiercely to the Captain, "What are you doing here? You're not supposed to be about."

"This is very worrying."

"It's all right. We have them in hand."

"You think you have. You don't know them. Did you really *have* to . . ."

"Fetch them?" Commander Preem looked at the Captain wryly, then quickly down at the sand. "I don't know. It's easy to ask after the event." The Captain heard him sigh and once again his stomach twitched with a queer sympathy for him. He's lost weight over it. I'm not surprised. I have, too. "Something had to be done," the Commander said. He looked over at the church, where a lamp glimmered, and burst out, "They didn't exactly help me, did they?"

"No," the Captain had to agree.

"You know, the priests don't own God—freedom's a bit of religion, too."

He's right.

"They live in a kind of bubble. I mean, they're insulated

200

from the world. It's a pretty cruel place." The Commander was trying to form words that would make sense, and something told him instinctively that nothing anybody could say would make sense. "They demand their private right to holiness—don't they see that it has to be defended? There are places where they won't let holiness live." And he said begrudgingly, "I wish they didn't bring in God so much. God has to be defended, too."

That's true. Isn't it a terrible world we live in? God has to be defended, too.

"Do you understand them?" The Joshua Islanders were making so much row that the Commander had to push his face right up against the Captain's ear to make himself heard.

"Yes," the Captain said. "And I understand you, too." The holy ones were such awful people to deal with—what was it Dr. Edmond had said? They never bend, all you could do with them in the end was burn them. And Commander Preem was too kindly and sincere a man to burn them.

"I've tried. I can think of fifty commanders who wouldn't have stood for half of what I've taken from them," he said. "My Jesus, *how* I've tried. But they never gave me a chance."

You know what? the Captain addressed himself intimately. I'm glad I'm going. I don't know how this can possibly end.

"I'm pulling out," he told the Commander.

"You are? Lucky you," the Commander said.

"I don't like this weather. Something is blowing up."

"I've already had everything blown at me," the Commander said.

"Have you had any more storm warnings? How far off will it pass?"

"It's veered a little."

"What? Farther off?"

"Nearer."

Why am I wasting time? the Captain thought with alarm. The hairs on his neck crept at the Joshua Islanders' chant.

201

He noticed the sailors beginning to gather into defensive groups. What a peculiar, tuneless, shuffling rhythm. However did they survive the dinosaurs? He said, "Keep an eye on them. They're like bad children. You never know what they can get up to next."

"Don't worry. We'll let them blow off steam a little, then drive them back to their camp."

"Well," the Captain said, thinking as he looked at the Commander, I don't suppose I shall ever see him again. He was wrong. "I have to say a few good-byes and get back to my ship." He didn't know that he would never set foot on it again.

He hurried round the shelter of the dark beach to the banana plantations, where he could see Father Joseph working with a few islanders in the light of a kerosene lamp. They were chopping down palm trees, the crisp trunks cracking easily in the strokes of the axe. Jamming them up against the leeward side of the copra drying-sheds, planting the stumps deep in the ground. Filling sacks with sand, thrusting them between the trunks to form a dyke. "What are you doing?" the Captain asked.

"We have to be ready," Father Joseph said cheerfully, and put down his axe to wipe the sweat off his face. "We have had it before. This is the best and strongest place to hold us all. The sea has never come up this far."

*This* far? the Captain thought with incredulity. They were a quarter of a mile up from the beach. He heard then the sea hissing up the sand. The tide was supposed to be going out, and it was *coming* in. He looked at the islanders and muttered, "The curfew . . ."

"Oh, the Commander is a good man. He will forgive us. He knows it is an emergency."

"I'm leaving."

"You are?" Father Joseph turned to listen to the sea that had suddenly rumbled in from that far-off disturbance, knocking like an impatient bailiff on the reef. Another of those little oven-hot blasts of wind—the palms leaned over and the fronds pattered, and, looking up, the Captain saw the froth of the haze thicken into cloud and blot out the moon.

"You will be safe?" Father Joseph asked anxiously.

Safer than here, the Captain thought. He suddenly realized how dreadful it would be for the old, old *Heinrich van Reyn* to be trapped in the lagoon.

"We will miss you," Father Joseph said, and dropping his axe he embraced the Captain impulsively. "When will we see you again?"

God knows, the Captain thought. Do you think even *He* knows? He doesn't seem to see much of what is happening down on this earth. His eyes went ridiculously damp and he said to Father Joseph, "Stop it. It isn't for ever. I'll be back."

"Take care of yourself."

"I will."

"And don't worry about us." It didn't occur to the charitable Father Joseph that the Captain might only be worrying about himself. The Captain turned guiltily—they make me feel *terrible*—and as he went he heard Father Joseph call after him emotionally, "God bless . . ." but the palms began to rattle again in the arriving squall and killed his voice. The Captain saw him for an instant with his hands outstretched, looking like St. Francis feeding the birds, and then the moon was finally doused and he didn't see him again.

He went right round the banana plantations, keeping away from the street, which resounded riotously with the aborigines' hoots, and he arrived tiredly and irritably at the church. He looked in at the vestry. He heard raised voices—first Dr. Edmond's, then Mother Hubbard's—and he wondered what all the emotion was about. Dr. Edmond saying, "She needs him. We have to help her," Mother Hubbard breaking in, "No, no. Nothing would forgive it. She must not . . ." and Father Ho, unbelievably stirred, wringing his hands, "It would be so wrong." The Captain saw Belle-Marie watching them calmly, her eyes going from one to the other with a kind of inner amusement. He thought, the heavens are falling in on us—the Vandals are out on the rampage—and all they can talk about is Belle-Marie.

The door almost blew out of his hand in a hard shove of the wind. He either had to go in or be shut outside. He went in.

Dr. Edmond said defiantly to Mother Hubbard, "We sometimes forget what it is to be young."

"Yes. I have long since forgotten," she sighed.

The Captain started to say, "Well, I'm off . . ." but Dr. Edmond glared at him. "She pines for him," he said.

"It would still be unforgivable," Father Ho said.

"She is pregnant with him. You know that."

"Nobody can be sure."

"I am. So is Belle-Marie. Look at her face." The Captain looked at it, too. So she is, he thought.

He tried again, "I'm leaving . . ." and Dr. Edmond interrupted him, "Be quiet." The vestry door rattled. The Captain turned to it anxiously. Listen to what is blowing up. "He will soon be gone. Let them be together for a little while," Dr. Edmond said.

Father Ho twisted his fingers. "How can you suggest it? Without marriage in God's . . ." and Belle-Marie spoke for the first time. "Of course he will marry me," she said.

Dr. Edmond looked at her with astonishment. "He hasn't asked you."

"I will tell him to ask me," she laughed.

"You seem very sure of him."

"Yes, I am very sure of him," she said.

Mother Hubbard said softly, "Ask him to come . . ."

"I have already sent for him," Belle-Marie said.

The Captain forgot his anxiety in his curiosity. "Where is he?" he asked.

204

Dr. Edmond said innocently, "In your ship. Didn't you know?" The Captain gagged. "China Tom put up a hammock for him in the engine-room."

The Captain was so enraged that he didn't even want to say good-bye. He marched to the door. The warm tremulous blast met him. He stood for a moment, breathing hard, in the dark porch. *That China Tom. It is more than insubordination. It is derision. I am not even master of my own . . .* but he was aware of the sea coming in great heaving thumps over the reef, and now he had no time to be anything but worried. *I have to get back before it is too late.* He put up his collar and went shoving out into the darkness, and before he had gone ten paces a sailor came round the corner of the church and stopped him. It was a Filipino.

He said, "Where are you going? The curfew," and the Captain felt himself propelled back into the porch.

"I have to . . ."

"Please. The curfew."

"It doesn't apply to me." He couldn't make the man understand. The Captain cried, "I have to get back to my ship . . ."

"It is not safe." The sailor's dark uneasy eyes rolled obtusely over towards the street. They were yelling there. The Joshua Islanders. "It is an order. You should not be out. The curfew, please. Go back," and the Captain, horridly aware of the rifle in the man's hand, his throat tightening, let himself be pushed back.

*My God, I cannot be stuck here. In half an hour it may not be possible to cross the lagoon.*

They were still talking in the vestry. But there was another voice now, and the Captain, his mouth puffed out petulantly, could guess whose it was. He opened the door a crack. He saw Red looking at Belle-Marie with a fond slant. "The first good sleep I've had for a week," he was telling her blandly, "and you had to call me over to make an honest woman of you." What in this dire situation, the Captain wondered, can there possibly be to laugh at?

"Not a minute too soon, either," Belle-Marie laughed back.

They like each other. I am bewildered. Who, but a foolish adolescent, could *like* that vagrant? I am surprised at Belle-Marie.

"Take a month or two to think it over," Red said.

"I have thought about it. Here and now will do," Belle-Marie said.

"It's usual to wait for the man to make the suggestion."

"Our child will be of marriageable age if I wait for you to make it," Belle-Marie said.

Father Ho recoiled and the Captain saw Mother Hubbard, watching them keenly, make a reluctant gesture to him to be still.

"You're not a very modest woman."

"You're not such a delicate man," Belle-Marie said.

"You think I'd make you a good husband?"

"You could be trained. At least, I would try to make a good wife and mother," Belle-Marie said.

The pair eyed each other humorously and speculatively. The wind was vibrating the windows of the vestry. The lamp jumped in the draught. Dr. Edmond began suddenly to chuckle. He approves, the Captain thought sourly. He will be sorry, too.

He turned to look down the street. The shouting had become angry and aggressive. It had the edge of violence. The sailors were advancing in line, sticks up, and the aborigines were streaming away from the huts. About time. Thank God. Get those raw primitives back to their camp. And his anxiety redoubled, looking up at the sky, watching a star appear fleetingly through the scurrying clouds, the palms flapping, branches sailing knee-high past the church, the sea booming in over the atoll: for a moment there was a glitter of a mad moon, and in its light he saw that the reef was hidden. Just

**206**

the boil of foam, as if vast quantities of detergent had been poured into the lagoon. My poor, poor *Heinrich*. Insured or not. I feel for her. I hope the anchors hold.

It made him angry at such a time, his ear back at the crack in the door, to hear Red's voice, "I might beat you . . ."

And Belle-Marie replying demurely, "Women do not feel themselves respected unless they are beaten now and again."

"Get it over with," Dr. Edmond said.

"I have no ring," Red said.

"Here." Mother Hubbard took something off her finger and passed it to him. "It was my mother's. I don't think she would approve of you. But still," looking at Belle-Marie with fierce affection. "Take this."

"Come to the altar," Father Ho said.

Not quite a shotgun wedding. Not quite a romantic idyll, either. One good thing about it. I'm finally rid of him. The Captain, peering in, saw them go into the church. He listened with mixed feelings to the first whisper of the service—Father Ho's sweet clucking voice—thinking with wry humour, I'll bet it's something *he* never expected: to be married by a Chinese priest.

There was some scuffling in the dark distance beyond the huts. He heard the pained hoot of a native—they had chests like drums—he couldn't see things too clearly, just a buck prancing in front of the sailors. Like a militant shop-steward expressing mass-indignation. Meaning sexual frustration. Were they throwing stones? They'd expected certain fringe benefits. Women. Their trade-union should have written it into their contract, the Captain thought. It wasn't very funny, and he was nervous, his breath hissing in his throat—he had the sudden feeling that the aborigines had broken up into scampering bands. But they weren't returning to their camp, they were retreating to their canoes.

They *must* be enraged to want to depart in this sea. They will never make it, he thought. Again a quick blaze of light

207

from that terribly refulgent moon: he saw a few canoes dancing like matchboxes in the lagoon, and then the moon went, and he tasted salt in the blast of the wind, and a shadow at his elbow became a man and he jumped at the voice.

Lieutenant dos Vargas. He drew breathlessly into the shelter with the Captain and said, "Good riddance. They're off."

"You should never have . . ."

"Don't start that. Thank God for small mercies." The lieutenant remembered that he was in the porch of a church and crossed himself. "I'm not sorry to see them go."

"How can they live in this sea?"

"Savages like that have no regard for human life. Not even their own."

The sand, coming up from the beach, was spattering the walls. Lieutenant dos Vargas drew back even farther. Hearing the murmur of voices he glanced into the church. The light was low, the lamp jumping fitfully; his eyes weren't adjusted to it, and he seemed not to give it a second glance. He said intimately to the Captain, "We have bigger worries. This bitch, Carlotta. She's going to be the mother of all hurricanes . . ." and suddenly, as if his mind had registered a double-take, he looked blankly at the Captain: and then back into the church.

The Captain didn't breathe. He watched the lieutenant's eyes freeze with incredulity: looking past him covertly to the altar, where Red and Belle-Marie stood, Dr. Edmond and Mother Hubbard the quietest of witnesses, Father Ho murmuring his blessing . . . who but the most charitable, the Captain wondered, could bless a union like that? I'm not even going to lie about it. There he is. Take him. He saw Red kneel awkwardly, as if it were a posture he would never get used to, Belle-Marie with him, and he thought: take his wife, too. God has made them one.

Lieutenant dos Vargas said in a high unnatural voice, "We

are right in the bitch's path. If it gets worse we may have to leave." He had turned his head back to the beach.

"You think it'll be that bad?"

They were making false conversation.

"Worse. If the anchors drag. It will be dangerous for the fleet to be trapped in the lagoon."

I *am* trapped, the Captain thought. Who is going to get me back to my ship?

"You said a hundred miles off . . ."

"I was wrong." The Captain could see the lieutenant trying hard not to look back into the church. "I can be wrong about other things, too. About one's duty, for instance. Humanity is a duty, too." The lieutenant's eyes roved up at the piled black sky, then down at the canoes shoving through the racing surf. He said loudly to the Captain, "Don't you agree?"

Keep me out of it, the Captain thought.

"We are civilized human beings. There are times when orders can be unnaturally cruel." The lieutenant stared right into the Captain's face and said recklessly, "Sometimes one has to be like Nelson and turn a deaf ear to them."

The Captain corrected automatically: blind eye.

He was aware of a high keening screech in the sky. The trees leaned as if they had been slapped. Here it comes. And only the beginning. The sea heaved like a mattress and flooded up the beach. The palms were root-deep in water. The Captain looked back into the church and saw that the wedding party had gone. The lieutenant was watching him intently. He said carelessly, "By the way, did you hear voices in there?"

The Captain licked the salt off his mouth. "No."

"I just wondered. It must have been our echo," the lieutenant said. He braced himself to go. "I'd dig in if I were you. It won't be long now. God *is* in a bad temper. I wonder what we have done?" He lost his hat; it skittered off madly in

209

the gale and he shouted, *"Adios,"* and ran after it. The Captain never saw if he caught it. The sand blinded his eyes.

He went into the church. They'd gone into the vestry. To sign the register: as if it were a proper spiritual marriage. I suppose, in a way, it is. The nearest thing to marriage *he* will ever get. Red looked at him amusedly, then at Belle-Marie and his eyes shone. She'll never keep him. Nothing will tie him down. The windows banged. Father Ho looked at them anxiously. In a violent gust the lamp blew out.

Dr. Edmond relighted it. He said to Red, "Take my cottage. It's yours for the night."

Bridal quarters, too, the Captain thought. He was all on edge. Do they expect *me* to give them a wedding present, too?

"Go on," Dr. Edmond said to Red. "With my blessing. Don't worry. You'll see, everything will turn out all right for you." He's surer about it than I am, the Captain thought. "Go round by the plantations," Dr. Edmond said. "Keep away from the beach. They may still be looking for you, you know." She has married a man with a price on his head. Dr. Edmond kissed Belle-Marie and patted Red's hand. The Captain felt something was expected of him and he shook Red's hand, too.

"I wish you luck."

"You're all right," Red laughed. "If only you'd stop being so stuffy. You're waiting for me to say I'm grateful. Well, I am."

I wonder.

"Give my love to our friends." Kanaka Tom presumably. And China Tom. "I'll remember the *Heinrich*. Why don't you do right by the old lady and put her out to stud?"

He won't be serious about anything. For an instant the Captain had a petrifying vision of a harbour filled with baby *Heinrich van Reyns*.

Red said softly to Belle-Marie, "Well, then, Mrs. . . ." hesitating. She looked at him with a short strange laugh and said, "I do not even know my name."

How had he signed the register? The Captain saw Father Ho look at it confusedly. Then shrug.

"Does it matter?"

"No," Belle-Marie said. "The label doesn't matter. The goods are solid enough for me."

"If you're ready," Red said almost excitedly, "why wait for the threshold?" And he laughed and picked her up and carried her out.

The Captain's last thought about him was: he's wearing the torn shirt in which he arrived. There must be some hidden moral in that.

Mother Hubbard began with an old woman's anxiety, "I hope he will . . ." and Dr. Edmond interrupted her, "He'll never let go of her. Don't worry. He's a better man than we think." The wind hissed under the door and again blew out the lamp. "We may have to evacuate the hospital," he said. "Now I must get back."

He went out, letting in a gust that shivered noisily right across the vestry and through the church. Who will evacuate *me?* the Captain thought.

Just at this moment he was solely concerned with Hurricane Carlotta's gathering fury, the risk of dragging anchors and what might happen to the *Heinrich's* strained old plates. Later he would piece together the night's frightful events and then he would think: there are more violent things than the elements. For instance, men.

❀        ❀        ❀

Dr. Edmond had no time to waste and he went straight to the hospital, walking quickly and angrily down the street. The ground was littered with stones and some hurt-looking sailors were posted alongside the huts. The thatch torn by

211

the aborigines flapped in the gusts. Dr. Edmond glanced into one or two of the huts. The people looked back at him silently. He didn't know what to say—we taught them that the meek inherit the earth and all they've inherited is shame and shock. One of the sailors approached him and he began to simmer: just let him slap that curfew on me . . . but a voice behind him said, "It's all right," and the sailor, rubbing a swelling on his face, went off.

Dr. Edmond looked round at Commander Preem. "So they've gone, have they?" he said.

"That's right. They've gone."

"Anybody hurt?"

"Nobody's hurt."

Dr. Edmond felt like saying tartly, "It would have served you right if somebody was," but all the belligerence was worn out of him. The Commander looked gaunt and exhausted, too. Something rather strange happened in that instant. A sympathy sprang up between them. We've harassed the guts out of the poor man, Dr. Edmond thought.

He never thought the time would come when he'd say, "We've given you a bad time." But he said it.

"That you have," Commander Preem said.

"You must hate us."

"No, no. Nobody hates anybody."

"I wish I could say we're sorry. But we'd still do the same," Dr. Edmond said.

"So would I. Do the same. Maybe a little more ruthlessly," Commander Preem said.

Something was going on in the boiling lagoon. One of the destroyers flashed on its searchlight—they saw a canoe tossing in the surf about the reef, trying to get through the gap, but the swell squirted through it, and lifted the canoe on a tall soapy wave and cracked it like straw. Heads bobbed in the water, and then another great lift of the sea sucked them outside the reef, and though the searchlight probed for them

212

it was all over: there was nothing but foam on the sea. Dr. Edmond turned his head away quickly and crossed himself. He said with pity, "You know, it only takes a couple of generations to teach them to love God . . ."

"It could only take a couple of hours for the whole world to lose God," Commander Preem said.

"Yes." Dr. Edmond gave him a troubled look. "I know what you mean. I still think human beings ought to be able to handle these things better," he sighed. He looked up. He couldn't tell what it was that was so peculiar about the sky. The black riffled clouds, like the flock of a torn mattress, hurtling along under the watery-looking moon—yes, I know what it is. Everything up there racing hell-for-leather and nothing down here but those queer little oven puffs. The palms had suddenly stopped rustling. Stiff and erect and nervous. Listening out. "It's taking its time," he said.

"It'll come."

"Yes. We'll start getting the hospital cleared."

"If we can help . . ."

"Oh, it won't be the first time. We can cope."

"I'd get well dug in."

"We collect our people in the copra sheds. They've stood worse." Grinning reluctantly, "That is, if you don't mind lifting the curfew . . ."

"Forget it. Just scream out if there's anything you want."

"Yes. Thank you." They stood looking at each other intently for a few moments. Dr. Edmond made a small useless gesture. He put out his hand. The Commander looked astonished and shook it. "Well. Until after the blow," Dr. Edmond said, and went off.

The wind began again suddenly—this time a hard, steady blast, and he had to lean against it, stumbling in the dark, knowing that this time it was here to stay. The palms strumming like telegraph wires. A frond cracked loose, and the gale took it as if it were a feather and sucked it into the sky.

He saw the hospital windows gleaming. He hurried. With Belle-Marie gone there was only one nurse on night duty and she would be feeling lonely. He heard a soft muffled scream as he came up and thought, the wind: it came again, and somehow the shrill bitten-off gasp didn't sound like the wind, and he grew very nervous and ran. He saw a black fuzzy head pass the window and he thought with horror, they haven't all gone. He looked inside. There were five of them; one held the nurse, hand locked over her throat, and they grinned with an insane desperation, and they didn't stop grinning as he ran in. But they were frightened. The children in the inner ward were awake and crying, and Dr. Edmond let out an enraged yell. The natives looked at him. They let go the nurse and ran.

He smelled them as they passed, a sexual smell, as animal as a hog's pen, and he tried to grab hold of the black greasy skin of one of them, but the man twisted out of his grasp. Blundering into the nurse's table, upsetting the lamp.

It streamed in a pink lick across the floor. It caught the curtains and the next moment—swept by the draught from the open door—ran up the bamboo like crackling red ants. The thatch took fire. Dr. Edmond would never have thought it could happen so quickly. He started to tear down and beat at the curtains, and burned his hands, and knew it was useless; the nurse ran to the door to scream, and the wind raced in and turned the room into an oven. He heard the children whine.

He thought, keep your head: and said to the nurse in a dry blustering voice, "Get them out. Quickly." She stopped crying and they picked the nearest from the cots and ran out. Then back, but by now the roof was well alight, and they'd seen it at the camp and sailors were running up. Father Joseph, too. From the copra sheds. They came in and out through the front, desperate and silent, wheeling out the cots of the permanently bedridden, clattering iron against the door jambs, rocking wildly across the veranda like a Keystone Comic, but it was deadlier than that: and one blazing wall was eating up the door and the lintel began to fall. They had all the children out, except from the far ward, and Lieutenant Darling was smashing away the distant wall with an axe, letting the gale drive in and whip up the flames. But there had to be another exit, and now they were taking them out at the back as well as the front. Breathless and smoke-blinded, a sailor crying with momentary terror as sparks rained down and ignited his hair. The Keystone Comic touch again: someone slapped it out with a cruel flurry of hands.

The wind gulped at the hospital ruthlessly and the flames streamed into the sky. Lieutenant Darling said, "They're all out," but the crackling was in Dr. Edmond's ears and all he could hear was his own whooping breath—perhaps a cry from within, not quite sure, and he said, "Yes," vaguely and nervously, and ran in. He had—he knew it as soon as he was in the middle ward—gone into a trap. There was nobody there, the overturned cots smouldering, the floor getting hot, and the smoke was frightful and he couldn't breathe. Couldn't see. He made for the smashed back wall, but it was a criss-cross of flame. Then for the door, but the roof sagged suddenly under the weight of the wind: it was banging at it with cruel enjoyment and as he swivelled blindly on his feet for a few moments, choking with dismay, he knew that he would never get out.

And a rafter fell on him—and then nothing. He didn't feel the hot blanket of the roof come down.

＊　　　＊　　　＊

Red and Belle-Marie were in the dark fringe of the plantation when they saw the sparks of the hospital funnel into the sky. They didn't know it was the hospital; they guessed it was either that or Dr. Edmond's cottage; Belle-Marie began

**215**

to tremble and Red said, "Come," painfully squeezing her arm. He had an uneasy instinct. He thought he'd caught something, a whisper, a crack of twigs. Perhaps an odd smell, and they ran, and then—they came on them suddenly. As one meets a picnic party scampering out of the rain. The five childlishly scared aborigines who'd just fled the hospital stared at them in the clearing, not moving, and Red and Belle-Marie stared back. Listening to each other's breathing, and the natives' eyes shone with nervous guilt. Then they looked at Belle-Marie, and transparently the guilt became something else.

Red saw the change of expression. He didn't stir; he knew they were very frightened; knew that fright had made them doubly unstable. He caught again the same nauseous smell of desire that Dr. Edmond had caught and it made him sick. He moved Belle-Marie gently behind him. She was as cold and rigid as a stick. One of the natives stirred tentatively and moved round. Now he had them at all points of the compass, and he rotated uselessly, watching them, trying to keep all expression out of his face, in case his fear should embolden them—and then Belle-Marie shook unendurably and the native closest to her made a lunge.

Red chopped him down with both hands locked. He had three on him now, and he kicked, searching technically for groins to disable them, but he couldn't grip the black oily skin, and the hard fingernails rasped at his face. He heard Belle-Marie's cry; twisting his head he saw the native choke it off with his hand, and he went mad. They tumbled on him, pegging him flat to the earth, and he rolled from under them, tearing at them, seeing Belle-Marie borne down, seeing the quick greedy fumble of the native's hands, and in his rage—as if spitting at God—he spat into the black face crushed to his.

They clubbed him hard. And the pain leapt down his neck. And that was all.

216

Later some sailors found Belle-Marie whimpering like a kitten in the undergrowth. They were Filipinos and they called Lieutenant dos Vargas. He told the Captain:

"She had his head cradled in her lap, as if she were a mother rocking a child to sleep, but this man of hers was already sleeping—and sleeping hard. The blood was matted on his head. She had been torn a little. You understand? Her clothes. One breast bared, a nipple . . . it might have been the picture of a mother feeding her baby, but no baby would ever have scratched her like that. She had no thought for herself. She was terrified only for her man.

"He was coming round as we arrived. He was in great pain. At first he saw us all as strangers, nothing penetrating his brain, then he remembered and looked up at her. At Belle-Marie. At the ripped blouse and the bared scratched breast, and I would have expected tears and pity: the man stared at her, and it soaked in, and he just looked at her with a kind of sick revulsion, and Belle-Marie began to cry.

"She said to him pitifully, 'Try to imagine I have been bruised a little by some animals, don't think of it as worse than that.' He said nothing. That man, who no doubt had been free with endless women in his life, just watching her with wryness and horror, and then he rolled away from her.

"And finally surprised me. The tears *did* come. He began to cry."

❋      ❋      ❋

The wind was the final cruelty. It swung hard north, coming like a bombardment; they could hear the shells of its artillery screeching in the sky. It was time to collect the children in the sheds. The Captain wanted to help, and he and Father Joseph led the first batch, faces wrapped against the stinging sand, along the beach. The sea was all thunder and spume. An old palm that had withstood many hurricanes fell with a creak; the water grabbed greedily at its exposed roots and dragged it out into the lagoon. Something else, not less spectacular, though the Captain couldn't see very clearly, was going on a short distance along the beach. The destroyers were aware of it, too; an inquisitive searchlight flashed on. The five aborigines—the guilty ones—were trying to launch a canoe. The sea lifted it, the outrigger tilted, and the canoe came skidding skew-wise back along the beach.

They tried again. Then again. It would have been farcical if they hadn't been so determined. Each time the outrigger reared up like a startled horse, the natives shoving hip-deep in the surf, and the sea rumbled beneath it and flipped it back. The natives saw them watching from the beach and shouted and waved. One of their number lay in the sand. "He is hurt," Father Joseph said.

The Captain said in a loud voice, "Wait."

"But he is . . ."

"You mustn't go down there."

"He is hurt," Father Joseph repeated obstinately, and the Captain tried to grab at his soutane but he was gone. He wouldn't follow. He was too scared. He shouted. His voice was a squeak in the wind. They seemed suddenly to grow anxious in the destroyer, too, for another searchlight flashed on. The Captain knew what was going to happen; he averted his head so that he shouldn't have to see it; when he looked back the natives were shoving madly at the canoe again, and the soutane lay like somebody's abandoned washing in the surf.

They got the canoe miraculously launched. But a long sea hissed in like a biblical threat, and took it and cracked it, spilling the natives into the water; the surf sucked at them revengefully, and they were gone, and the Captain, straining his eyes for Father Joseph, saw the soutane rolling in it for an instant and then that, too, was gone.

**218**

# 9

Carlotta was almost here. She was about eighty miles off, trailing her windy skirts across the Pacific. She'd spared the Matarakas with feminine humour, for nobody lived there; seeking landfall for a little mischief she trimmed her direction so that she wouldn't miss Christ's Island. And the choking sultriness of her bad breath went ahead. The Captain sweated in it. I am so fat that I suffer for two men, he thought. The glass in the vestry had dropped so low in the last half-hour that he regarded it as a meteorological impossibility: he refused to believe the evidence of his own eyes.

It was now coming up to midnight. And dark with the darkness of Exodus "which may be felt." The air whining like a cageful of tomcats in heat.

They'd finished buttressing and sandbagging the copra sheds. They looked like medieval castles prepared for a long siege. The transfer of the whole community had begun. The hospital had already been emptied; the wind had scattered its embers, nothing was left of it but a few glowing stumps. They were now vacating the old people's home. Those who could walk walked, those who had to be wheeled were wheeled. The chairs went rattling at a smart pace over to the sheds—

it reminded the Captain of one of those annual processions of automobile crocks. They chirped like senile sparrows. He thought, I suppose when you get old a little excitement is good for the glands. Because of the great darkness they'd lighted kerosene-soaked rags along the route and they ripped smokily in the wind: it looked like the beginning of a pagan rite.

The children next. A long string of the islanders carrying them as if they were bundles going to the launderette. The Captain didn't know what to do, and Father Ho saw him doing nothing and put one of the babies into his arms.

"Hurry."

"Who does it belong to?"

"Take her. Her mother will know."

Father Ho looked yellower, and bent. The Captain guessed that his heart was bleeding for Dr. Edmond and Father Joseph. He thought, my heart also bleeds for my poor ship. The navy was riding the vicious swell in the lagoon sturdily, but the *Heinrich* reeled in it like a nervous old lady assaulted by thugs. Her hour of travail has come, the Captain mourned. It didn't seem important to him that Kanaka Tom and China Tom were aboard, that their hour of travail had also come.

The sea was racing up the beach. Father Ho said to him anxiously, "I have never seen it as high as this."

"I've never seen the glass so low, either."

"We are in God's hands."

The Captain wondered agnostically why He couldn't do something to control that screeching virago, Carlotta. The baby was heavy in his arms and he hurried it to the sheds.

They were packed. There was room to sit, to lie as sardines lie in the tin, without false modesty. The air in each shed was close. They'd planked up the windows. The dark faces were tensed. The lamps flared and the shadows leapt eerily across the timber walls. They were still fetching in the stores of food, the kegs of water. Enough for three days—there was a known routine, a memory, a practical knowledge of the emergency, and they'd shuttered off toilet pans in the corner, and there was already that bitter ammoniac smell.

Time was pressing. They could hear the sea grunting with increasing temper on the reef. They'd refused—bitterly and misguidedly—the help of the sailors, and they were hurrying to rig up a dispensary, making the sick comfortable under the walls. The Captain watched with disbelief as Father Leon encouragingly wound up a museum-piece of a phonograph and a scratched disc, as ancient as Edison, rasped out. They all sang. Nothing will make me sing, the Captain thought.

In the corner Father Ho was arranging a tiny altar, spreading the vessels of the Mass. The candles blew out, and he relighted them three times. He looked finally relieved in the glow. God is here. Not too sure of it, the Captain climbed over the children to the door. He needed air.

There was nothing to do now but wait for Carlotta, and she was in no hurry. Her handmaidens—the squalls—were still banging outside. Mother Hubbard had just arrived. Two poles slung underneath her chair, borne like a sedan. She was very calm. The Captain thought, how can I be so calm? and began to worry about the *Heinrich* all over again.

Father Leon said to him sympathetically, "We have a mattress for you. You will not be able to return to your ship."

"You don't know what she means to me."

"Trust in . . ."

Oh, don't start that, the Captain thought. He said, "Believe it or not, I'm scared."

"Of course. So am I."

"You are? I thought priests were never scared. What of, dying?"

"Of not behaving with composure and grace. Look. They are all watching us. I would not like them to think me unworthy of their faith."

"So what do you want me to do? Sing?"

"That's right, sing," Father Leon said cheerfully. And he began, in an excruciatingly tuneless voice, to sing.

221

Suddenly three figures came up, like loose leaves blown out of the dark. Lieutenant dos Vargas peered at the Captain. He said with a gesture of recognition, "I've found you at last." He had Lieutenant Welch with him and a depressed-looking Filipino sailor. "The Commander wishes to see your friend." The Captain knew which "friend" he meant: he was tired of disclaiming the relationship. "He has sent Lieutenant Welch to fetch him," Lieutenant dos Vargas said.

"What for?"

"Probably nothing very drastic. Just a reasonable precaution. I imagine he would like him safely out of the way"—looking up at the sky—"while all this commotion is going on."

"Can't you leave him alone?"

"I am sorry."

"Hasn't the man got enough trouble?"

"Yes. I have just explained that to Lieutenant Welch."

Lieutenant Welch said sharply, "A naval duty isn't a matter of sentiment. I've been told to fetch him, and that's what I intend to do."

"My young associate believes in resolutely carrying out orders." Lieutenant dos Vargas glanced at him humourlessly.

Lieutenant Welch looked just for a moment less resolute. "He will probably kill you."

Lieutenant dos Vargas said to him, "So I have suggested that you might like to speak to him first. Persuade him to be amenable."

"I wouldn't go near him," the Captain said.

"I think you should."

He probably will, too, the Captain thought.

"Why should I interfere?"

"There has been enough violence."

"I don't even know where he is."

"In the church."

It surprised the Captain. "What's he doing in the church?"

"Certainly not praying. Does it matter? That's where he is."

The Captain hesitated. Lieutenant Welch said with a dis-

222

play of bravado, "I'm not afraid of him," but the Captain thought he was. I'd be afraid of him if I were you. He said unwillingly to Lieutenant dos Vargas, "All right," and regretted it the moment he spoke. "You can guess the state of mind he's in. I don't know what I can do. Just for a few minutes. I want to be back here before all that," looking up at the sky, too, "comes down."

"It's a pity about the girl."

"Yes." Poor Belle-Marie. "Do you have to remind me?"

"Hurry."

"Don't rush me. I must be mad to let you talk me into this."

The wind scooped them up and buck-shot them with sand. It hurt the Captain's face and he cried out. The Filipino's hat vanished; he made a futile grab for it, looking injuredly at his lieutenant. He was the most dejected Filipino the Captain had ever seen. He half turned to go back. Thinking, I'm the midwife of trouble: when will I learn to keep my nose out of everybody's business but my own? A single furious gust, booming across the atoll, swept them like chaff up to the church. It vibrated hollowly. The Filipino peered at the plaster saints, wide-eyed and religiously nervous, and hung back. They had left the candles burning on the altar. Is He here, too? In the leaping infinitesimal glitter the Captain saw Red up near the altar, doing nothing, merely sitting as if God might like a little company at this terrible time. The Captain made a gesture to the two lieutenants to stay behind and went in.

Red looked at him. The candles riffled over his face and the Captain couldn't quite make out his expression. He said carelessly, "I wondered where you were."

There was no reply.

"What are you doing here?"

Still nothing.

Then rather uneasily, "What is it? What's the matter? You shouldn't be here. You know it isn't safe."

There was some kind of echo and the last word "safe"

hissed back. The gusts slashed through the door and one of the candles blew out. Red looked at the Captain, his face shadowed, and said finally, "Where is it safe?"

"You know what's blowing up. They're all in the sheds."

"You go there, then. Good-bye."

It made the Captain angry. "What about Belle-Marie? You know the state she's in."

Red said something indescribably profane.

"She needs you. Don't you think you ought to be with her now?"

Red used the same disgusting words again.

"Remember where you are." The Captain half expected something scripturally fearful to happen. The church rolled disquietingly with sound. He felt his skin tingle. The Virgin watched them, pallid and compassionate. He looked back and saw the two lieutenants waiting secretly just inside the door. The air whined in and another candle went out. The Captain heard Red's breath. He said to him sternly, "You are married. It wasn't any fault of hers." Then with pity, "You mustn't think she's been despoiled. I mean, it wasn't anything like that. You have to think of it the way she said. Just imagine she was bruised by some animals . . ." and, without really seeing his face, the Captain thought with terrible consternation: surely he isn't going to cry. Is it possible that he *loved* her?

I must be out of my mind. What am I doing here? Why have I opened my big mouth?

Again a screeching gust and the last candle went out. The darkness froze the Captain. He thought Red was looking at him. He blundered on, "You can't blame her for what happened . . ."

But Red wasn't really looking at him. He had seen the lieutenants standing by the door. "I blame them," he said.

"It was an act of God."

"I blame Him, too."

224

The Captain said, "You're mad," and as he used the word he got a good look at Red's enraged tormented face and thought: he *is*. This man is dangerously insane.

He grew scared. At that instant a raven on his shoulder whispered, you had to stick your nose in: and you're going to regret it for the rest of your life.

Red said, "What are they doing here?"

"Nothing. It's all right."

Lieutenant dos Vargas had said, "There's been enough violence." And that dreadful bird of ill-omen whispered in the Captain's ear, the violence isn't over: it's going to be worse, oh, much much worse.

"Have they come for me?" Red asked.

"Well, yes. Let's be calm."

"I'm calm."

"That's good. It's only for a little while. Just go with them quietly . . ."

"Why don't they come in?"

"It's a church."

Red said, "We mustn't desecrate a church."

The Captain followed him to the door. Red looked from the lieutenants to the Filipino. "Three of you. Do I deserve an escort?"

Lieutenant dos Vargas watched him strangely. He said, pointing to Lieutenant Welch, "The Commander has sent him to fetch you." The Captain had the curious idea that he was dissociating himself from the affair.

"Couldn't he come himself?"

"Now that'll do," Lieutenant Welch said irritably. "We've waited long enough for you."

"You can wait a little longer."

Oh, God. Now we're going to see the end-product of all the violence. The Captain took three quick nervous steps back into the sanctuary of the church.

The Filipino's eyes rolled. He was frightened, too.

Lieutenant Welch said in his cold young voice, "We can do it without the fuss," and put his hand on Red's arm.

"Good."

"We don't have to hang around here to get wet."

"You think you can take me? Without your navy?"

"Just let's . . ." but the Captain never heard what Lieutenant Welch intended to suggest, for it seemed to him that, in the most demeaning fashion, Red had up-ended him. It happened so quickly that even the Captain, who'd been expecting something like it, was surprised.

Lieutenant Welch lay on his back, the breath dashed from his body. He looked dumbfounded. The Filipino made a husky sound. The Captain stared about for Lieutenant dos Vargas. He seemed to have retired discreetly into the church. The wind struck at them and Red ducked his head under it, making for the beach. Lieutenant Welch got to his feet with an outraged cry, went after him, and caught him up. The sky shimmered theatrically with lightning—it was a long way off—and the Captain saw them silhouetted against it, struggling. Heard them panting. Then caught an ugly sound like a breaking stick. He shuddered. He knew, without going to investigate, that Red had struck the lieutenant savagely to the ground. Then nothing. The air was alive with whining cats. The Filipino hadn't stirred. Again the lightning fluttered and the Captain saw—thought he saw—a figure running to the beach, but the jumpy glitter under the clouds made it all deceptive, and the darkness was back before his eyes.

He said to Lieutenant dos Vargas, "Why didn't you go after him?"

"He might knock me down, too. My government wouldn't like my uniform humiliated. This isn't my war. Also I am out of condition. I cannot run very fast." Lieutenant dos Vargas said briskly to his sailor, "Come. It's all right. We're not going to catch him," and they went, shielding their eyes against the stinging grit, a little way down the dark beach. The Captain followed. He saw them stoop to Lieutenant Welch.

Lieutenant dos Vargas said, "I hope his jaw isn't broken. He doesn't look very well." He got up, listening out for Red. "Animals behave like that." Then, almost as if accusing the Captain, "What did you say to the man? He is demented." But he didn't wait for a reply. He seemed to have heard something, and went plunging down to the sea.

The Captain wouldn't follow. He caught a thick mechanical putter; it seemed to come from the lagoon, but there were so many sounds in the wind that he couldn't distinguish one from another. Lieutenant Welch rose, holding his face as if it might come apart. He looked numbly at the Captain and lurched off. Presently Lieutenant dos Vargas returned. He was breathless. He had lost his hat.

"He has take one of the motor pinnaces."

"In this sea?" The Captain was bewildered. "It isn't safe. It doesn't make sense."

"Everything that man has done so far has made a kind of frightful sense."

"Taken it where?"

"Presumably to your ship."

"My ship?" The Captain stammered, "What for? Why would he want to do a thing like that?"

"Why ask me? You should know him better."

The Captain shouted, "I don't know him at all. I am frightened."

"Aren't we all? Look." The lightning gleamed coldly, broke like a glass sheet, then reappeared, as if someone were spattering a switch, and the Captain saw that half the sky was covered by whirling rumpled clouds. The other half, from the horizon right to the zenith, was the densest creeping black with a razor edge. He knew what it was. He had heard mariners talk with awe of "the bar of the storm," but he had never seen it himself.

227

Lieutenant dos Vargas said hastily, "I must get back to my ship. It may be necessary to leave the lagoon," waving to the Captain, "Come on," and he and the sailor began to run.

The air sighed sweetly: seemed to take a long breath. It detonated. It turned the Captain round solidly, shoving him hard against a palm, enveloping him in a warm wet blanket: there seemed to come out of its folds a rising yelp, and he thought in that moment of unspeakably comical terror that someone had trodden on a dog.

Carlotta was here.

* * *

The voice he heard complaining thickly, "This is dreadful. My God, what is happening?" was his own. He was embracing the palm as one embraces a lover, in the posture of sexual passion. But the passion was a living fear: the fear of being blown into the night like a straw. The wind that had been a moaning nag was—all in a staggering instant—a howling bitch. The sheer torrent of air, as if a dam had broken, shoved the breath right back down his throat. And he mumbled again, protesting to nothing that could hear—he couldn't even hear himself—"Don't, don't," half crying, not ashamed of his terror. The trunk he was clutching madly jerked under the onslaught. He heard palm fronds cracking. Saw, through a whirling stream of leaves, a great cluster of coconuts come crashing down like a bomb.

It is wicked. *Lieber Gott,* what have I done to deserve it? He shouted, "Wait. Wait for me," over in the direction Lieutenant dos Vargas and his Filipino had gone. "I am here . . ." but where *was* he? He went blundering after them, reeling from tree to tree, bouncing off them rubberily. Thinking for the first time in his life: it's a good thing I'm so fat. A thinner man would break a few bones. "Can you hear me? Where are you?" yelping out into the sucking gusts, but he

228

knew he wasn't really running: it was the wind trundling him along like a leaf.

The lightning glared all over the sky. He got intermittent glimpses of the carnage, the sand rising bodily in sheets up from the beach: palms leaning over at impossible angles, roots creaking, snapping like twigs. The sea surging mountain-wise over the reef. The ships tossing in the boiling kettle of the lagoon. And all the time he was bouncing along like a sail with the wind behind him, trying to grab at anything that would stop his rush, the branches ripping out of his hands: his mind racing as fast as his aching legs. I will crack into bits. I am not a stone. *Herr Jesus,* give me a rest, and he fell head first into a nest of bracken, and lay there, whimpering, feeling for bruises, mashed skin and torn nails.

I am lost. Nobody will ever find me. I will never survive this.

He called out for the last time to Lieutenant dos Vargas, "Where are you?" and the wind howled back derisively ". . . are you . . . ?" and he said to himself: save your breath. They have probably been blown out into the lagoon.

He could hear the surf rushing right up the beach. It is going to swallow the island. And this is just Carlotta's first mad puff. Bitch. Her lungs are dreadful.

He was under a dead load of palm fronds, and he felt as panicky as if he'd found himself in a coffin and heaved himself up through them into the night.

The sea is coming, he thought. Better to run than drown. God. You must be kinder. I am not a bad man. The Psalmist had said, "He leadeth me beside the still waters." Give me some still waters. I do not like the sound of that sea.

He told himself out loud, "Don't be afraid. It's all right. Just get moving." He might keep his sanity if he kept talking to himself. Run. Anything. You have to find your way back to the sheds. He got to his knees and started, head down under the blast. It waited just long enough for him to get ten steps along the fringe of the beach, then it had him again, playing with him, and he was reeling, hands out, shouting at it, "Stop it, stop it," and found himself making love again to a palm. His body squashed to it obscenely, and he wouldn't let go.

The wind made him. Peeled him off it cruelly, and bowled him along.

Something quite frightful happened. A corrugated iron sheet sailed out of the night, cut through branches knife-like, and thumped, bonging, a step or two ahead. One of the navy's huts had lost a roof.

And then the rain came. Not with a hesitant patter, but a great frothing torrent as if a heavenly toilet had been flushed. He was drenched in an instant. He floundered through puddles, still talking idiotically to himself—*keep* talking—"It's all right, you'll make out in the end." "Just stay alive." "Don't stop or you'll be drowned." He panted. It's no good, after all, to be so fat. I'm finished. The wind will take me into the sea, and the sea will take me to the fishes, and . . . he fell with a gasp, so exhausted that now he *wanted* to die. But quickly. Stop making a game with me. I give up.

And the rain lashed down, and rivulets ran off him, and the wind banged, and he lay with his sodden head in a puddle, seeing the great crackles of lightning reflected in it, scrabbling defeatedly with his fingers . . . and felt a curiously sharp edge. A door lintel.

He peered up wonderingly. He'd blundered right back to the step of the church. He dragged himself in, forcing the door to, and he'd locked the wind outside. The windows rattled and the church echoed cavernously, and the lightning blinded through the stained glass. Now I believe in miracles. One has just happened to me.

The four great stilts that supported the church creaked. He heard a hissing over his head. It was the air squirting in through the louvres of the bell-tower. He had a mad and terrible curiosity to look out: and he crept up the iron ladder, up and up to the bells, and brushed one so that the clapper made it hum. And then he looked out through the slits. It was frightful. The tower reeled noticeably with every blast. The lightning gave him a broken picture: the boiling sea, the reef emerging from it like a drowning man reaching for air, the ships struggling to ride it out in the lagoon.

He guessed that the naval vessels were manoeuvring desperately with engines and rudder to keep the anchors from dragging. As for the *Heinrich* . . . there she rolled, like a great cow, and he saw her with distress falling back. Her anchors *had* dragged. Her engines were probably full ahead, but she was making no way. The wind was stronger than her screws, and she floundered astern, the wheelhouse low to the sea, and he heard suddenly above the wind the wild bray of sirens.

The *Heinrich* was coming up to the destroyers. He heard the soft thump as she hit one, saw her rebound, saw the naval searchlights flash furiously. The Captain stared, mouth open. The *Heinrich* thudded again, like a waif buffeted by a hurrying crowd. They must be going mad on the destroyer. She blundered tubbily into a second, then her screws seemed to grip water and she manoeuvred herself clear. She got a little way off, bow into the wind, and held. Maybe at last her anchors had caught.

It was as if he had watched a horror film that affected him so sweatily that he couldn't bear to watch any more. He crept down into the church. He looked at the cross. He had a sudden pathetic yearning for company. He went over to the altar and lighted the candles. They flapped, but didn't go out. Now he had God.

And he went and sat tiredly in a pew, watching the guttering candles, listening to the raving wind, his head nodding, and . . .

. . . someone nudged him. He was as stiff as a board. Daylight was coming through the windows. Before his eyes were quite open he was listening nervously for the wind. Lieutenant dos Vargas and two of his Filipino sailors, cloaked in oilskins, gazed at him with wonder.

The Captain said, "I thought you were dead."

Lieutenant dos Vargas said, "We were sure you were. Where did you get to?"

The Captain wanted to say: where did *you?*

"Have you been here all night?"

"Yes," the Captain said. "What was it like?"

"You mean you slept through it?" Lieutenant dos Vargas stared at him as if he were a freak. "It was too frightful. We thought it would tear the island out of the Pacific like a bad tooth. And there is worse to come."

The Captain rose: every joint grating like a rusty gate. "Is everybody all right?"

"They've survived. So far. A little crowded," Lieutenant dos Vargas said cheerfully, "a little smelly, it isn't very hygienic in the sheds. There was a time when the sea came up to the sandbags. But I always say, if you have a couple of priests handy everything is usually all right."

The Captain, shaken by his own ordeal, could imagine the night's horror in those sheds: the whimpering children, the packed bodies, the sea crunching at the sandbags. I suppose a couple of priests are handy to intercede with God. And then he looked at the candles with a curious sense of gratitude: I had Him all to myself.

He listened. The wind seemed to have gone. "What is it? A lull?"

"We're under the 'eye' of the storm. We'll soon have the return engagement, Look." The Captain followed Lieutenant dos Vargas to the door. His mouth sagged. The lagoon heaved with floating palms. The beach had been stripped. Most of it was under water, surging soapily and restlessly, and where he would once have seen the school, the kindergarten, the

232

neat civilized rows of huts . . . was nothing. A few tilted posts, a mashed heap of debris: the navy's wooden buildings had collapsed like cards. His eyes rested on something totally inconceivable: a hut, caught upside down in the crotch of a tree, thatch and everything, like a bird's nest. Had the wind done that?

And then he stared across the lagoon. The naval vessels pitching, a destroyer with a dented bow (he knew how *that* had happened), and the *Heinrich* . . . the Captain's heart wept. She looked as though a meteor had hit her. Her funnel askew, the decks swept, the wheelhouse windows gone. He had always pictured her as a staunch and virtuous old lady, and the bitter notion that came to him was: she's been raped.

"She lost her anchorage in the night," Lieutenant dos Vargas said. "She hit the Pakistani destroyer. If we could have got her crew off we would have sunk her. She's nothing but a naval hazard." He saw the Captain grimace and said in a kindlier voice, "She's insured, isn't she?"

"Does that have anything to do with it? I love her."

"Even our loved ones have to go."

There was a strange watery halo round a peering sun. The haze flitted across it, driven on by something soundless in the sky: scarcely any wind, as if Carlotta were holding her breath. They were at the very centre of the vast tearing whirl. The outer radius had still to come. And there it was—the ominous black bar—creeping over the horizon.

"Hurry," Lieutenant dos Vargas said. "The fleet is leaving. This lagoon is a trap. We're going to ride it out in the lee of the island. If the anchors drag loose we can all end up on the beach."

"What about the *Heinrich* . . . ?"

"She'll never make the rest of the storm. Incidentally, your red friend is aboard. He has been seen. How he made it, God knows. Or why."

The Captain didn't know, either. Why *was* he aboard?

Maybe, if the poor *Heinrich* comes through it, one day I will find out.

"Now come on," Lieutenant dos Vargas said. "Let's get you back to the sheds."

"I'm not going," the Captain said.

"What do you mean, you're not . . ."

The Captain said stubbornly, "I've suffered enough, I'm not going to suffer any more." He looked at the altar. "Do you have any candles?"

"*Candles?*" The lieutenant was beginning to doubt his sanity.

"Never mind. I'm not stirring out."

Lieutenant dos Vargas said dubiously, "Well, I suppose a church is as safe a place as any." He looked at the Virgin. Carlotta began suddenly to press again, and the timbers creaked. "Here she comes." He beckoned hastily to the sailors and they went to the door with a rustle of oilskins. He shouted over his shoulder to the Captain, "*Hasta la vista,*" and they ran out.

The Captain was lonely again. He sat. He could see a blackness developing through the windows; the rain came like a frenzied slap, streaming on the glass, and the doors began their furious rattling, and then the church was all cave-like echoes and whistling draughts. He felt cut off from mankind. That was the worst thing: not *knowing* what was going on. He looked up into the bell-tower and climbed the ladder.

Again that sickeningly precarious motion: the tower swaying like a stalk in the insensate gusts. Each came with an identifiable yowl as if missiles were crossing that satanically-enraged sky. He could see the remaining palms bending, the tossing branches; the side of a naval hut, borne on the wind, vanishing out to sea. The procession of landing craft and pinnaces crossing the lagoon, making for their ships. Good-bye, he thought. And good-bye, too, my *Heinrich*. The navy will be back, but there is no resurrection for old exhausted ships.

The air, squirting coldly through the slits in the tower, made his eyes run with tears.

He heard, in a fleeting lull, the rattle of anchor chains. Saw the flotilla straining against the wind, coming round in the lagoon, all ordered very formally, like a fleet going into battle. The cruiser first, the destroyers line astern, the depot ship, the landing craft and ancillary vessels like terriers about the bulldogs. And they steamed slowly in their precise formation, semaphores flashing, making for the opening in the reef. He had hardly been aware of the *Heinrich*. She was moving, too. Like a fussy dowager determined not be left out of the action.

She must have been swinging about, steam up, before the others. She was well ahead of the fleet, shoving and rolling on her way to the reef. My *Heinrich*. I am proud of her. Let her die in the open sea in which she has lived; not like a rat in this hole of the lagoon. (There were human beings on board, but the Captain was temporarily too overwrought to think of them.) She butted on, leading the naval array, as incongruous as a scavenger's cart in the van of a royal procession. The wind struck at her and her bow disappeared in foam. She emerged, streaming, and the Captain's heart crept into his mouth. He had a bird's-eye view of it all: though no bird with a vestige of brain would have ventured out in that.

And then . . .

It must be the height: or perhaps I am seeing it from a strange angle. But she is doing something very wrong. It wasn't the wind; she was making a quite curious course; circling the edge of the atoll, which was in itself dangerous enough, to come slantwise at the opening in the reef. And that was when the Captain had what Shakespeare called "the pricking of the thumbs."

What *is* the matter with her? What are they up to? They will . . . and he knew, his arteries thudding, that they were going to, and he heard his own voice raving incoherently, "No, no. They mustn't. Stop them, God. I will never forgive You if You let them do this."

＊　　　＊　　　＊

The *Heinrich's* stern seemed to be chasing her bow. It was as if a giant finger was poked through the reef into the lagoon, flicking her about. The finger was Carlotta's: and she was out of her mind. The air had a mental-colony shriek. The Captain watched, like a Peeping Tom with his eye glued to a crack in Hell. Never, never—not in what are called the wildest dreams—had he seen seas like these. Whole watery Alps, stalking in out of an inky Pacific, green and oily at the base, staggering up to broken creamy peaks.

A Mont Blanc of a wave fell on the reef with the vast plop of an elephant dropping from a balloon. The Captain cringed in his swaying eyrie. And the *Heinrich* fell back from the explosive crunch. She went out of sight: simply lost in the walls of the sea. Time passed. Out of the trough she came, avalanching water. Her twisted smoke-stack at such a ludicrous angle that it seemed to belong to a different ship.

The Captain trembled: now she's in two pieces. She wasn't. Bent a little, but whole. She is wonderful. That pensionable old lady. I love her. Look at her: she bobs like a cork.

She hung tenaciously about the reef, like a terrier trying to get her teeth at the gap. Far back in the rain-stormed lagoon, the fleet watched her massively. Like departing theatregoers queueing up for the solitary exit. While the *Heinrich* rolled about the aisle they couldn't get through.

The Captain's eyes streamed. She is going to die. I know it. And what is more, she is going to die a terribly Wagnerian death. It is that man, that *unspeakable* man—why doesn't God stun him?—who is taking her ruthlessly to her death.

He shouted out into the wind, as if it might carry the mes-

236

sage to Red, "You will pay for this," and the wind, whistling back through the slits in the tower, mimicked him cynically ". . . pay, pay."

"He is a murderer. He is murdering my ship."

He heard the fleet's sirens sounding. They still don't know what he is up to. I do. The *Heinrich* took another sickening pitch into a trough—the Captain thought, she's lost her smokestack—but it was still there when she came up out of the grave of the sea. No grave can hold her. We Dutch, he thought with tearful pride, know how to make ships. And her tired engines seemed to summon up a little strength: she made a second slantwise run at the opening in the reef.

She met the sea squirting through the gap. Her engines full-ahead, the combination of wind and weight of water swilling her off. That *man* is inhuman. Has he no pity for her? She was actually retreating bodily. Like a runner going back a few steps for another sprint.

They were mystified in the fleet. Getting impatient. The cruiser began furiously to flash a semaphore at the *Heinrich*. Clear the passage. The Captain thought, don't bother: there's nobody on her who can read it.

Something very strange was happening to him. He'd lived with the *Heinrich* for half a lifetime—he was as sensitive as a cat to anything that happened to her—and suddenly, in a kind of waking dream, he was present in the wheelhouse. He knew—saw with his own ghostly eyes—who it was that was steering her. Red, of course. The Captain wanted to cry out, "Get down. You have no right there," and in his stupor Red just looked at him callously and laughed. During the voyage to Christ's Island he'd spent his lazy hours up there. Kanaka Tom—in defiance of the Captain's strict orders—had occasionally let him take the helm. Now we're all going to pay for it. He knew just enough about it to steer the *Heinrich* where he meant to take her—in his imagination the Captain reached out imploringly and seemed to hear Red say to him coldly, "Take your hands off the wheel."

"Please. Don't do it. I beg you not to . . ."

"Get out of my way."

The Captain thought, let me wake up. I do not want to dream this dream.

The rain heaved thunderously through the smashed windows. Kanaka Tom reeling from bulkhead to bulkhead with each wild pitch, hands up to protect himself, watching Red with a baffled, stupidly hypnotized grin. He was terrified. Too terrified to interfere. He opened his mouth once to say huskily, "You'll kill us . . ."

And Red said, "You? You're indestructible. Shut up. Nobody's going to be killed."

The Captain, in his nightmare, saw the sea swinging up dizzily, as the ground comes up to a roller-coaster, and the green wall lapped into the wheelhouse, boiled about the floor, ankle-deep. The *Heinrich* shuddered. The Captain heard every old rivet in her sigh. What was China Tom doing down in the engine-room? Had he no *will* of his own? Had that red maniac, with his lust for revenge, hypnotized him, too? The *Heinrich* swirled about, got her bow over to the opening in the reef, and tried to get to it again. Back there, clouded by the rain, the great shapes of the naval vessels loomed distantly. Waiting, waiting: for what? The *Heinrich's* cavorting must be driving them mad. The cruiser's semaphore flashed. A destroyer came shoving up angrily out of the murk, a loud-hailer braying, and an officer yelled, "Get to hell out of the . . ." but the WHEE-WHEE-WHEE of the wind drowned him, and the *Heinrich* rolling uncontrollably alongside scared him. The destroyer drew off.

Kanaka Tom said to Red faintly, "I didn't bargain for this. It can't be done."

"We're doing it, aren't we?"

"Draw off." Then in a strangled voice, "Watch that . . ."

238

. . . the beaky coral jutting out of the sizzling foam, a thin hard squeak as it rasped along the *Heinrich*'s bottom like a slate-pencil on a blackboard: again the torrential flow of water through the opening elbowed her back from the reef.

She slewed about doggedly to try again.

It can't go on for ever. The ship will come apart: roll right over, and the last anybody will see of her will be the barnacles on her keel. How can a man *not* pity her? She shouldn't be allowed to suffer like this.

Red said, "Next time . . ." the stinging rain on his face. Drenched. He looked mad . . . as, of course, he was: frozenly, furiously, dangerously mad. My ship is given over to a demon, the Captain thought. Look at him. If he were only frightened. As I am. The crotch of my trousers wet, my belly sodden with fear. Look at Kanaka Tom. Who would have thought that unfeeling barbarian could go *nigger-green?* One of those mountains of water, riding over the reef, fell on the *Heinrich* and embraced her like a greedy lover. The shock was stunning. Red half lost the wheel, clung to it, spitting out salt; a raging fist of sea slapped at him, and he disappeared in it briefly, wetter than a sponge floating in a bath. Little kettles boiled out of the gratings. The sea retreated from the wheelhouse, leaving a saline haze. The shock had done damage. The steering-gear leaked steam. The binnacle blinked like a ghost-lighted face in a fog. And the lamp went out.

The Captain saw the *Heinrich* broaching to. The boiler maybe drowned and the engines dead. More likely it was the monstrous rush of water piled on her stern by the wind.

Kanaka Tom's enfeebled voice crying, "She won't answer."

Red saying, "She'll answer," *willing* the ship to answer. Who does he think he is: God? He seemed to have some divine connection, for the *Heinrich* came staggering upright, shedding the drowning weight of water. And again, her engines thudding—would she never give up?—her bow was pointed to the gap in the reef. She went at it bull-like.

The flotilla was drawing up behind. They couldn't wait for ever. And the enraged sirens blared. Red looked at them, and then he looked at Kanaka Tom, and laughed.

"Bastards," he said. "They'll wait."

Kanaka Tom whispered, "You are frightful."

The Captain thought dreamily: yes, just look at that frightful face.

They must have realized then what he was up to. The Captain saw a boil of foam about the fleet. He sensed—as only a ship's master can sense the panic of another—the convulsion of terror that ran from bridge to bridge, as infectious as typhoid. The sky was all inky whorls, the wind bearing down with orchestral frenzy; he thought, they have to get out, and quickly, or end up on the beach. He saw the cruiser go threshing forward, as if into combat, to intercept the *Heinrich*. Maybe to ram her. They've left it too late. The *Heinrich* sprawled like a carcass about the opening in the reef. Perhaps Red had judged it better—fool's luck more likely—he'd waited for the torrential ebb of water out of the lagoon, and the *Heinrich* went with it. The Captain heard the crunch of her bow on rock and felt as if one of the strings in his heart had torn.

The old ship wallowed, half wedged on the reef: then the waves picked her up and plomped her obliquely in the gap. The Captain saw her break in two with the rending sound of a collapsing bridge. The smoke-stack toppled, bonging audibly. The wheelhouse fell. I hate him: I hope he is dead in it, the Captain thought. The cruiser sheered off. The *Heinrich* lay brokenly on her side, belching steam, the engine-gang rushing up like ants.

And the Captain, weeping in the perch of the swaying tower, thought: he has done it. He has trapped them in the

240

lagoon. He has made them pay for Dr. Edmond and Father Joseph and Belle-Marie. No one, in the whole history of mankind, single-handed, has ever had such a terrible revenge.

❖      ❖      ❖

A destroyer nudged precariously up to the corpse of the *Heinrich*. They were going to try to blow her up. They got a line over to her. And men aboard. The Captain watched intensely. You'd better hurry. Your time is running out. Was there anyone left on the *Heinrich* to be taken off? He thought —it was like looking through a crack in frosted glass as the rain squalls momentarily broke—that they'd crawled out and wedged themselves in crevices in the atoll.

The explosion jarred the *Heinrich*. Her halves separated; her derricks groping like dead fingers, the sea rumbling hollowly through her horizontal smoke-stack. And then she settled, if anything more firmly, in her bed in the gap in the reef. The Captain thought with fierce pride: we built ships in those days, not welded cans. You're not going to have a second chance.

There was a weird purplish hue in the sky. Electrical sheets sandwiched it to the sea. The Captain couldn't take his eyes off it. This is what the lightning in hell is like. They were coming under the teeth of Carlotta's buzz-saw. The air pressed on the church tower. It leaned. As the Captain stumbled he saw—no, this is an optical illusion—a landing craft go skittering back, borne on a vast sea, dropped on the beach like a toy tossed out of a baby's bath. He grabbed at something. Anything. Thinking . . .

❖      ❖      ❖

. . . Armageddon is here. It was almost too dark to see anything. And if I do see it, and live to tell about it, who will believe me? Lightning sparked from clouds to sea. Those

**241**

mountains from the Pacific staggered in and, peering down, the Captain saw water flooding about the base of the church. The depot ship lost way, struck the reef, was torn off, and lifted up on to it. It stayed, perched like an iron nest. The landing craft were all gone: fluttered back through the surf, and when it retreated they were up on the beach among the stumps of the palms. This is what a daft Nature thinks is funny. It clattered the destroyers together. And they went together, deposited far beyond the highest tide-mark there had ever been. Or would ever be again. The cruiser was struggling to beach herself. The wind helped her with the sound of delirious animals locked in a tin vault. She lay crooked in the surf, her side exposed, and the Captain thought: I have seen enough.

He crept down into the church like a very old man.

He looked at the altar. He thought in a trembling rage, punish him, and God knew who he meant, shouting it out loud, "Punish him," but nothing happened, just the timbers making snapping noises, the darkness rumbling, and he went and sat, totally beyond caring, cold and wet and frightened, no longer interested whether he lived or died.

*     *     *

Ten days later the Captain sat on the deck of a light aircraft carrier in the lagoon. The sun was wonderful. It was hard to think that the sweet breeze was a daughter of Carlotta: now happily deceased. But the signs of her dreadful visitation were all about. The cruiser lay tiltedly in the shallows, the destroyers grounded up among the splintered palms. The landing craft washed so far up the beach that they looked as though they'd grown there mushroom-fashion. The depot ship was the most disconcerting sight of all. It was still perched, nest-like, on the reef, as if the children of giants had been playing with it and had dropped it there while they scampered off to lunch. Every time the Captain looked at it he had to rub his eyes.

The *Heinrich,* of course, was gone. They'd blown her up to clear the passage. The bits of her lay in the deep water of the atoll. "Of her bones are coral made." But something of her remained. Her smoke-stack, by some freak of the explosion, had landed squarely on the reef, wedged there to brave the eternal storms.

She has a memorial. The Captain got a fierce consolation out of it.

He had an attested report of her loss from the navy. Her insurance money was safe. But he grieved for her terribly and whenever he looked at the smoke-stack he told himself woundedly: "I will make the underwriters pay double for that." Red and Kanaka Tom and China Tom were held down in the carrier's brig. The Captain couldn't even begin to think of them rationally. I will make the underwriters pay for them, too.

The aircraft carrier, that would drop the Captain at Hawaii, had arrived a week ago with her attendant frigates to clear up the mess. They were all American, as hard and shinily efficient as a Detroit car-plant, and with them was a junior deity of an admiral who seemed to have more authority than God. He had a square red face and wintry eyes. This was no Commander Preem. Poor Commander Preem. He had departed. It had been his bad luck to cross swords with an antagonist as merciless as Red.

The Captain would never forget the Admiral's stupefied expression when he and his aides inspected the calamity. It was unbelievable: to be able to walk round warships as if they were gasworks. The Captain was on the beach at the time and one of the aides whispered to the Admiral. He looked sharply at the Captain and came across.

He said bleakly, "What made him do it?"

The Captain sighed. It would be too long a story. They

243

would have to bring Dr. Edmond and Father Joseph back from the dead, and undefile Belle-Marie.

"You fetched him."

The Captain bridled. Are they blaming *me?*

The Admiral gave another stunned look at the stranded fleet and said, "One man did *that?*"

"There were others. My Papuan crew . . ."

The Admrial said faintly, "Papuans. Jesus God."

"My engineer, China Tom . . ."

The Admiral grimaced.

"That primitive." The Admiral looked at the Captain with revulsion and went on.

They would start refloating the cruiser in a few days: salvage what could be salvaged of the destroyers. The landing craft might make good beach shelters. They were lucky not a single life had been lost.

It had taken the Captain a little while to bring himself to visit Red. He was led along gleaming corridors in the bowels of the carrier, as sterile and busy as a crowded hospital, and he was shown into a small clean compartment, coolly lit by a fluorescent lamp. It didn't smell like a prison. Red lay on a bunk, doing nothing. He'd already done enough, hadn't he? The Captain was surprised that the sailor who'd escorted him didn't even bother to relock the door.

Red said gravely, "Sit down."

He looked pale. He should, shouldn't he? He'll look even paler before they're finished with him.

And the Captain began suddenly to tremble. "How can you bear to *speak* to me after what you've done?" he burst out.

"I'm sorry."

"They will make you pay for it."

"That's all right."

"They will court-martial you, or something. You and Kanaka Tom and China . . ."

244

"If it makes you feel better."

"They have an expression: they will throw the book at you . . ."

"Now you've got it out of your system," Red said mildly. "Sit down."

The Captain licked his lips. He sat. "You have lost me my *Heinrich.*"

"Better than the boneyard. She died heroically, didn't she? You'll always be able to remember that."

"Why did you do it?"

Red said, "It had to be done. Somebody had to protest. I protested: the only way I knew." He looked enervated. Drained of all his vital fury. "I'm sorry now. But it's done. It's all burned out of me. I'll never do anything like it again."

Then the Captain asked him the question that had disturbed his mind since they'd first met. He'd asked it before without getting a satisfactory answer. Now he asked it again. "Weren't you frightened?"

Red said emptily, "I've never been frightened of anything in my life."

And, staring at him with shock, the Captain finally understood him. "The fear of the Lord is the beginning of knowledge." Fear made a man whole: its total absence crippled him.

He felt deflated. He muttered accusingly, "Five navies have been lost." (A little dramatic licence.) "They'll do something terrible to you."

Red looked at him and said softly, "They won't do anything at all."

"*What?*" The very notion outraged the Captain.

"They don't want me as a witness. They just want me hushed up. There'll be questions asked. In parliaments, places like that. Navies are supposed to be indefatigable." Red looked through the porthole. "They aren't supposed to end

245

up on their butts on a beach. Like old railcars. They'd be a laughing stock. They'd give anything to be rid of me."

No, no. It wasn't possible. There would be no justice left in this world.

Would he ask after the community? Belle-Marie? Red said seriously, "How are they all?"

"They are leaving. They are going to start again on another island."

Red nodded. He called after the Captain, "Would you leave me a cigar?" and the Captain's hand went automatically to his pocket. He remembered just in time that that was how it had all started—with a cigar in Captain Malaise's ship—and shuddered and went.

In the next compartment he saw Kanaka Tom and China Tom playing cards with the door wide open. He said resentfully to the sailor who was escorting him, "Don't you *guard* them?"

"That laundryman and the fuzzy-wuzzy? Hell, what for?" the sailor said pityingly. "They're bone-simple. They didn't know what they were doing."

That's what you think. Kanaka Tom laughed. The Captain retorted, "You're both fired."

China Tom said blandly, "You owe me a month's pay . . ."

"Sue me," the Captain said. He had had the last word.

That was several days ago. Now he was sitting on the aircraft carrier, waiting to watch the community leave. They'd crated their precious possessions: schoolbooks and altar ornaments: right down to the church bells. A frigate would carry the heavy stuff for them, but with a kind of stubborn pride they insisted on travelling personally in their own canoes. The island looked scraped; it would never be the same. Nothing was left standing but the copra sheds that had sheltered the people, and the church tower. Even that leaned precariously. The Captain thought with awe: I was safe in the House of the Lord. He felt the pulsations of four quick

246

launchings. He was on a vast power-house, as complex as Cape Canaveral, the subtlest product of man's brain, and he watched the jets circle the lagoon silkily and land. They'd laid a temporary airstrip. Huts and stores and servicing pads were springing up. The navy had effortlessly absorbed the island. It had even reverted to its ancient name, Matsutura. Christ had lost His lease on it.

And, there on the quarterdeck of the carrier, in that queerly emotional and fuddled state, the Captain heard the frigate's siren sound, saw it manoeuvre for departure, saw the canoes that had been massing all morning form up behind.

The Admiral watched thoughtfully. He looked almost sad. He said, "We'll do the best we can for them. We'll start them off on the right foot," but he wasn't sorry to see them go. The navy and the religious made bad bedfellows; he had a difficult enough job. An officer came up and whispered in his ear. The Captain caught the words . . . "wants to watch them go," and he guessed instantly who it was wanted to watch. The Admiral's face went twice as wintry. He was going to refuse. Then he surprised the Captain by looking at him carefully and saying to the officer, "All right. Fetch him up."

"Here, sir?"

"Here."

"What are you going to do with him?" the Captain asked.

The Admiral said coldly, "What the hell can we do with him? Nothing. He can talk his way out of it. He can say that ship of yours was in peril. He had the right to try and leave the lagoon. He misjudged the passage through the reef. We know he didn't: but *prove* it. The hell with him. I know what I'd like to do with him," he said harshly. "Tie four fathoms of chain to his feet and drop him over the side."

That was when the Captain realized that Red might be right. They wanted to be rid of him.

"There'll be a Congressional inquiry," the Admiral said.

247

"Christ, there'll be no end of trouble. You think we want that man subpoena'd by the Naval Finance Committee? It's a hard world. This navy has to look after itself."

Then Red appeared, followed by Kanaka Tom and China Tom, escorted by the officer and a sailor, and the Admiral glared at him: the Captain thought for a moment that he *would* give the order to tie four fathoms of chain to his feet and toss him over the side.

The Admiral beckoned the officer off.

Red went to the rail and watched the frigate shepherding the canoes towards the reef. They trailed behind it in four thick formations, avoiding its wake. The Captain, blinking hard, tried to distinguish faces—he'd already said good-bye to Mother Hubbard, to Fathers Ho and Leon and Belle-Marie—but his heart thumped painfully: I would like to see them just once again. He turned so that he could get a glimpse of Red's face. He looked strained. He has lost something irretrievable, the Captain thought. Why do I feel so sorry for him?

And suddenly he was on edge for no apparent reason. He felt a tension. Red seemed to feel it, too, for he turned to look measuringly at the Admiral. The Admiral said in a careless voice to the escort sailor, "Ask the OOD to join me on the quarter-deck."

There was a phone on the bulkhead behind him; he could have achieved the same thing in ten seconds through the loudspeakers. Red was also aware of it, and he looked at the Admiral again. "Sir," the sailor said obtusely . . .

"Go on."

"Sir . . ."

"Son, nobody argues with admirals. Didn't they tell you that?"

The sailor went. The Admiral looked through Red as if he were thin air and moved absently ten feet away from him along the rail. The Captain followed him. Something is going

to happen. I want to be out of the way. He saw only out of
the corner of his eyes that Red had gone over the side. The
Admiral seemed not to notice. But the ships had noticed. The
Captain heard the hard rasping of alarm klaxons, the quick
patter of feet, saw two gigs leave a frigate with a spurt of
foam and race for the head almost lost in the sheen of the
lagoon. The Admiral went to the phone and said into it irritably, "Belay that. When I want action I'll call for it. Now
slacken off. Recall those gigs."

The loud-hailers brayed and the boats meandered about
bewilderedly and returned. The Admiral said with a cold
chuckle, "Only admirals can do that." The Captain watched
the man swimming towards the canoes: he thought, isn't it
strange? he always seems to be swimming somewhere. This
time he isn't going to make it. Then they saw him from the
canoes—someone waved—one of them broke formation and
turned towards him.

"They can have him. Good riddance," the Admiral said.
But he seemed puzzled. "What made him want to go along
with them?"

"I think when he first arrived here he felt he'd come home,"
the Captain said.

"The man's violent. Whatever will they do with him?"

"They will teach him fear."

It was lost on the Admiral. He watched the canoe reach
Red—the whole fleet watched, too—the head lagging ex-
haustedly in the water, the canoe dragging him aboard, turning to rejoin formation, and the Captain could no longer see
clearly. Someone waved again—Father Ho? Belle-Marie? who
could tell?—and he felt deprived. He couldn't speak. The
frigate was through the reef, the canoes streaming after it
into the open sea. The Captain's eyes (what an emotional
state I'm in) brimmed with tears. I shall never see them
again. I shall miss them. It has been a rewarding experience

249

to know them: at least, for a little part of my life, I was nearer to God.

The Admiral was watching him curiously. "Why, you're mushy. You're weeping."

The Captain said defiantly, "Nelson wept, too."

"He did?"

"Yes, he did," the Captain said.